"YOU'RE HIDING SOMETHING, HAL."

"I'm not holding out on you, Barbara. I've just been trying to keep you and the others here at the Farm in a safe, plausible deniability zone."

"It's not like we've never been attacked before," she stated. "And with the new setup operational, we're even better equipped to defend ourselves."

"Not against an attack originating in the Oval Office," he reminded her. "The Man controls our destiny, and we can never forget that."

"We can always go into an Alamo Protocol until you can get us cleared."

"No, Barbara, that's the one thing we can't do this time. We can protect ourselves from attacks from other federal agencies, but we can't go to war with the President. That's called treason."

"Even if he's working for the enemy?"

DON PENDLETON'S

MACK BOLAN®

STONY MAN®

DOOMSDAY DIRECTIVE

THE
ARMAGEDDON
PROJECT

BOOK II

A GOLD EAGLE BOOK FROM

WORLDWIDE®

TORONTO • NEW YORK • LONDON
AMSTERDAM • PARIS • SYDNEY • HAMBURG
STOCKHOLM • ATHENS • TOKYO • MILAN
MADRID • WARSAW • BUDAPEST • AUCKLAND

First edition February 2001

ISBN 0-373-61935-9

Special thanks and acknowledgment to
Michael Kasner for his contribution to this work.

DOOMSDAY DIRECTIVE

Printed in U.S.A.

DOOMSDAY DIRECTIVE

CHAPTER ONE

Uganda

David Merkov was running for his life. Before being released from captivity, he had been stripped naked and lashed until the blood flowed from his back and chest. Then he had been given a half-hour head start to reach the western border of Uganda sixty miles away. If he could make it through the jungle into the Republic of the Congo, he'd be safe.

When Merkov had last been in Tel Aviv, his name was Hersh Wizemann, and he was an agent of Shin Bet, the Israeli secret service. He had flown to Uganda on assignment posing as a radical Zionist who wanted to join a mercenary force composed of fellow Jewish radicals. The state of the so-called Middle East peace process was still fragile, and the Israeli government needed to know what this group of expatriates was planning to do. He had barely settled into his role as a mercenary when his cover was blown and now he was a fugitive.

Merkov was in his early thirties, well fed and exercise-room fit, but that didn't mean much against the realities of the African jungle. Not when he was naked, bootless and had no way to carry water. He had no realistic chance of escaping his pursuers, but he was still alive so he would run.

Coming across a muddy pool along a game trail, he staggered to a halt. Falling to his knees, he scooped up the thin muck with both hands and sucked it down. He was aware that he had just infected himself with at least half a dozen rare and exotic diseases that would surely kill him if he didn't get medical attention in the next couple of days. But his more immediate concern was living out the rest of the hour, to say nothing of the day. What he would do after he reached the border with the Congo was a dream he didn't dare think about until he had it in sight.

By the third handful of muck, Merkov started to gag, but he continued to suck it down. His only hope of retaining his strength was to keep himself hydrated. Having been born in a semiarid land, he'd had no idea that one could get dehydrated in the jungle until he had gone through a quickie Shin Bet jungle survival-course back in Israel. Along with the desert, the Israelis knew the African jungle.

By an odd turn of history, the Israelis and the Ugandans shared a long history. More than a hundred years earlier, the first Zionist leaders searching for a Jewish homeland had seriously considered settling expatriate European Jews in Uganda, at that time a British colony. Although that plan never came to pass, the connection continued after the Jews created their nation out of what had once been Palestine. The first Israeli foreign-aid program had been to teach Ugandans how to farm kibbutz style.

It was only when the former police sergeant turned nationalist leader Idi Amin Dada proclaimed himself president of Uganda for life that the relationship broke down.

In the post-Idi Amin era, Uganda had drifted into the endless cycle of tribal warfare, pitting one warlord against the other, that was ravaging so much of Africa at the time. Thirty years later, European companies were starting to operate in the country again, but Uganda was still a hellhole.

EX-SOUTH AFRICAN Major Bernard Hart led the forty-man patrol that was tracking David Merkov. There was no hope that the spy would be able to escape, and had Hart wanted, he could have put an end to him within the first hour. But tracking him through the jungle was good training for the mercenaries under Hart's command. He wouldn't be leading them into action in a jungle, but a good soldier needed to have his combat instincts honed under all conditions.

The man in the command group wearing the Land's End safari suit, with the scoped 7 mm bolt-action rifle slung over his back, was in his late forties, but he wasn't having much trouble keeping up with the younger men in jungle camou uniforms accompanying him. Not only was he fit, but also he was their paymaster, so the mercenaries weren't about to let him get lost or lag too far behind. It just wasn't good business practice, and even though they were driven by ideology, they were still businessmen. Part of their pay included being able to live on their own lands in Israel again, and that was worth far more to them than money.

MERKOV THOUGHT he was hallucinating when he saw the sky-blue-and-white flag flying over the outpost in the distant clearing. Wiping the crusted sweat salt from his eyes, he realized that he wasn't seeing things; it was a United Nations flag.

Summoning the last reserves of his strength, he headed for the small compound. He had long since lost the feeling in his feet and didn't know that he was leaving a blood trail with every step. Even if he had known, he would have kept stumbling toward the safe haven the flag represented. If he could just reach it, the mercenaries chasing him would have to let him go.

DR. RACHEL FERGUSON peeled off her surgical gloves at the end of her afternoon rounds. Instead of the gloves being discarded, as they would have been back in her home hospital outside of Manchester, they were dropped into a plastic bucket of disinfectant to be cleaned and used again. A second bucket held hypodermic needles and syringes that would also be re-used. She could afford to waste nothing in this remote jungle outpost.

Taking the charts from her nurse, she headed for her office to write her progress notes. Those notes, however, would be brutally brief. There was little to record when most of her patients were dying and there was no hope of saving them. The Slimming Sickness, as AIDS was called in this part of Africa, was rampant. So were a couple of mosquito-borne fevers that acted a lot like dengue. When she was honest with herself, she knew that she was running a hospice, not a hospital where people came to be healed.

Ferguson put her head down on her desk for a long moment to refocus. The last thing she needed was to give into the despair that was so prevalent in this part of Africa. It was more deadly than the diseases. Sitting up, she reached for the first of her charts.

She had just started to write on the second chart when she heard shouting from outside her hut. Going to the open door, she saw several of her black staff running out into the clearing by the main road. Looking beyond them, she saw a naked white man, or at least he looked white under the layers of mud and blood, stumbling toward them.

Laying her charts aside, she rushed to see who this unexpected visitor was.

By the time she caught up with her two orderlies, they had the man between them and were walking him to the clinic. The man's eyes focused on Ferguson, and he croaked, "Are you UN? I need to get to the UN."

"This is the Wulanda clinic. We work under the UN, but we're a private organization, Doctors without Borders."

The man's eyes went wild. "Do you have any troops here?"

"No." Ferguson was puzzled. "Like I said, this is a clinic."

"Oh God." Tears sprang to the man's eyes.

"What's wrong?" she asked.

"They're coming," he said, grabbing for her hand, "and they'll kill us all."

"Who's coming?" Ferguson asked.

"The mercenaries."

Compared to much of the rest of Africa, Uganda was a fairly tame place. But compared to any civilized nation on any other continent, it was an unremitting hell that gave a new definition to the concept of anarchy. From what she knew, mercenaries were a thing of the past simply because there wasn't anything in Uganda worth paying professional fighting men to defend. Beyond the troops of the national factions, there were roving bands of thugs, but that was about it. There hadn't been mercenaries, black or white, in Uganda for a long time.

"Let's get some food and water into you, and then I'll see to your injuries."

WHEN THE BLACK tracker came back, he reported to the major. "He says the blood trail leads to the clinic." Hart relayed the information to the man in the Land's End safari outfit, American industrialist Grant Betancourt.

"What clinic?"

"There's a small AIDS clinic not far away run by some international do-gooder agency. About all they do is warehouse the dying, and then burn the bodies. It's a complete waste of time, but you know how those people are."

"Are there any UN troops there?"

"Not to my knowledge."

"Take them out," Betancourt ordered.

"The Europeans, too?"

"All of them," Betancourt answered. "It will be good training for the troops."

Hart didn't argue with his paymaster. He was being paid enough for this assignment to finally be able to retire, and he wasn't going to jeopardize that for anything. If the whites who came to Africa didn't understand that it was a harsh land, that was their bad luck.

Hart had no fears that there would be repercussions for what was about to happen here today. When they were done, they'd just pile the bodies in the buildings and torch them. It would be weeks before anyone came to see why the clinic had been out of contact. By that time, the rains would have obliterated their boot prints, and there would be nothing to suggest anything other than another routine rampage by one of the nameless bandit gangs that ravaged the countryside.

Hart barked orders over his throat mike to his subordinate leaders, who relayed them to their units.

A SHOT OF PRECIOUS Demerol put the man to sleep, and Dr. Ferguson was cleaning and suturing his wounds when one of her African assistants burst into the clinic. "Doctor! Soldiers come!"

"Government soldiers?" she asked as she carefully drew a cut on the man's foot closed.

"No. White soldiers."

She finished her suture before stopping. "Bandage this," she told her nurse, "while I see what's going on."

"Yes, Doctor."

Like all foreigners working in Africa, Ferguson tried to keep abreast with the latest local political developments. It was an important part of her personal survival program. Even so, she hadn't heard of any movements of white troops into the region, UN or other.

When she walked out, she saw armed squads in jungle camouflage closing on her little compound from all directions. They wore face paint and floppy jungle hats unlike anything she had ever seen before. When she spotted what had to be their command group, she started in that direction.

BETANCOURT HAD GOTTEN a radio report from his base camp and knew that this medical outpost was run by an Englishwoman under the Doctors without Borders program. The woman hurrying toward him had to be Dr. Rachel Ferguson.

"You're not UN," she said without introducing herself. "Who are you?"

"Who we are is none of your concern," Betancourt said smoothly. "We're looking for a dangerous fugitive, a murderer in fact."

"What does he look like?"

"At last report, he was naked."

"I haven't—" she started to say when she saw a half a dozen soldiers break off and head into the clinic.

"You lot!" she called out to them. "Stay out of there!"

When the mercenaries ignored her, she turned back to Betancourt. "Tell your people that they can't—"

Major Hart was listening to his earphone and broke in, "They have him."

"Do it," Betancourt ordered.

The major spoke into his throat mike and the firing started. When Ferguson started for the clinic, Betancourt grabbed her arm. "You should have stayed in England," he said as he pulled the trigger of the 9 mm pistol he held against her left side.

She gasped as the first round ripped through her and turned to face her attacker. She was trying to ask why when the second round tore through her heart.

BLACK GREASY SMOKE stained the clear blue African sky over the clinic, but Betancourt didn't fear that anyone would come to investigate its cause. Smoke often was seen on the horizon of Uganda, to say nothing of almost every other nation in sub-Saharan Africa, and people had learned not to be too curious when the fires were still burning. It was better to wait until those who had set the fires had moved out of the area. That was the time to come and steal what hadn't been burned.

Although Betancourt had enjoyed the exercise of the two-day hunt, he saw no reason to waste more time walking back to his compound. "Major Hart," he called out, "send for my chopper."

"Yes, sir."

"And, Major, the exercise isn't over. Keep them tactical all the way back to the compound."

"Yes, sir."

CHAPTER TWO

Uganda

On the flight back to his compound, Grant Betancourt was well pleased with how his troops had performed over the past two days. But then, he had expected little else from them. Every one of them was a veteran of the Israeli army, and the Jews had proved that they knew how to fight. Not all of the men were actual combat veterans, but almost all of them had been under fire at one time or the other. Living in a land where the enemy was all around you was a good training ground for mercenary soldiers.

That was also why he had hired white South Africans to fill most of his cadre officer and NCO positions. They, too, had come through the fire and hadn't been weakened by the liberal crap that passed for modern thinking. In a force composed of militant Jews and South Africans, there would be none of the "all points of view are of equal importance" garbage blinding their thinking when he finally gave them their target.

The Project he had worked so long to create was back on track, and he smiled.

THE MEN WHO MET Betancourt's chopper at the mine's landing pad knew him as a high-level security officer of their parent corporation, and they thought that his name was David Brown. This mining operation wasn't under his BII corporate name. Instead, one of his three-times-removed European cover companies, Wagner Metals Ltd., was the operator of record. The mercenary force he had recruited was in the guise of being the company's security force for the mine. Businessmen who wished to hold on to their investments in that part of Africa had better come equipped with a well-armed security force. If they didn't, they and their investments would soon be bloody history and their bones would bleach in the sun.

"How did the mission go, Mr. Brown?" the manager asked. Of all of the Wagner staff, he was the one who was the most concerned about local unrest because he had the most to lose.

"It went fine," Betancourt said. "That's a very professional force, and I don't think you'll have to worry about a thing here."

The manager knew nothing about Merkov, nor did he know that the tactical exercise had been anything other than another routine training mission. All he wanted to hear was that his mine was well protected.

"Great." The manager beamed. "The home office

will be pleased. The stockholders expressed concerns about local unrest in the last meeting.''

Even with the unprecedented risks of doing business in East Africa, the rewards were also unprecedented for high-tech resource-recovery companies. The Wagner Metals Ltd. operation was remining a played-out chromium mine that had been abandoned years before when turn-of-the-century mining techniques were no longer able to produce usable ore. Modern mining equipment, however, had turned the mine around and the price of chromium had never been higher. If this mine could operate unmolested, everyone who had invested in it would become very wealthy.

The Wagner compound was a fortress ringing the mine head. Built like a Vietnam-era firebase, but with modern security sensors and weapons, it would take a well-armed, brigade-sized attacking force to even get close to the outer wire defenses. To breach the wire, it would require armor.

Betancourt smiled. ''You can tell the investors that their money's safe here.''

The manager returned the smile.

WITH HIS INSPECTION tour of the mine's security force completed, Grant Betancourt took the company chopper to the Ugandan national airport at Entebbe and boarded a business jet licenced to another one of his holding companies. A quick flight across the South Atlantic would land him in the Cayman Islands, where he would take his personal plane back to his BII headquarters in Phoenix, Arizona.

On the long flight, Betancourt updated the plan that he called the Project. After the frustrating debacle of the first incarnation of the Project, turning to mercenaries this time looked to be working and working well. And now that he reflected on the earlier failure, he realized that he should have used the blunt-force mercenary option from the very beginning.

His first plan had been too complicated to provide the depth of the cutouts he had needed to safely distance himself from the action teams. But he should have given greater consideration to the fact that he had been working with flawed materials. The action teams had been composed of men who'd all had strong personal motivations driving them. But they hadn't been professionals, and their thirst for personal revenge hadn't been enough to overcome their lack of experience. In each instance, they had made a good start, but hadn't been able to complete their missions.

He was still trying to put together the details of how and why the first attempt had failed, but the picture still wasn't clear. From what he did know, the nerve-gas attack on the Vatican had been foiled by a visiting Mexican priest, as unlikely as that sounded. In Jerusalem, some kind of radical terrorist group had stopped the neutron-bomb attack right as the weapon was being emplaced. Exactly which of the three religions the attackers belonged to, or why they had acted, he still didn't know. In Mecca, a slight accident with the propane refueling station in the lower levels of the Kaaba had apparently tipped off the Saudi authorities to the danger of using propane-powered equipment.

While frustrating in themselves, these failures had also worked to make the task of trying again even more difficult. The authorities at the three target sites were now at a state of heightened alert, and that was why Betancourt needed professionals like the Israelis and the other two mercenary groups he had hired if he was going to try again.

Even with the setbacks he had suffered, Betancourt was confident that his Project would be successful this time. And for the good of humankind, it desperately needed to be. The planet couldn't survive another thousand years of the same squabbles over what name to call God and how to pray to him. Now that the religiously driven were armed with modern weapons, sectarian fights simply couldn't be allowed to go on anymore, particularly in the Middle East.

The last hundred years had been the most successful century in the entire history of the human race. Humankind had taken a giant leap out of the slime of ignorance and was poised to take the final leap that would allow humanity to fulfill its destiny. But while the age-old forces of darkness had been pushed well into the background, they hadn't been defeated. They stood ready to nullify the unprecedented scientific achievements that had been made in the twentieth century. And for reasons he couldn't even begin to comprehend, they seemed to be getting stronger.

After decades of struggling toward the light, wishful thinking, superstition and religious mumbo jumbo were on the rise again. It was almost as if humankind had a death wish or yearned to live back when people had been barely thinking animals. For the bright light of reason, rationality and science to prevail, the fortress of the darkness had to be defeated once and for all.

Even after the successful destruction of Mecca, the Vatican and Jerusalem as religious centers, there would still be those who would cling to the old antiscientific mind-set. But they would start dying out, and a new generation could be born who wouldn't have their minds warped by ancient lies and mythology.

This quantum leap in human progress would also be made easier because his business empire was poised to move into the Middle East as soon as the blood dried. Once the Jews and the Arabs had finished killing one another, the survivors could be brought into the modern world, and the area's abundant resources, particularly oil, would be made available for the betterment of humankind.

Betancourt believed that if could pull this off, he would go down in history with the other great men ho had fought to bring science and rationality into forefront of human affairs. But he hadn't worked for years and spent a fortune on the Project for his personal fame. He thought of himself as just another foot soldier in the eternal war between good and evil. Just one more man who had found a way to strike a blow against the darkness that had caused so much bloodshed and misery throughout the world for so many years.

Other men had struggled before him, but for many reasons they had lost the fight. The fact that he was one of the richest men in the richest nation in the world gave him a greater chance of success. That his wealth came in large part from defense industries was an additional important factor. So was his longtime friendship with the most powerful man in the world, the President of the United States.

It was true that the President had no idea that his old college buddy was remaking the world. It wasn't the kind of thing that he was known for. At least not yet.

Istanbul, Turkey

MACK BOLAN HATED to leave loose ends hanging; it offended his sense of order in the universe. He was only one man, and he had no illusions that he could bring order to the chaos that was so much a part of human affairs. He could, though, impose his personal code of justice on those parts of the world that he decided to become involved with at any given time. His interest right now was focused on a man who had once gone by the single name of Miller, and that interest had taken him to Istanbul, Turkey. Miller was now calling himself Derek Sanders, but it was the same man and the man was evil.

Bolan had no doubt that his target's current name wasn't any more valid than Miller had been back in L.A. From what little background Aaron Kurtzman and the Stony Man Farm crew had been able to put together for him, this man had used a number of names over the years. But he had always been in the same business. Sanders was an action man for hire. If a person was willing to pay to get something done, he could do it. The thing that made him different from any number of street thugs was that he was a pro and didn't work the nickel-and-dime trade. No matter how much money was offered, petty Mob and drug squabbles or husband-and-wife problems weren't his style.

If, however, a person needed a politician to commit suicide or a rival drug lord to be dragged from his home over the bloodied bodies of his wife and children, Derek Sanders was the man. He also specialized in high-tech penetrations of secure areas, military or civilian, the destabilization of governments, the hostile takeover of industries and anything that had to do with high-grade gemstones.

Bolan didn't yet know what had brought Sanders to Turkey, but he had come to insure that Sanders paid the price for the bodies he had left behind in L.A. One of those dead had been a woman under the Executioner's protection, and she had died trying to help him. Sanders hadn't pulled the trigger himself, but that didn't matter.

The Executioner always squared the accounts when he had given his word.

DEREK SANDERS HAD long ago learned to roll with the punches that came with a life lived to the fullest. Being Grant Betancourt's primary action man had been a damned good job. The pay had been princely, and the work had usually been interesting to him. His last-minute attempts to provide security for the Rainbow Dawn operation in Los Angeles, however, hadn't been one of his better professional moments. He didn't see the failure as being his fault, however. Had he been in charge of that affair from the first, it would have ended differently. As it was, he'd been called in well after the situation had turned to shit. That was never a good position to be in, and that time it had been a first-class disaster.

Not that he cared anything about the death of Roy Givens or any of the rest of his nut job Rainbow Dawn followers. The man had been a simple tool, and he hadn't been up to the task he had been given. Miller didn't bother to wonder why Betancourt had brought in Givens; that wasn't his area. But the man had screwed up big time and had caused a lot of trouble for Miller's employer.

For that failure, Miller had shot him in the back of the head and had left him where he fell.

The worst thing about the fallout from the L.A.

fiasco was that he'd had to drop his long-established Miller persona and take up his life again outside the United States as Derek Sanders. Sanders was a good persona, though, as it came with dual papers.

The Sanders name was on a genuine Canadian passport, but also on a valid U.S. green card. That combination gave him access he might not have had posing only as a U.S. citizen. Everyone loved the Canadians because they weren't seen as posing a threat of any kind to anyone. They were also seen as being antagonistic to the United States and that was also a plus on his current job.

It was a long time since he had been in Istanbul. The last time had been to secure a group of high-grade diamonds that had come out of Iraq. In the aftermath of the Gulf War, the market had been flooded with valuables looted from the war zone. Much of the treasure of the Kuwaiti royal house had ended up in the bazaars of the Old City, and it had been a buyer's market. That last visit had seen him walk away with a fortune, but he'd made enemies doing it, which was why he had stayed away for so long. Now, enemies or not, he was back and he was after something a little more expensive, but still for sale—as everything was in this part of the world.

Istanbul had been a major market city for several thousand years. Founded by Greeks, it had passed first into the hands of the Romans, then the Byzantine Christians, followed by the Muslims and now the Turks. After each conqueror settled in, the buyers and sellers buried their dead, rebuilt their burned and looted stalls and resumed business.

Not everything bought and sold in the city consisted of high-end goods, but treasure of all descriptions had always played large in the history of the Istanbul markets. Today, the definition of treasure had changed and now included what Western politicians and the media loved to call "weapons of mass destruction." Even though the city was in a NATO-aligned nation, its geographical location made it the perfect place for those with nuclear weapons for sale to make their transactions.

The city was also the nexus of far-flung smuggling networks whose history went back as far as the first Greek markets. For the past forty years, drugs had been the smuggler's cargo of choice. But, as lucrative as that trade had been, the collapse of the Soviet Union had created a new king of contraband—military hardware of every description.

Most of the weapons that changed hands were infantry small arms, ammunition, light artillery, the odd tank or two and even a few jet fighters and choppers. The money to be made in this trade was good, usually better than dealing drugs, and the payments were often made in gold or jewels, which could be resold to boost the profit margin even higher. The big money, though, wasn't in slightly used Russian AK-47s or T-72 tanks. The dealer who could get his hands on a Russian tactical-missile nuclear warhead could retire on the profits.

Even though the status of the old Soviet nuclear and chemical arsenal made the headlines in the West every month or so, hundreds of portable missile warheads weren't accounted for. And many of them were in the hands of nationalists in breakaway former Soviet republics who didn't have any real use for them. Tribal warfare didn't lend itself to the deployment of nuclear weapons.

They were, however, a very good means of raising needed funds for other projects. And that's where Derek Sanders came in. He was a buyer with ready cash.

CHAPTER THREE

Stony Man Farm, Virginia

The violent but very satisfactory Stony Man conclusion to the Rainbow Dawn plot to destroy Jerusalem, Mecca and the Vatican hadn't settled the matter in Aaron Kurtzman's mind. Even though most of the men involved were dead and their weapons of mass destruction had been rendered harmless, that wasn't the last of it for him.

Like Hal Brognola, he, too, was certain that the wealthy industrialist Grant Betancourt had been the single driving force behind that atrocity. But, unlike most of the situations that he investigated, the perp's bloody fingerprints weren't all over the evidence this time.

In this case, everything that had survived the Stony Man solution pointed to the late Roy Givens of the now defunct Rainbow Dawn New Age cult in Los Angeles as having been the brains behind this outrage to the world's three most prominent religions. And with Givens dead, there was no way that obvious assumption could be disproved. As far as the media and the President were concerned, the case was closed, but that didn't sit too well with Kurtzman.

The main thing that tied Betancourt to these attacks was the fact that he had put up the money to fund the three UN-sponsored cultural projects that had been used as cover for the plotters. But, as the man himself had explained, he was a well-known philanthropist who spent millions on worthy causes. When he had been approached by the UN and asked to contribute to the World Heritage Commission, he had agreed to fund it. He claimed to have had no input as to who had been hired with that money, and the UN backed him up on that claim.

There was also the small matter of the security firm Roy Givens had hired to protect his L.A. Rainbow Dawn headquarters. It turned out that Security Plus was one of Betancourt's many BII subsidiary companies, but it was a matter of record that the request for their services had come directly from Givens himself. Again, on the surface it looked as if the big man was clear there, too. But that was only on the surface. Any fool could dummy up a letter with Givens's signature on it and put it in the files of Security Plus.

The truth, if it was out there, would only be found in cyberspace, and that's where Kurtzman was looking.

His attempt to penetrate Betancourt's computer security systems was turning into a mainframe-versus-mainframe cyber battle in the invisible realm of cryptotechnology. Or in layman's terms, the guy with the bigger number cruncher was going to win this one. Kurtzman's new hardware in the Annex included some of the most advanced mainframe computers in existence. But in the warped world of cyberspace, that didn't necessarily mean much.

Computer technology didn't march to the beat of the same calendar as did the rest of the technological world. A single programming advance could make "currently in existence" instantly obsolete. While that was true for every aspect of the cyber world, it was doubly true for computer security systems. Confounding the problem was the fact that another one of Betancourt's subsidiary companies on contract to the federal government was the creator of the highest-level cyber security programs that had ever existed.

Every U.S. government agency from the Atomic Energy Commission to NASA and the military used Betancourt's crypto systems to guard their cyber information. The upside of that was that in an age of international cyberspace espionage, what America needed to keep secret was being properly safeguarded. The downside was that to the man who owned the codes, as Betancourt did, they weren't really secrets.

Cracking cyber crypto systems was one of Kurtzman's favorite pastimes. Anytime he needed a break from the mind-dulling routines of Stony Man Farm, he would play with secret computer codes the way most people worked the Sunday crossword puzzles.

Attempting to crack Betancourt's codes, though, wasn't just fun and games for him. Kurtzman was deadly serious about it. But, after having been able to crack into the Rainbow Dawn's systems, he wasn't making much progress with the real threat.

While Kurtzman had been totally absorbed in the BII cyber code problem, Hunt Wethers and Akira Tokaido were minding the store. The best thing about their new Annex facility was that taking care of business was so much easier now. The new equipment gave them what computer geeks always wanted from their electronic toys—bigger, better, faster.

Wethers was working on the weekly terrorist update when he ran across a report from a deep-cover Israeli agent in the Islamic Brotherhood's action arm, the Sword of God. He reported that someone was trying to recruit mercenaries from the smaller Islamic radical groups. The agent ended by saying that he was going to try to volunteer for this force and would report more later.

Wethers bookmarked that report for several reasons. One was that the Brotherhood's long history of terrorist violence made it essential that Stony Man knew what it was doing. The second was that this report of mercenary recruitment tied in closely with two more such recent reports. Mercenaries had long been a fact of life in the trouble spots of the world, but the decade of the nineties had seen a dramatic drop at least in non-Islamic soldiers-for-hire.

To have mercenary activity on the rise again didn't

make sense to him. But all that meant was that he didn't know enough about what was going on. And being a naturally curious and very methodical man, he didn't like to be in the dark on anything.

HAL BROGNOLA WASN'T flying down to the Farm three times a week because he was tired of the view from the window of his D.C. Justice Department Building office and wanted to rest his eyes on the rural vistas of the Shenandoah Valley. It was true that Washington had long since lost its charm for him. But while he had seen it all, far too many times, he had a reason for taking the time out of his schedule to make the ninety-mile chopper flight three times a week. He was tracking what he felt was one of the most serious threats to the United States that he had seen in years.

Unlike most of the threats the leader of the Sensitive Operations Group targeted, this man wasn't hidden; he was out in plain sight. In fact, when Brognola had left Washington less than an hour earlier, the target had been in the Oval Office talking to his good friend, the President of the United States. From there, he was scheduled to go to the Senate chambers to testify in front of the Armed Forces Committee about the new antiballistic-missile defense system one of his companies was working on. And that was why Brognola hadn't simply ordered Grant Betancourt taken out.

This threat wasn't only the President's old college

roommate and an old hand in the halls of the Capitol; Betancourt was one of the wealthiest men in the nation. Along with the electronics companies that had gotten him started, he headed the largest defense-industry conglomerate in the Western World. There was hardly anything in the American military inventory that didn't have Betancourt's BII logo on it somewhere. If not on the final product, at least on the components.

Even if you were the head of the nation's most clandestine strike force, you had to move carefully against a man who walked a trail like that.

As BROGNOLA'S PILOT FLARED out to land on Stony Man Farm's chopper pad, he saw Barbara Price waiting for him. As the Farm's mission controller, she was his right-hand woman. He could disappear in a puff of smoke and he'd never be missed. She would just keep doing what she did, and SOG would continue to soldier on. If she suddenly dropped out of sight, however, things would start coming unglued real fast.

When Brognola stepped out of the chopper, Price saw that he was starting to show the wear and tear of his commuting schedule. But he didn't yet have the grim set to his jaw that came with bad news.

"Isn't this getting a little old, Hal?" she asked. "You're wearing yourself out."

"It is a bit wearing," he admitted, "but this is the

only way that I can keep close enough to the investigation.''

"You don't have to fly down here to do that," she said. "We can send you hourly updates if you want."

"I need the flight time." He smiled. "When I get enough federal frequent-flyer miles, I'm going to book myself onto the space shuttle. You know, do a week in space station Freedom, relax, float around in zero grav, drink a little Russian vodka with my orange juice."

"'Fed in Space,'" she said, laughing. "I love it."

"Besides," he said, turning serious, "a fax printout just isn't the same. I need to see the raw data on the Bear's screen and watch him working on it. It's the feel I need more than the polished information."

Price understood that. Reading the conclusions on a hard copy was bloodless in that it didn't convey the undeveloped hunches and leaps of faith that went into the final intelligence product.

"Have you had any lunch?" she asked as they walked to the farmhouse door. "I can have the cook whip up something for you."

He glanced at his watch. "I don't have much time, but maybe a sandwich."

"Roast beef on sourdough with light Dijon, no horseradish, no onions, right?"

He smiled wistfully. "I used to love horseradish. And onions. Someday I'm going to take three days off and eat all the onions I can stand."

"Let me know when you're planning on doing that. I want to be out of town that week."

"That's okay, because I'll be spending two of those three days in a hospital getting a stomach transplant."

Price laughed. It was nice to see Brognola in a better mood for a change.

INSIDE THE FARMHOUSE, Price led Brognola downstairs to the old Computer Room to take the tram to the Annex. Although the War Room had been preserved in the old farmhouse, Brognola liked to conduct his informal visits on-site in the new Computer Room. He still couldn't get over the new facility. The lights and the spacious surroundings were so alien to what the Farm had been for so long.

An informal briefing room had been set up around the common coffeepot where they all could sit, have a cup of coffee and go over the latest information. After grabbing a clean cup, he headed for it.

"All I have to report," Hunt Wethers started off, "is that we've come up with yet another mercenary unit apparently being formed."

"Where is it this time?" Brognola asked.

"Uganda, and they're being recruited from militant West Bank Israelis to guard a mine site."

When Brognola frowned, Kurtzman broke in. "That's not as odd as is seems," he said. "The Ugandans and the Jewish people go way back. The Entebbe raid kind of strained relations for some time, but that's over now. There's a European-backed mining operation starting up there. The Israelis make good soldiers, and the Ugandan warlords trust them."

"But don't the Israelis have antimercenary laws on the books like we do to keep a handle on that kind of thing?" Brognola asked.

Kurtzman laughed. "When has that ever stopped a young man with a yen to see the world and shoot people? Plus, with the land giveback that's in the mill for the West Bank, there's a lot of angry young Israelis right now. They've lost their homes and don't want to have to fight their own people to get them back. It's easier to go somewhere else and take it out on foreigners."

"Nonetheless," Wethers said, "that's three mercenary units that are being formed at the same time, and except for guarding the mine in Uganda, I can't find that many trouble spots that need those kind of troops. And that's saying nothing about people who can afford to hire and outfit them."

"How about the breakaway Islamic republics?"

"They've got the cause, but they don't have the money to hire formal mercenary units. Plus, they get enough recruits who'll sign on for a holy war and will fight for their daily issue of food and ammunition."

Brognola consulted his laptop. "What's the status on that so-called Army of the Lord group in the Caribbean you came up with?"

"That's another odd one," Wethers said. "The

FBI and ATF are all over them, but they're not coming up with anything more than they usually do when they try to infiltrate the Christian militias. Beyond that first report, as skimpy as it was, there hasn't been much more that we've been able to get on them. All we know is that some well-known figures from the militant right have vanished from their usual haunts.

"And," Wethers added, tapping his briefing paper, "I'm not talking about the militia blowhards and the rabble-rousers you see on the TV news exposé shows. From what we know, these are mostly younger men with military backgrounds who ran into trouble when they were in the service. You know, the sexual-harassment or racial thing more than criminal activities. Some of them have been connected to known militant organizations, but others have been loners."

"You have IDed their camp, right?"

"Right," Wethers replied. "It's in Costa Rica."

"Do we have oversight on it?"

"Not yet," Wethers replied.

"Don't make a project of it," Brognola said. "But I guess it wouldn't hurt for us to know what they're doing down there. They can't be up to any good."

"That's a fact," Kurtzman broke in. Even though the advent of Y2K had mostly been a nonevent in the United States, there was still a core of millennialists who refused to give up their dreams of the apocalypse. "Anytime I hear about something like that, it always gets under my skin."

Brognola knew better than to disregard one of

Kurtzman's hunches. The exposure of the Rainbow Dawn millennialist plot had been largely the result of one of his hunches about the same kind of group. No one, not even him, though, had expected what that hunch would turn into.

"What do you think we ought to do about them?"

"As you well know," Kurtzman said, shrugging, "the problem is the old church-and-state number. As long as they don't start playing with bombs, whatever they're doing is off limits to us. But I think that we do need to know what they're doing. It's one thing if that Costa Rican camp is a big tent meeting where they're just trying to get closer to Jesus. But if they're planning to praise the Lord on full-auto, we need to know about it.

"Either way," Kurtzman continued, "at least we need to try to find out who's paying the bills. That sort of thing doesn't come cheap."

"You're thinking Betancourt?"

"Even though I can't prove it yet, I still believe that he fronted Rainbow Dawn. And if he was willing to pay that bunch of fruitcakes to further his plans, he might be playing that card again. But this time he's doing it in a country that won't ask questions as long as he makes the right payments, if you know what I mean. And the money means less than nothing to that guy."

Brognola turned to Price. "What's Phoenix Force doing right now?"

"Not much," she answered. "What do you have in mind?"

"See if T.J. wants to join the Army of the Lord," Brognola suggested. "He's got the right skin color and the proper background to blend right in with a Bible-thumping militia."

"T.J. might want to play," she said. "I'll call David and give him a briefing."

"Remember that it's just a recon. You know we have to walk lightly around the religious groups, the Constitution and all of that."

"Until we find them building bombs," Kurtzman added.

"But we have to find the bombs first."

CHAPTER FOUR

Istanbul, Turkey

One of Istanbul's largest tourist draws was the glittering Grand Bazaar. Spread over acres of the ancient city, it was the place to buy any of the ten thousand trinkets that visitors loved to lug home and show off as trophies. It had also been the backdrop to dozens of thriller novels and movies of sexy spies and international intrigue. Nonetheless, Bolan knew that despite the crush of buyers and sellers, the real action in Istanbul didn't take place in the stalls and alleys of the Grand Bazaar.

His objective today was a couple of blocks away in a dark, dingy rat's warren that hadn't changed much over the past thousand years. Known to the locals as the Thieves Market, this was where he hoped to make contact with the man he had come halfway around the world to talk to.

Even so, he knew that he wouldn't find a cramped stall in the Thieves Market full of Russian tactical nuclear warheads hidden among the well-worn, handwoven rugs and dusty, dented brass pots. That wasn't the way that the big-ticket items were handled in places like this. As with the other high-quality goods on sale, they would be safeguarded elsewhere. He was just looking for the initial contact man.

If he could pass muster with that man, he would then be handed off to another, and possibly several more, middlemen until he reached the man who actually had the goods in his possession. Every step of the journey from this shabby market to the final destination, would be a minefield, and Bolan would have to tread carefully. But along the way, he expected to find traces of Derek Sanders, if not the man himself.

The man he was looking for today went by the single name of Mustapha. Since that name was as common in Turkey as Bob was in the States, this Mustapha was nicknamed "the Black". Bolan didn't know if that was for his hair and eyes, though most Turks had dark hair and eyes, or for his mood. As with the rest of this plan, he would have to stay loose, wait and see.

Bolan had walked some of the most dangerous ground on Earth in his long career, some of it ground that no one else had ever walked. But every time he entered this half-lit realm of ancient intrigue, he felt danger. The treasures of many crushed and sacked empires had passed through this rat's warren in the past two-thousand-plus years, and the transactions hadn't all been peaceful. If all the blood that had been spilled onto these stones could speak, it would tell tales of greed, murder and plunder on a grand scale.

Even in modern-day Istanbul, it could be worth a man's life to make a misstep in this place. A wrong word to the wrong person could result in a slashed throat and one more body sinking to the bottom of the Bosporus. Though the Turks in general were a generous, warm, hospitable people, the inhabitants of this place had no loyalties except to one another. Here, a stranger always remained a stranger, but that didn't bother Bolan. He was always a stranger no matter where he went, but it did make him cautious.

His information was that Mustapha the Black kept a stall deep inside the market. That was smart, as it would give him early warning of anyone who might be looking for him with evil intent. Were a stranger to make an inquiry, he would know of it almost immediately and could decide whether he wanted to be found. To activate the primitive early-warning system, Bolan stopped at the first stall he came to and asked for directions.

Even after getting a verbal map, it took him fifteen minutes to navigate the twists and turns to reach his destination. A man was standing outside the stall he had been told to find, but if he was Mustapha the Black, his nickname was a cruel joke. His hair and most of the skin of his face was a dead-fish-belly white.

When he got closer, Bolan saw that the discoloration was from the kind of burn scars that resulted from a gasoline explosion. Molotov cocktails were a common way to resolve disputes in this part of the world, and Bolan could well believe that this man had made an enemy or two in his life. Mustapha was a big man, bigger than Bolan, and in Turkey, big men had to fight to keep what was theirs. If they didn't, they soon lost it.

THE MAN WATCHED Bolan as he approached. "My name is Mike Belasko," he said, "and I am looking for Mustapha the Black."

"At your service." The Turk sketched a bow. "What may I do for you?"

"May we speak privately?" Bolan eyed the interior of the stall.

"Certainly." The Turk motioned for Bolan to enter and take a seat.

"Now," Mustapha said as he seated himself across from his guest, "how may I help you?"

"I'm in the market for a certain item of Russian manufacture."

"And that would be?"

Bolan locked eyes with the Turk and said, "It's called an RD-45, and it fits on the top of an SS-10 tactical missile. I've been told that you can help me."

Mustapha didn't quite know what to make of this tall, blue-eyed man with black hair. That he was a warrior wasn't in doubt; his eyes told that much. They were watchful—and who wouldn't be in the Thieves Market—but they were confident. That confidence was also evident in the man's bearing. He had walked in danger before many times. This time, though, he was treading more than a dangerous path. He was starting down a one-way road to an unmarked grave.

"You talk of dangerous things," the Turk said. "I am not a coward, but I would be afraid to speak of such things myself. The wrong people might overhear, and they would think that I am a terrorist. I am sorry, sir, but I cannot help you."

Bolan looked to the side to scan the other stalls. "Is there another Mustapha the Black in here?" he asked. "I was told that I would meet a real man by that name, not a timid shopkeeper."

Bolan's studied insult didn't strike home. Mustapha knew that he was being tested, as he had just tested the stranger. His estimation of this Belasko went up considerably. It took courage to tell a Turk that he wasn't a man. Usually, that comment called for blood to be spilled.

Mustapha laughed to defuse the situation. "My women think that I am man enough, American. But they also know that I am not foolish."

When Bolan didn't reply, the Turk continued. "You know, maybe I underestimated you. Maybe I thought that you were one of those Jews or even a UN man. They come in here sniffing like dogs after bitches in heat hoping to find a big bomb. Them I usually send to meet with the police informers so they can tell their tales to them."

Mustapha shrugged his massive shoulders. "The ones who do not leave me alone? Well, they go away, too. But not to a place as comfortable as the jails."

"No wonder you're so poor." Bolan looked around the sizable but shabby stall. "You're getting too old to know who your real customers are. Maybe you have a smart, ill-favored daughter who could run your business for you?"

"Be careful, English," the Turk snapped. "We Turks do not like outsiders to talk about our women."

"My mistake." Bolan's blue eyes stared down his host. "My information was that you were a Gypsy."

It was true that Mustapha's great-great-grandfather on his mother's side had married a Gypsy. But she had brought a dowry worth a king's ransom, and there was no dishonor in that. There had also been pleasure in the match, as the girl had been a renowned beauty. Even so, that fact was known to few, so it served as a password. But even after hearing that, Mustapha didn't let his guard down.

"If I were a Gypsy," Mustapha said, "I would meet my customers in the dark."

"Since Gypsies often sell things that aren't approved by the government, that is probably a wise precaution," Bolan agreed.

"Do you know the old Hippodrome?" the Turk asked.

Bolan nodded. The old horse-racing track was one of the few landmarks left over from Byzantine times.

No one raced there anymore, and it was now a popular public park.

"I'm told that the Gypsies meet there at night."

"What time?"

"Call it after ten."

Bolan got to his feet. "I guess that I'll look for my man there then. God be with you."

"And with you," Mustapha answered.

THE TURKISH arms dealer watched Belasko walk away. It was odd that an American was using what sounded like a Russian name. But, as he knew well, it wasn't the man's real name. His instincts told him that he would have to be very careful with this one and should probably have him killed immediately just to be safe. But another part of him saw the stranger as a real man, and there were few real men left in the world. Even in Turkey.

He sighed as he pulled out his cell phone. He would set up the meeting, but he would also have enough men on hand to take care of this Belasko if a threat materialized.

BOLAN ARRIVED at the meeting place at nine. Only a complete fool would walk into the park without making a recon. As he had expected, Mustapha had put out a man to guard the area. The Turk was wearing unremarkable civilian clothing and had no weapon that Bolan could see. He was doing a poor imitation of a man taking an evening stroll in the park and checking all the good ambush positions in the shrubs.

As the meeting hour approached, Bolan saw the man answer his cell phone. He didn't have to speak Turkish to know that the guard had reported that everything was quiet. That was the signal for Bolan to make his move.

The takedown went smoothly. Bolan let the man walk past him before springing out and slamming the blunt pommel of his Tanto fighting knife behind the sentry's right ear. Stunned, the man slumped to the ground.

Bolan slapped a set of plastic riot cuffs on the man's hands and feet, and a strip of duct tape over his mouth secured his silence. After dragging his prisoner back into the shadows, Bolan made sure that he was comfortable before he left him. He might have to work with these people later and didn't want to make an enemy.

Back in his ambush position, Bolan didn't have to wait long for the curtain to rise on the main act. If nothing else, Mustapha was punctual; there was no missing the swatch of white hair. The Turk walked down the path to the cleared circle without bothering to look around. His men were surrounding the park, and his sentry had just given him the all clear.

In a flash, Bolan had Mustapha in a headlock and the chisel tip of his Tanto fighting knife pressing into the arms dealer's jugular vein. Feeling the knife, the

Turk didn't even try to struggle as Bolan backed up to a tree using him as a shield.

"You should have sent that smart daughter, Mustapha," Bolan whispered in his ear. "I don't think she would have walked into a trap."

"Tell your people to come out where I can see them," Bolan told him. "They're to put their weapons in a pile and back away from them. I don't need to tell you what will happen if even one of them decides to try to play the hero. You won't be alive to reward him."

With the razor-sharp point of the knife poised to rip his throat open, Mustapha had no choice but to obey.

"My sons," he called out in Turkish, "the American has me. Come out and put your weapons down and be very careful about it. This one is serious."

Eight men materialized from the underbrush, being careful not to make any sudden moves. They laid a variety of pistols on the ground and backed away from them.

"Now tell them to go away while the men talk business," Bolan said.

Again Mustapha gave his orders in Turkish, and his men started down the gravel paths out of the park.

"One of your men doesn't obey well," Bolan said as he slowly turned to keep the Turk between him and a particularly dark patch of shrubbery. "Tell him to come out slowly and with both hands in the air."

Mustapha sighed. "That is not one of my men,"

he said. "That is that 'smart daughter' of mine you have insisted on speaking of. I am afraid that she has taken a strong dislike to you because of it."

"Explain to her that I don't make war on women, but I also don't allow them to become involved in my business."

"Tell her yourself," Mustapha said. "She speaks better English than I do. And—" he shrugged carefully "—if you want to deal with me, you will have to deal with her, too. She owns half of the family business."

A slight figure in a black combat suit walked into the open. She, too, held her hands out in plain sight as she walked up.

"Careful, daughter," Mustapha said in Turkish. "His knife is sharp."

"I hear that you find me ill-favored," she said in slightly British-accented English as she slowly reached up to her face cloth. "I have never heard that said of me before."

When the woman dropped the veil, Bolan saw that she was far from ill-favored. What he had intended as a goading insult to keep the Turk off balance had been well off the mark. Her hair was copper-red, and her eyes a deep green. Even in her baggy black combat suit, he could see that she moved with well-trained grace.

This was an Amazon warrior, and he had better put an end to this before someone got hurt.

"My sincerest apologies," he said. "But your

beauty doesn't keep me from seeing that you're still armed. If you tried to use the knife in your sleeve, it would pain me greatly to have to kill you, but I would.''

"Put it down, Yasmine," Mustapha said in English. "Do not fool with this man."

"What do we do now?" she asked.

"What we do now," Bolan said as he withdrew his knife and released Mustapha, "is act like honorable men and women who are conducting business. I came here hoping to buy information, but I was set upon by thieves."

"We are not thieves," the woman snapped. "Men come to my father all the time trying to implicate him in the trade of nuclear weapons. We have to protect ourselves."

"She is right, Mr. Belasko," Mustapha said, rubbing the small spot of blood on his neck. "This is a dangerous time for a man like me. Everyone thinks that because I sell weapons I would traffic in such things." He spit on the ground.

"I do not care if men kill one another," the Turk said. "That is the way the world should be. But I draw the line at weapons that are used to destroy cities and kill women and children. I once bought a Russian missile warhead, yes. But I bought it to keep it out of the hands of fanatics. I also sent it back to the Russians with a note telling them that they should be more careful with their goods."

Bolan smiled. He had heard that story but hadn't

known that this was the man who had done that. The crate had been addressed to the RSV headquarters on Lubinka Street in Moscow and had been flown there on an Aeroflot jet liner. When the crate had been opened, a full-blown panic had ensued.

"So to answer your question. No, I do not sell such things. And I will not put you in contact with those who do. Kill me if you must, but I will not help you."

"But you know who they are?" Bolan asked.

"I know many things."

"Good, maybe you can still help me, then. What I really want to find is a man named Derek Sanders. He's the one who wants to buy the warheads."

Mustapha glanced at his daughter. "I did not know that he was back in Turkey."

"You know him?" Bolan asked.

"Yes, we do," Yasmine answered for her father. "We once had dealings with him."

"I take it they weren't satisfactory."

"I was kidnapped to insure delivery of his purchase at his offered price."

"I take it that his offered price wasn't the original asking price."

"Not quite."

"What is your business with Sanders?" Mustapha asked.

"If possible, to question him." Bolan met his eyes squarely. "If not, I'll kill him."

"Please come to my house, Mr. Belasko," the Turk said. "I think we can talk business after all."

CHAPTER FIVE

Stony Man Farm, Virginia

Barbara Price hadn't failed to notice that Hal Brognola hadn't mentioned Mack Bolan in their meeting, nor had he even asked about him as he usually did. Considering how far back those two went, it was a bit surprising. Unless, of course, the big Fed and the Executioner were working an operation on their own again.

She knew that Brognola was very concerned with the fact that it looked as if his nemesis Grant Betancourt had the President in his hip pocket. And while the Man had learned the hard way to hold what he knew about SOG missions very close to his vest, this was a special case. Brognola had taken the risk and had pushed the envelope when he sent Phoenix Force and Able Team to interrupt Betancourt's Armageddon attacks on Jerusalem, Mecca and the Vatican without Oval Office sanction.

He had gotten away with it so far. But in the

quickly shifting sands that were the arena of clandestine operations, that was always subject to change.

Knowing both Bolan and Brognola as well as she did, she knew that there was a good chance that the two of them had something cooking. Normally when they went hunting together, Brognola filled her in FYI if nothing else. That way she'd know not to figure Bolan into her mission planning. But, if those two did have something in the fire, she knew who was stoking the flames.

WHEN PRICE WALKED up to Kurtzman's workstation in the Annex, the man was busy as always and completely oblivious to everything else going on around him.

"Aaron?" she said.

He glanced up. "Hi, Barb. What's up?"

"Did you assemble that information Hal asked you to get for Striker?" she asked him.

"You mean that info on Miller?" Kurtzman automatically replied before wheeling his chair around to look at her.

"Gotcha," she said.

"Oh, shit." He looked stricken. "Hal's going to kill me."

"What's going on, Aaron," she asked, "and why don't I know about it?"

"He's having Striker take care of a loose end for him and he doesn't want us involved."

"Because…?" she prompted him.

"Because he's afraid that Betancourt's going to penetrate us through the Oval Office."

"It's that bad?"

"He thinks it is. He even talked to Buck Greene about getting us ready to go into a security lockdown."

That bit of information infuriated Price. "Did he mention why he didn't think that I wasn't a big enough girl to be told about this? I'm either the mission controller around here or I'm not, and I'm not going to have some—"

"Barb," Kurtzman interrupted her, "it's not like that at all."

"Tell me what it's like, then."

"He's trying to protect you," he said, "and all of the rest of the Farm crew at the same time. Only Buck and I know what he has going down because we volunteered to be expendable."

"But that's insane," she said.

"He's afraid that if Betancourt gets a hint of us, he'll manufacture some kind of federal investigation and blow us out of the water."

Price frowned. "Surely the Man wouldn't let something like that happen."

"What if Betancourt leaked us to a Senate Committee or something like that?" Kurtzman replied. "He could put the word out to the bleeding-heart media crowd and create quite an uproar. We work for the Man, but don't forget that, first last and always, he's a politician. He has to think of his 'legacy' and all the rest of that crap.''

She snorted. '''Legacy' is just a fancy word for covering his fat, lily-white ass.''

"It is," he agreed. "But that doesn't mean that he won't turn on us if he starts getting pressure from Congress and the media. Something like this could easily turn into impeachment material. The President running his own little strike force without the knowledge or consent of Congress, *yada, yada, yada.* Shades of Nixon's plumbers and all that. You know how the liberals will make it sound. He'll be compared to Hitler with us playing the role of the SS.

"That's why Hal's trying to protect you," Kurtzman went on. "If Mack can pull off his mission, we should be able to shut down Betancourt once and for all."

"What's the plan?"

Kurtzman sighed. He'd warned Brognola that they wouldn't be able to keep this a secret from her. They had worked together far too long.

"Striker's in Turkey on the track of a man named Derek Sanders," he said. "When the target was connected with Rainbow Dawn, he went by the single name of Miller, and Betancourt had sent him to L.A. to be Givens's security chief. When they tagged the bodies after Striker finished clearing the Dawners' building, he wasn't among the dead. It looks now as if he was behind the death of both the senator and his daughter.''

"How the hell did he get to Turkey?"

"That's the easy part," Kurtzman said. "He just switched passports. We think that he's trying to make contact with the arms dealers in the region who have access to what the press loves to call 'weapons of mass destruction,' specifically a couple of nuke warheads."

"Betancourt's going to try it again, isn't he?"

"That's what Hal thinks."

She got a faraway look on her face. "It's never going to end, is it?"

"A lot of that's up to Striker."

That, too, was something she was very familiar with. Some day, some time, Mack Bolan wouldn't be able to do what had to be done. What would happen then she had no idea, and she wasn't sure that she wanted to know.

"You'll keep me informed, won't you?"

Kurtzman grimaced. "Okay."

WHEN THE MOTORBOAT carrying T. J. Hawkins rounded the end of the cove and headed for the beach, he thought that he'd been sent to Club Med instead of a mercenary training camp. The sand was white enough to star in a cruise-line commercial, and the palm-leaf roofs on the white-washed buildings were pure travel-brochure material. The two watchtowers with sandbagged platforms on top at either end of the beach weren't anything he'd ever seen in a Club Med pamphlet, but maybe they were for the evening light show.

It was only when he got closer that he saw the figures moving around the compound were wearing camouflage uniforms and some of them were carrying weapons slung over their shoulders. But, beyond that, nothing betrayed the military nature of the camp.

When the boat tied up to the dock, a squad of six men in OD T-shirts and camou pants double timed up the dock. They were led by a man who looked every inch a battle-hardened mercenary from a Hollywood movie. He was in his early forties, but was more than health-club fit. He wore a buzz cut, and his faded blue eyes had the look you had to earn by being there and doing that.

The mercenary stared at the new recruits for a few seconds. "Fall in," he said.

Hawkins and three of his four traveling companions immediately got into a line on the dock, standing motionless at the position of attention an arm's distance apart. The fourth man looked around for his cue before posting himself at the end of the line.

The mercenary immediately zoomed in on him for the mandatory introduction-to-hell scene so familiar from every foreign legion and Marine Corps movie.

"You look lost, boy," the merc said, his face an inch away from the recruit's. "Are you sure you belong here and not at a Boy Scout camp?"

"No, sir," the man had the presence of mind to say. "I belong here."

"What's your name?"

"Ah...Bob," the recruit said. "Bob Gratton."

"Well, Bob, where are you from?"

"Lawrence, Kansas."

"The only thing that comes from Kansas are steers and queers, and I don't see any horns on you, boy."

Hawkins kept his head and eyes locked on the horizon throughout the entire tirade. He'd been there, done that, far too many times to get sucked in. He was playing a veteran who knew the score, and veterans knew not to interrupt the sergeant when he was in full rant.

After ragging on Gratton for a few more minutes, the mercenary slowly walked down the line and stopped in front of Hawkins. "Name?" he snapped.

"Burton," Hawkins answered, keeping his eyes locked straight ahead. "W.L."

"You've done this before, Burton," the mercenary said.

"Yes, sir, I have."

"What was your rank?"

"Staff sergeant."

"I'm the only sergeant here, so you're a private now."

"Yes, sir."

"Move these people to Building D for processing."

"Yes, sir."

Hawkins took one step forward, faced right and commanded, "Right face. Forward march."

Again three of the four recruits executed the command perfectly and marched off. The fourth man had to look around before following the rest.

As Hawkins marched his men down the dock, he could feel the mercenary's eyes on his back. This wasn't a good start to this exercise, and he would have to be careful.

BUILDING D WAS the headquarters and supply room for the camp. It looked, however, like the rest of the buildings, a slightly tawdry Club Med look-alike. Hawkins was sure that this had once been a beach resort before the corporations moved into the resort business and lured the customers away from the smaller operators. The processing of the mandatory paperwork went quickly. The recruits signed labor contracts made out to a company called Sunshine Distributors and filled out insurance forms. After these few formalities were over, Hawkins took his impromptu squad around to the back of the building to draw their equipment.

Hawkins was somewhat surprised when the clothing and equipment he was issued turned out to be brand-new current U.S.-issue BDUs, jungle boots and field gear. All of the tags had been removed, but he had worn the same gear when he was in the Army.

"When do we get our guns?" the awkward recruit asked.

The supply man looked at him and smiled, but there was no kindness in it. "When you earn them."

When everyone had stuffed his gear into his duffel bag, another mercenary showed up to take them to their new quarters. The barracks huts were summer-camp-style and big enough to accommodate twenty men, but only half of the bunks were made up.

"Find a place to park," their guide said, "and get your gear squared away. Evening formation's at 1800 hours, chow's at 1830."

"What's the exact time now?" Hawkins asked.

"The mercenary glanced down at his watch, "It's 1538."

Hawkins adjusted his watch. "Thanks."

As Hawkins stowed his new issue away in his foot locker and made up his bunk Ranger style, the awkward recruit walked up to him.

"Hi," the man said, putting out his hand. "I'm Bob Gratton."

Hawkins shook his hand. "Burton."

"What do they call you at home?" Gratton asked.

Hawkins smiled. "Those who don't call me shithead, call me Dub."

"Dub?" Gratton pressed. "What's that short for?"

"*W*, my first name."

Seeing that he was getting nowhere with that line of questioning, Gratton changed tactics.

"This sure isn't what I'd expected it would be," he said. "I mean you never see anything like this in movies."

"What kind of thing?"

"This camp. It's like some kind of posh resort, not an Army camp."

"Maybe that's because this ain't the Army," Hawkins offered.

"That sergeant, or whoever he was, sure seems to think it is. Man, I don't know what his problem is."

Hawkins knew exactly what the mercenary's "problem" was, but he wasn't about to waste his time trying to enlighten this guy. It was becoming readily apparent that whoever this Bob Gratton really was, he was a ringer. More than likely he was FBI and a young agent with very little field experience at that. There was no way that he'd be able to save the man without risking his life, so he wasn't even going to try. He was going to be busy enough covering his own ass to have time to cover anyone else's.

"Maybe he didn't have enough coffee this morning."

"Man—" Gratton shook his head "—he sure missed something. I'm really going to have to watch myself around him, that's for sure."

Hawkins gave him twenty-four hours, max.

AFTER GETTING his gear squared away, Hawkins dressed in a set of BDUs, jungle boots and floppy jungle hat. He debated wearing the field belt over his jacket, but decided to wait to see what the uniform of the day was around here. It was part of the IQ test that was being given here, and he didn't want to fail it.

In his line of work, life was a constant IQ test. And unlike life in the civilian world, there were no prizes awarded for second place in this business. If he screwed up, he'd simply be shoved into an unmarked jungle grave. Whoever was behind this mercenary force wasn't about to let anyone go free once he had seen what was going on.

He was on the parade ground five minutes before the scheduled formation. The other men started arriving shortly thereafter. At precisely 1800, the mercenary sergeant who had met him at the dock took his position and called the formation to attention. Bringing up his clipboard, he started calling the roll.

"Adams."

"Yo."

"Baker."

"Here."

"Burton."

"Here," Hawkins answered.

When Gratton's name was called out, Hawkins heard the recruit answer as he ran to make the formation. The sergeant didn't pause in calling out the names.

When everyone was accounted for, the sergeant gave his announcements. "Tomorrow's training schedule has been posted," he said. "Read it. A beer ration will be available tonight. Dismissed."

As the formation broke up, the sergeant zeroed in on the hapless recruit. "Do you have a watch, Gratton?"

"Yes, sir," Gratton answered.

"Then I suggest that you use it. This is your last warning."

"Yes, sir."

WITH CHOW AT 1830, Hawkins was at loose ends until then, so he took a quick walking tour of the camp. Beyond the two towers on each end of the beach, there were no defensive positions. The camp, however, had everything one would expect to find in a battalion firebase. Along with the headquarters and barrack buildings, there was a latrine and shower building, an aid station, a radio shack and the mess hall that he was sure doubled as the club for off-duty pastimes. The only thing that seemed out of place was the chapel with the whitewashed cross on top of a small spire.

The layout was military, but the location on the beach still gave it the Club Med feel Gratton had commented on. He would have to meet the rest of the men and take a look at the quality of the weapons and the training program before he could assess how big a threat this unit posed. If there were too many men in the unit like Gratton, however, he'd have a hard time taking this seriously.

If, however, Gratton disappeared, that would tell him something else.

CHAPTER SIX

Istanbul, Turkey

Mustapha's house was in an expensive quarter of the European side of the sprawling city. It didn't look like much from the outside, but when Bolan was invited in, he found that it was palatial on a small scale. That was an ancient tradition in Istanbul—look poor to the outside world so as to not incite envy and be very careful who you invite into your home.

As was the custom anywhere in the Middle East, once they were inside the house, Mustapha's daughter disappeared and refreshments for the guest were the first order of business. Tea and fresh almond cookies were brought into the reception room by another redhaired beauty, this one barely a teenager. As Bolan expected, she wasn't introduced, but she could only be another of his host's daughters.

"You are a soldier," Mustapha stated after they had both sipped tea and satisfied the ritual of hospitality.

Bolan nodded. "I have been, yes."

"What has brought you here to find Derek Sanders?" the Turk asked, getting straight to the point.

"I believe that he's going to try to purchase nuclear warheads for a terrorist group."

"The Brotherhood?"

With the financing of Osama bin Laden behind them now, the Islamic Brotherhood had moved to the head of the list of active terrorist organizations in the Middle East. Unlike many of the other groups that were primarily nationalistic or Arab based, the Brotherhood was a pan-Islamic group. It supported radical action anywhere in the Muslim world as long as it was aimed at destroying the influence of the West.

"No," Bolan answered to Mustapha's surprise. "This group is led by an American."

"But why?" The Turk was puzzled. "You Americans have no cause to destroy things. You are the richest nation on Earth, and every one dances to your tune. I do not understand what any American could hope to gain from doing something destructive like that."

"This man thinks that he can gain from a major disruption in this region."

Mustapha shook his head. "He is as mad as the rest of the destroyers."

"That's why I need to catch up with Sanders to stop him."

"I will help you with your quest," the Turk decided. "But it will take a day to make the necessary security arrangements for you."

"I've done this before. I'm pretty good in hostile territory."

"I am sure you are," Mustapha said. "But since my daughter will be going with you, I want to make sure that my security is in place. You know how fathers are about their daughters."

This wasn't what Bolan had in mind. "It would be best if I do this alone," he suggested carefully. He needed this man's contacts and didn't want to offend him. "There's going to be bloodshed before this is over."

"Do not worry about her," the Turk said. "She was nineteen when she killed her first man. He was one of Sanders's kidnappers, and she killed him with his own knife. She can take care of herself."

Mustapha clapped his hands, and Yasmine joined them. Gone was the combat suit; she now wore traditional women's garb.

"Mr. Belasko," Mustapha said. "This is my oldest daughter, Sofya."

"You should call me Yasmine," she said as she stepped forward and extended her hand. "Sofya means 'the wise.' I do not want the people we will have to deal with to think that I am too clever."

Bolan smiled to himself as he shook her hand; calling her clever wasn't even scratching the surface. This was as competent a woman as he had seen in a long time.

She sat and outlined her role in the mission. "For the first part of this trip, I will be one of those Westernized Istanbul women who travel with men. Once we get into the mountains, though, I will go back to wearing Turkish dress and will be my father's daughter again.''

"What does that make me?" Bolan asked.

"You will be a businessman. I think a Canadian because the man you are looking for is using a Canadian passport. You can say that you are a countryman of his. That will go better with the men I must talk to.''

That made sense to Bolan. In the Middle East, nationality and ethnic grouping were everything. With that covered, he moved on. "How difficult will it be to obtain weapons in the interior?" he asked.

"We will take what we need with us," she answered. "We will be driving one of my father's Mercedes cars, and they all have storage compartments.''

Bolan knew that she was talking about a smuggler's car with hidden compartments. In her line of work, it was an essential business tool.

"We can discuss the rest of the details in the morning,'' Mustapha said. "It is late and we will have much to do tomorrow.''

DEREK SANDERS KNEW that he would have to watch his backtrail while he was in Turkey. Stolen nuclear weapons were always a hot topic in this part of the world. The last-minute Russian recovery of a wayward tactical nuke destined for Islamic rebels in Chechnya hadn't made the news, but it had been nonetheless real. The Russians had sent an elite commando team on a predawn raid to recapture it.

Since the Russians had provided adequate air cover for the paratroop assault, the fight had been brief. Most of the casualties had been among the smugglers and their Islamic radical customers. The man they had most wanted to bag, however, had managed to escape yet again. It was that same man that Sanders would be meeting.

Karim was a Kurdish warlord who specialized in making trouble for anyone he could in his spare time. When he was paid, though, he would also work for anyone. At one time or the other, he had allied himself with the CIA, the Iraqis, the Syrians, the Turks, the Russians and any number of Islamic radical groups. At other times, he had worked against all of them and more, including his own people. He had no ideology beyond doing what pleased him at the moment.

From the Turks to the Saudis, almost everyone in the Middle East wanted to see him dead. Except, of course, for the party he was currently working for. And, since that changed so often, it gave him quite a bit of cover when he needed it.

Another of Karim's sidelines was smuggling anything of value, but with his part of the world being the way it was, he dealt mostly in weapons. That was why Sanders would be meeting Karim at the end of his journey. And, with half of the intelligence agencies in the world looking for the smuggler, as well, it wouldn't be an easy journey. Karim never slept in the same bed two nights in a row.

Along with governments, other people had an acute interest in finding Karim, including fellow smuggler Mustapha the Black. Sanders knew Mustapha well, how well the Turk had no idea. The kidnapping ten years ago of Yasmine hadn't been a fluke; it had been an inside job. One of Mustapha's most trusted cohorts, a cousin named Gamal, owed Sanders big time and had arranged the snatch. In return for a lifetime obligation of service, Sanders had once saved the man from being killed. He had rarely called upon the man since that time, but he had activated him for this mission.

Mustapha was the biggest danger he faced. The man was like an octopus with a thousand tentacles. Little went on in the shadow world of the black market that he didn't know about, and he was bound to hear that Sanders had returned to Turkey. He also had his tentacles into the Turkish officialdom. Though he was known to the authorities, he was so useful to them that they left him alone. Covering both sides of the coin, as he did, required that he walk a fine line. But Mustapha came from a family with a long, successful history of doing just that.

Because of that, Sanders had activated his mole agent to keep him informed if Mustapha picked up his trail. If the Turk decided to stick his nose into something that was none of his business, Sanders would have to kill him this time. That, however, would be only a last resort. Killing Mustapha would result in a vendetta he couldn't win, but allowing the man to track down Karim through him would also result in his own death.

It had been some time since Sanders had played the dangerous game of working the Middle Eastern arms black market, but he hadn't forgotten the ancient, unwritten rules of the game. The first rule was to trust no one, and as long as you didn't forget that first rule, none of the others mattered.

In that regard, he had stacked the deck in his favor by hiring a pair of European bodyguards. One of them was an ex-Stasi officer, Heinz Holmann. The second guard was a South African, Ian Vanbauer. Both had extensive Middle Eastern experience as guns for hire and were as trustworthy as any professionals he could hire.

His second tier of protection included a small army of well-paid informers. His tactic was always to pay them a little up front, not much more than expense money, but to promise a fortune if they came through for him. They were scattered along his route like so many trip flares so that anyone who followed him would have to run into them.

He half expected that someone would get on his trail, but he was confident that he had taken adequate precautions to keep them from impeding him.

BOLAN AND YASMINE LEFT Mustapha's compound at first light when traffic was light. Crossing the Bosporus to the Asian side of Istanbul was like driving into a impoverished version of the bustling city on the other side. The European Istanbul didn't really look European, but it was clean, and the well-kept historical buildings gave it a grandeur worthy of its great tradition. The Asian side of the city looked like any Middle Eastern slum. It could easily been the bad part of Cairo or Calcutta.

"It is all the immigrants from the small villages," Yasmine explained when she saw Bolan closely checking his surroundings as they passed. "They flock to the city looking for work, but most of them never find a stable life. Most of them go into thievery or join criminal gangs. It is making life very difficult for all of us."

That was the universal story in almost every large city in the world, not just in Turkey, and the solution was elusive.

"We have a tail," Bolan said as he glanced into the side mirror. "It looks like a white Audi."

"That's probably either the police or the secret service," she answered as she checked her rearview mirror. "My father pays all the right bribes to the right officials, but that does not always guarantee that he will be left in peace. They should fall off once we leave the city."

"And if they don't?"

She smiled widely. "Then you will get to experience German engineering at its very finest. The engine in this car was race prepared by AUG in Munich, and it can go 250 kilometers per hour. Nothing in Turkey can catch it.''

"Except a radio or a helicopter." He didn't want to pop her bubble, but even the fastest cars had their limitations.

"The police almost never have radios in their cars," she replied. "And as far as helicopters go, they cannot follow me at night. I drive with those goggles the smugglers use to see in the dark."

Bolan didn't bother to point out to her that chopper pilots could wear NVGs, too, but he would take an active advisory role if the situation got sticky. In fact, as soon as he knew that he actually was on Sanders's trail, he intended to send her back to Istanbul. He didn't want her blood on Betancourt's score card like the last woman who had tried to help him.

He wasn't going to tell her that now, though.

When the outskirts of the city thinned out to the odd shack well off of the side of the road, their tail was still in place. Reaching over to the door handle on his side, Bolan pushed it forward and pulled it out to release the cover of the compartment hidden inside the door panel. Tucked inside was his Beretta 93-R and his .44 Magnum Desert Eagle, with spare magazines.

Taking out the powerful pistol, he racked back on the slide to chamber the first round.

Yasmine glanced at him but didn't say anything.

THEIR TAIL TRIED for the takedown ten miles farther down the road. After having hung back several hundred yards for most of the way, the white car accelerated and started rapidly closing the distance between them.

"Do you want me to lose them?" she asked.

"No," Bolan said. "If we have to deal with them, I'd rather do it now and this is a good place for it."

Just before the car got into his blind spot, Bolan rolled down the window, leaned out and fired a single shot from his .44 pistol into the middle of the Audi's grille. After punching a hole in the radiator, the heavy slug drilled through the spinning fan blade, destroying it before exploding the water pump.

Though the front of the Audi was blowing steam, the driver didn't back off. If anything, he tried to speed up. One gunner leaned out the passenger window, and two others stood up through the sunroof and opened fire with AKs. The Audi was swerving erratically from side to side, throwing their aim off, but when Bolan heard the first two slugs drill into the Mercedes's bodywork, he knew it was time.

Switching weapons, he flicked his 93-R to burst mode and steadied his hand against the back of the window frame. "Pull into the left lane!" he shouted.

Yasmine snapped the wheel to the left, and the speeding Mercedes jumped out in front of the pursuing Audi.

With his line of sight cleared, Bolan targeted the two men standing in the open sunroof. Two 3-round bursts caught them both in the upper body and took them out, punching them back inside the car.

His next two bursts swept from right to left across

the car's windshield, punching into the driver, who slumped over the wheel.

With a dead man at the wheel, the Audi careened off the road and rolled down the embankment before coming to rest on its wheels.

Without being told, Yasmine stomped on the brakes before snapping the Mercedes around expertly in a bootlegger's turn. Driving past the wreck, she turned again, pulled off the road and stopped close to it.

Bolan had changed magazines in the Beretta and was ready when he exited the vehicle and climbed down the bank to reach the Audi, but all four men were dead. None of the bodies showed anything unusual. All wore nondescript civilian clothing and bullet holes. He quickly went through their pockets, but came up with little more than cigarettes, spare change and a few tattered lira notes.

When Yasmine joined him he asked, "Do you recognize any of them?"

"No. From their clothing, they are petty criminals. The class that will do anything for the right amount of money."

"Who do you think could have hired them?"

"My father has many enemies," she answered truthfully. "But this also might be Sanders's work."

Bolan looked both ways down the highway. He didn't see anyone approaching from either direction yet, but it was a major highway. "We need to get back on the road," he said.

Yasmine didn't even look back as they climbed the bank.

AFTER TRAVELING ten miles, Yasmine turned the vehicle onto a dirt road leading up to a small wooded hill. When the car was out of sight of the highway, she pulled up under a large tree. Reaching into the car's glove box, she produced a three-inch roll of black plastic tape and a pair of scissors.

"I have to make us look better," she explained.

Getting out and going around to the back of the car, she found three bullet holes in the bodywork. Pulling out a piece of tape, she cut off a square and slapped it over the bullet hole in the left rear fender. The color and sheen of the tape was an exact match with the Mercedes's glossy black paint.

When the other two holes in the bodywork were patched, she stood back and smiled at her work. "There," she said. "Now it doesn't look like we were shot at unless one stands close."

"You've done this before."

She smiled. "That's why each of our cars carries a roll of this tape matching the paint color. The police like to stop cars with bullet holes in them."

"While we're here," Bolan said, "I want to get out one of the submachine guns."

"That should be safe to do now," she said. "We won't have to worry about being stopped by police until we get closer to Ankara."

CHAPTER SEVEN

Costa Rica

Dinner at the mess hall was good and plentiful, a mixture of fresh and preserved food prepared by a locally recruited kitchen staff. Mercenaries were no different from any other troops when it came to their groceries. Soldiers liked to eat, and keeping them happy in the mess hall was simply good management of valuable resources.

After clearing his own mess tray, Hawkins drifted over to the coffeepot for a second cup. Being in Costa Rica, he wasn't surprised to find that the coffee was first-rate. That was also a big part of keeping the troops happy. If they had to choose between coffee and beer, getting their caffeine would win out every time.

"Hey, newbie," called a smiling mercenary sitting at a table with two other men.

Hawkins grinned back. "Yeah."

"Grab wood and tell us about the outside world."

Hawkins carried his cup over and took the available seat on the bench.

"W. L. Burton," he said, introducing himself. "And I'm here to tell you that the outside world is still there. But—" he shrugged "—why you'd want to trade it for this, I'll be damned if I know. I used to have to pay good money to go to places like this."

"But the places you paid to go to had women and bars, right?" a man at the end of the table asked.

Hawkins laughed. "You've got a point. But we're having a beer ration tonight, right?"

"Two cans." The man didn't look pleased.

Hawkins laughed. "Sounds like the Army in Saudi."

"Who were you with?"

"The Seventy-fifth Rangers," Hawkins replied. That wasn't a cover story, but the rest of the military record these people would be able to access on him was. The revised version of his 201 file had him being court-martialed for involvement in a racial-harassment incident. It was nothing major, but had given him a general discharge. That and cyber membership in a number of extremist groups had allowed him to make the cut with the recruiting screeners back in the States.

"I was in a mech battalion with the Third AD on Bradleys," the mercenary said.

Hawkins managed to look impressed. "Were you with those guys who made that three-day sweep? That was one hell of an operation."

The mercenary grinned as if it had been his very own tactical plan. "Old Stormin' Norman's Hail Mary play? You better believe it! And man, was that fun. I shot the barrel out of my 25 mm mike bagging ragheads. I just wish the hell they'd have let us go all the way to Baghdad. Man, we could of torn them a new asshole and we wouldn't be fucking around with them now."

"You got that right, brother," Hawkins said, and the man did have it right. Prodded by the UN and the liberals, Bush had taken a risk by ending the war early, and it had blown up in his face. After all these years, Saddam was still in power, and someday somebody would have to try to take him down again.

"We should have bagged all them sorry-assed bastards over there and left them to rot," another coffee drinker said. "There's not a single one of those people worth a bucket of cold spit."

The political discussion quickly broke up when the beer ration arrived. Each man got his two cans, and they were cold, and they went back to a general BS session with the main topics being the universal military topics of women and drink.

When the beer was gone, the men started drifting out of the mess hall in ones and twos, and after a few more minutes of small talk, Hawkins made his exit, as well.

On the way back to his barracks, he checked the board and saw that the next day's training was an urban-assault course. He hadn't seen much that could be called urban around there, so that raised his curiosity. Urban training meant that their target was in a built-up area. It also indicated that it was going to be a suicide mission. No fifty men could take out a city and get away clean.

AMONG GRANT Betancourt's many subsidiary companies was a small manufacturing firm called Powerdyne Tech, which specialized in the production of exotic batteries. If you were planning to build a deep-sea submersible and needed batteries that were able to withstand the crushing depths, you went to Powerdyne. When the Jet Propulsion Lab designed the Mars Rover, Powerdyne built the solar rechargeable batteries that had powered its exploration of the Red Planet. Other customers included the aerospace firms that built deep-space satellites, for both commercial and military use. But by far the largest purchasers of Powerdyne's product line was the military, and it was followed closely by NASA.

Though Betancourt kept his fingerprints off the management of his subsidiaries, he always went through the NASA and military purchase orders as a matter of course. They were the best source of classified information he could get without having to make any effort at all.

Running down through the list of equipment the batteries had been ordered for, Betancourt was surprised to see a Keyhole satellite in the lineup, a K-12, serial number 2039D. That was more unusual than finding the proverbial nun in the cathouse. The classified K-series birds were always resupplied under NSA or military contract, and the entire operation, to include the supply procurement, was top secret. The purchase orders always had the classified information about the end use removed by the Defense Procurement Agency before they were sent to Powerdyne. This time, though, the purchase orders had come from NASA and the end-use applications were listed.

With the space agency's funding under heavy fire again from the Congressional liberals, they were trying another grandstand play for their critics. The aim this time was to show how they could get more work out of the expensive, one-billion-dollars-a-shot shuttle launches by servicing civilian communication birds along with the classified spy satellites on the same missions.

It was a good idea, but as with all too many good ideas, the implementation hadn't been well thought out.

Betancourt probably knew more about the nation's fleet of spy satellites than anyone who wasn't in the military, NSA or the NRO. Since he provided so many components for them, he was cleared to know what they did, how and when right down to the last rivet and sensor head.

Clicking on a menu, he brought up a list of all the active spy satellites in orbit and found that the K-12 39 Delta wasn't supposed to still be in service. It was in a midorbit and had been superceded by the new deep-orbit birds and abandoned. But if someone installed a new set of batteries in it and refueled its thrusters, it could be brought back on-line. To do so would require some fancy, and expensive, orbital maneuvering burns, as well as a lengthy space walk by the shuttle crew, but it could be done.

The first question wasn't why it had been done, but rather who was paying for it.

The answer could only be that someone with unlimited funding had authorized the work. And the only agencies with that kind of money to toss around went by the initials NSA, CIA, DIA or NRO.

While it would difficult, but not impossible, for him to find out who had taken over this bird, it would be easy enough for him to find out what 39 Delta was being used for. Among the various technological marvels at his disposal, Betancourt had access to one of the best deep-space radar arrays at another one of his subsidiary companies DSI, Deep Space Imaging. This high-tech company was part of the new network of radar and telescope arrays that had recently been brought on-line to watch for NEO—near Earth orbit—objects.

NEO objects translated into meteors, asteroids and comets that might be on intersecting trajectories with Earth. Now that technology could keep a more accurate eye on the heavens, the dangers of extraterrestrial collision were being taken more seriously. Recent geological proof positive that a giant asteroid had wiped out the dinosaurs and brought on an ice age had pointed out the need for early warning.

Part of the information DSI needed to track incoming space projectiles was a radar map of all of the satellites and space junk orbiting the earth. The map was generated by the NORAD command center in the Cheyenne Mountain complex, but DSI had a constant feed from them. If the orbit of an object changed, they would have the change sent to them within minutes of NORAD updating their plot.

It would be no trick to have DSI track 39 Delta for him.

THE DEEP SPACE Imaging technician on duty in the company's command center didn't know who Grant Betancourt was, but he knew that he needed to be as helpful as he could because the DSI president had called and told him to.

"That's odd," the technician said as he checked on the satellite in question. "The 39 Delta was tagged as being derelict. It had a thruster malfunction a couple of years ago that threw it so far off station that it wasn't worth spending the fuel to recover. But we just got an update from NORAD saying that it's changed orbit. I hope the alien mother ship didn't power it up to spy on us."

"Where's it at now?"

"It's back in a geosync orbit parked over the western Caribbean. I can get the exact coordinates for you if you'd like, sir."

"That's okay," Betancourt said. "What I'd like you to do is keep me informed any time it changes position."

"Can do, Mr. Betancourt," the technician replied. "I'll lock it in the tracking system so it will kick out with anything more than a one-degree shift."

"Good. Tag it priority and send it to me immediately."

"Will do."

BETANCOURT HADN'T needed to get the exact coordinates of the target 39 Delta was watching because he knew what it was looking at. The only thing of interest to anyone in the shadow world of intelligence gathering in that part of the Caribbean was his mercenary training camp in Costa Rica. The only question was who was doing the looking and why.

So far, the Costa Rican operation was the only one of his three camps that had gathered undue notice. The Ugandan camp was covered by the mine-security story, and the Sudanese camp was just one of hundreds of such sites in that war-ravaged nation. Recruiting militant Americans and creating a cover story for the Caribbean camp, though, had been more difficult.

Since Oklahoma City and Ruby Ridge, the FBI, along with nearly every other federal, state and local agency, was keeping a close watch on what was being called the militia movement. That grouping included many organizations that had once been regarded as churches and had been off limits to federal spying.

But with these organizations taking public antigovernment and antiglobalism stances, they, too, had now become fair game.

Recruiting for the Costa Rican camp had been done completely by word of mouth. But with the number of informants and infiltrators in these groups, the formation of the unit couldn't be kept secret. The cover story was that they were on a spiritual quest to get back in touch with their Biblical role as husbands and fathers. It had worked for the Promise Keepers, and he had thought that it would work for him, but apparently not. With the satellite overhead, it was time for the men to go into hiding.

GOING INTO HIS private office, Betancourt opened his computer menu that controlled his communications network and selected Tight Beam. Tight-beam communication was expensive, but it couldn't be intercepted. The radio signal from Betancourt's headquarters was beamed up to one of his geosync relay satellites and, from there, it was retransmitted to a ground station.

Since he controlled a far-flung business empire, no one would think twice about why he used such a complicated and expensive way to keep track of his affairs. Almost all large multinationals were using tight-beam messaging to keep their competitors from listening in. For the same reason, no one would question why he was encrypting his transmissions.

The message he sent was simple—implement code name Looking Glass. That would instruct the camp's cadre to have the mercenaries change back into their civilian clothes. The main purpose of the uniforms and military discipline was to form the men into a cohesive unit. The rest of their training could be done in resort clothing.

When he was notified that the message had been received, he switched menus to deal with the greater problem. Before he went much further, he needed to find out who was watching him and why.

This was a multifaceted question that had lingered in the back of his mind for some time now. Particularly, the part of the question that dealt with the demise of Rainbow Dawn had never been answered to his satisfaction. The consensus was that whoever had gone on that killing spree in the Dawners' L.A. headquarters had been taking vengeance for the death of Senator Bowers's daughter.

The facts as he knew them, however, didn't necessarily fit that scenario.

He knew for a fact that the young woman's mother hadn't hired anyone to take that vengeance. And with the daughter's boyfriend dead, as well, there was no one else who had an interest. Or at least not that much of an interest. Hiring someone like the professional who had cleaned out Miller's security unit wasn't cheap, and it wasn't the sort of thing one could do by letting his fingers trip through telephone listings.

Whoever that shooter had been, he'd been a pro, and Betancourt felt certain that he'd been connected the team that had been conducting surveillance on the Dawners. One of the other questions he had about the L.A. action was the identity of that surveillance team. They, too, were still a mystery.

Betancourt hadn't gotten to where he was by not being able to find answers to his questions.

"ON YOUR FEET!" The sergeant's voice rang out in the darkness of the barracks. Rolling off his bunk, Hawkins glanced at his watch. The illuminated dial told him that it was 0430, an hour earlier than their scheduled wake-up time.

"There's been a change in the uniform of the day," the sergeant said. "Until further notice, you are to wear your civilian clothing. Any questions?"

"How about our boots?" Hawkins asked.

"You can wear your issue boots."

When there were no more questions, the sergeant turned to go. "Chow's been put forward half an hour, so get busy packing your issue except for your load-bearing equipment."

As the men packed their uniforms back into their duffel bags, Gratton kept up a steady chatter, posing hypothetical questions about why they had been ordered not to wear their distinctive camouflage uniforms. He received no answers, though. Following Hawkins's lead, the other mercenaries were giving him the brush off, as well. They, too, smelled something funny about him.

AT THE AFTER-BREAKFAST formation, the cadre sergeant gathered the unit in a circle around him instead of in their military ranks. "Okay," he said. "From now on we get to act like we're on vacation. Until further notice, do not wear your uniforms, not even the boonie hats. Got that?''

After a chorus of "yes sirs", the sergeant went back to the rest of his announcements. "Today's training has been changed to a tactical exercise without weapons. The assembly area will be in the clearing right inside the jungle. Carry your field gear to that location, and we'll move out from there."

The sergeant's eyes swept over the troops. "Any questions?"

Hawkins wasn't surprised when Gratton spoke up. "Ah...why can't we wear our stuff, Sergeant? I mean, we're supposed to be soldiers in the Army of the Lord, right?"

Hawkins hadn't heard any of the mercenaries use that name for the unit. There were some serious believers in the camp, but that was a little too hokey for most Americans, even a holy warrior.

The cadre sergeant didn't change expression. "Gratton, fall out and report to the headquarters building."

The man looked around as if for support, but didn't find it. "But what did I do?"

"Move out."

The sergeant's eyes followed the recruit until he disappeared around one of the buildings.

"Okay, you lot," the sergeant snapped, "move out."

CHAPTER EIGHT

Costa Rica

David McCarter never liked it when one of his men was off somewhere flying solo. Phoenix Force was a team, and it worked best when everyone was together. As with any good tactical unit, the synergy of the team made the whole greater than the mere sum of the parts. And it wasn't that he had any doubts at all about T. J. Hawkins's ability to take care of himself. The ex-Ranger had proved more than once that he had the right stuff to handle anything that came his way.

But McCarter knew that even with Hawkins's Southern charm working for him on this assignment, he would be dancing a real fine line. The backers of this armed Bible-study group had to know that they were being watched. After Waco, Heaven's Gate and Rainbow Dawn, the authorities had learned to keep an eye on anyone whose religious devotion was off the far end of the normalcy scale. The leaders of this group would be professionally paranoid and would be keeping a sharp eye out for ringers.

The fact that he and the rest of Phoenix Force were less than an hour away by high-speed boat didn't do anything to calm his fears, either. If Hawkins was discovered, he could be dead long before that hour played out. All they'd be able to do would be to exact vengeance and recover his body.

"I'll tell you what," Rafael Encizo said after hearing McCarter voice his concerns for the third time that morning. "Why don't me and Calvin get us a local boat and go on a diving trip?"

"And leave Gary and I sitting on our asses here?" McCarter said. "Why can't we all go?"

Calvin James grinned. "Just look at yourself in the mirror, man. You and Manning are a little too whitebread to blend in with the locals in this part of the world. Rafe, he's a local. And me? Well, in case you haven't noticed, there's a bunch of blacks in the 'hood around here, and I speak enough Spanish to get along."

"I don't like splitting up the bloody team even more," McCarter muttered.

"If you and Gary go with us," Encizo said, "we might as well fly a big U.S. flag off the stern of the boat and all wear those nifty little blue nylon jackets with the big yellow FBI letters on the back. Those guys are going to be on the lookout for the Feds. But if Encizo and I are spotted in a beat-up old fishing boat, we'll look like just two more locals wasting our time."

"Okay, okay," McCarter said. "Do it."

"Actually," Encizo stated, "the boat's almost ready. Calvin and I found it yesterday, and we've worked out a deal with the owner."

"I like being kept informed of what's going on, dammit!" McCarter snapped.

"I just told you." Encizo grinned.

"Get out of here."

WHEN HAWKINS'S mercenary unit returned from training that afternoon, they looked like any group of recreational hikers. All of their military equipment had been left in a storage shed well hidden at the edge of the jungle. The only thing uniform about them was that were all still wearing jungle boots.

Back in his barracks, Hawkins noticed that Gratton's bunk had been stripped and rolled. The group leader had called the man from the training briefing before they moved out and had told him to report to the headquarters building. He hadn't returned by the time they moved out, and Hawkins had forgotten about him until now.

Finding that all traces of the man had been removed didn't sit well with Hawkins. He had little doubt that Gratton was a plant, and finding him gone could only mean that he had been found out. What would happen next wouldn't be what a naive Gratton could have possibly expected. That was the biggest problem about signing on with any mercenary force—the power of life and death was always in the hands of the paymaster, not in an established military court system.

At the best, Gratton was being held prisoner somewhere, but that was a long shot. More than likely, he'd been taken out into the jungle and forced to dig his own grave before being shot in the back of the head. It was a shame that the man hadn't been better trained for the job he'd been given, and it was a harsh reminder to Hawkins not to screw up.

Dying in combat was no big thing; he expected it to happen to him sooner or later. Being shot in the back of the head as he knelt beside a hole in the ground, though, just wasn't on his dance card.

EVEN THOUGH he knew the dangers of being marked down as being too curious, when Hawkins ran into the mercenary sergeant on the way to the mess hall, he asked what any man would have asked. "Hey Sarge, what happened to Gratton? When we came back, his bunk was empty."

The mercenary locked eyes with him. "Not everyone is well suited for this business," he said. "He didn't work out, so we sent him back to the mainland."

"I'm not surprised," Hawkins said honestly. "He'd have never made it my army. I don't know how in the hell he got past the screeners in the States."

"That's not my end of it." The mercenary shrugged. "I'm just to shake you people out and train you."

"When do we get the mission?" Hawkins pushed his luck again and ventured to ask.

The mercenary studied him closely. "You'll get it when the principal wants you to have it."

"No sweat," Hawkins replied casually. "I know the drill. But some of the guys have been tossing ideas around, and I was just curious."

"Don't be," the sergeant cautioned him. "You're here to train and if I want you to think, I'll tell you when I want you to do it."

Hawkins laughed. "I've heard that before."

"You'd better hear it this time, then."

"Yes, sir."

THE FIRST BATCH of photos Aaron Kurtzman got in from 39 Delta weren't very helpful. Apparently, someone had tipped off the mercenaries that they were being spied on from deep space. The only figures he could see in the photos were dressed in mixed civilian clothing, and there was no sign of military equipment anywhere.

There had been a glitch getting the satellite back on-line after it had been refueled and maneuvered into position to keep an eye on the camp. The optical sensors hadn't wanted to wake up after their long sleep in the cold of space. By the time they could be unfrozen, the images they were sending back weren't showing him what he wanted most to see.

A few images later, though, there was a shot of about forty men running down the beach. The date-time group showed that this was an early-morning shot, and the men weren't jogging like a gaggle of civilians. They were running in a four-man file formation like troops out for their morning PT run.

"Gotcha," Kurtzman muttered.

It was time to bring Yakov Katzenelenbogen in on this and get his take on it. The wily ex-Israeli had more experience with this than most people in the business.

WHEN PHOENIX FORCE HAD been deployed to Costa Rica, Katzenelenbogen had been called back to the Farm to take up his tactical-operations post. So far, there had been little for him to do until now.

"This looks like bullshit to me," Kurtzman said as he displayed the hard copies of the satellite's images. "There's no way that place is a 'spiritual retreat.' Everyone's wearing civilian clothing now, but their activities are a little too regimented for your average Bible-study group. That morning run in formation isn't the only thing they do like soldiers. Even though I can't find the weapons, the military stamp is all over that place."

"There's one way we can find out what their intentions are," Katz said. "Call the dogs in on them."

"What do you mean?" Barbara Price asked.

"Well, if the Justice Department were to send an unofficial 'heads up' to the Costa Ricans, telling them that they've got a mercenary unit training in their backyard, they might want to look into it."

"Don't you think that whoever's behind this has applied enough grease to the right palms to make sure that doesn't happen?"

"I'm certain that's the case," Katz agreed. "But I'll bet there's some army colonel down there who's a straight shooter and has the loyalty of the men of his battalion backing him up. He's probably worked with us before on drug-smuggling ops and has his eye on higher office. That's the oldest story there is in that part of the world. If he could show that the powers that be are corrupt, he can catapult himself into the presidential palace."

"Do you know of such a man?" Price asked.

"Not off the top of my head," he replied. "But it shouldn't take us long to find him if he exists. Aaron and I can go through the DEA files pretty fast and find out who they've been working with down there."

"Do it," she said.

GRANT BETANCOURT HAD no doubt now that someone was actively working against him. The back-channel communication to the Costa Rican army's Black Panther Anti-Drug Task Force was clear proof that someone was at least onto the Costa Rican unit. It was true that of his three camps, it was the one that was the most exposed, but turning a deep-space spy satellite on it wasn't happenstance. The only question was the identity of this opposition, and the answer to that lay in his finding out who had reactivated Keyhole 39 Delta.

Before he did that, though, he had to get those mercenaries out of their camp. That would be relatively easy, as he had already leased the tramp steamer that he intended to use to transport the unit and its equipment to their jump-off point in the Red Sea. The ship was standing by up the coast, ready to sail, and he could have it alongside the training camp's pier ready to load out right after nightfall. He would send the troops to the Sudan ahead of schedule, and they could finish their training there.

The satellite would be overhead during the load out, but for someone who knew how spy satellites worked, there were ways for a ship to get lost on the open sea.

BARBARA PRICE WASN'T surprised when Hal Brognola's chopper flared out over the Farm's pad for the second time in the past three days. Since he was trying to keep Bolan's mission secret, he had to come down in person to stay informed. Now that she knew what he had cooking behind her back, she had decided to give everyone a taste.

"How's Striker doing?" she asked casually as they walked to the farmhouse.

"Oh, not too bad," Brognola started to answer. "He made the contact in Istan— Dammit, Barbara!"

"But Hal, what's wrong? I just asked you a question about our old friend."

He shook his head. "I'm not holding out on you, Barbara, I've just been trying to keep you and the others here in a safe plausible-deniability zone. We're not clear of the minefield on this thing yet. I'm still afraid that Betancourt's going to try to torpedo us."

"It's not like we've never been attacked before," she stated. "And with the new setup, we're even better equipped to defend ourselves."

"Not against an attack originating in the Oval Office," he reminded her. "The Man controls our destiny, and we can never forget that."

"We can always go into an Alamo Protocol until you can get us cleared."

"No, Barbara, that's the one thing we can't do this time. We can protect ourselves from attacks from other federal agencies, but we can't go to war with the President. That's called treason."

"Even if he's working for the enemy?"

"That's not what he's doing this time," he said. "And, even if he was, we'd have to have hard evidence on that before we could take action. Even with that in hand, we'd have to bring Congress in before we could move."

"So what do we do?" she asked.

"We hope that Striker is able to pull off his end of this operation."

"And that is?"

"To keep bootleg Russian nukes away from Betancourt. If he can do that, I think we'll be able to take care of the rest of this ourselves before too much longer.''

"Does Katz know about this?"

Brognola looked a little sheepish. "No. I've been trying to cover for him, too."

Price paused at the farmhouse door. "Hal, I know you're trying to do what you think is best for all of us. But we've been through all of this so many times before. I don't understand what makes it different this time."

"I guess what concerns me this time is the closeness of the relationship between Betancourt and the President. I know that I've mentioned it many times before, maybe too many times. I know you're tired of hearing it and I'm sure as hell tired of saying it, but I can't get it out of my mind. I might be making too much of it, but outside of you all here, I don't have close friends like that, and I don't know how much influence he might have on the Man."

"Whatever influence he might have," Price said, "I think we can counteract it and I'd like to bring Katz fully into this, too. It's hard to beat him in the dirty-tricks department."

"Okay," he agreed. "I guess if we're going to be one, we might as well be a big red one."

She smiled as she opened the farmhouse door. Hal was mixing his metaphors again, but the message came through loud and clear. Stony Man was going to war again.

"I'll get the War Room ready."

Brognola automatically reached into his coat pocket for his antacid tabs. It was starting again.

KATZENELENBOGEN HADN'T been as uninformed as Brognola had thought. As it was with Price, it was a full-time job trying to keep things hidden from him. Even though he had only recently arrived back at the Farm, it hadn't taken him long to find out that Bolan was on a solo mission in the Middle East. He had no concerns about that; Striker always worked best in his lone-wolf mode. But it was curious that Brognola hadn't seen fit to fill in the entire team on the mission. But since this entire post-Rainbow Dawn follow-up operation was being done off the books, he wasn't surprised.

Brognola, Price and Kurtzman were waiting when Katz walked into the War Room. Since the big Fed was seated at the table instead of the podium, Katz walked up to it.

"Let's see, now," he started. "Why are we having this meeting? We have one Justice man dropping in on us almost every day on his lunch breaks. We have Striker unaccounted for, and we have a lot of furtive glances being thrown around every time I walk into the Annex. I'd say that our man Striker is off on a secret mission, and where could he be? Let's see, is he—?"

"Okay, Katz," Brognola said. "You got me.

Mack's in Turkey chasing down Betancourt's overseas buyer so he can do an intercept.''

"And the items on the market this time are former Russian nuke warheads, right?''

"That's what it looks like,'' Brognola admitted.

Katz shook his head. "Why is it that this shit never ends?''

CHAPTER NINE

Turkey

Yasmine's Mercedes had covered a lot of ground since the abortive road ambush. She hadn't been kidding about the engine under the hood, and her driving skills were up to handling the raw power. Even so, they were entering a region of questionable roads, so it would be more than another day before they reached their destination in the southeasternmost tip of Turkey, where it bordered on Iran and Iraq. This was the region that was often in the headlines because of what was being called the Kurdish Question. The unrest in the area, though, made it the perfect place for smugglers and black marketers to operate from.

Yasmine and Bolan approached a small town right after nightfall, and she pulled the Mercedes into a service station. After fueling the car and checking the oil and tires, she had it washed by the young sons of the station's owner.

''It is best if we do not look like we have come a

long way in a hurry," she explained. "We Turks like to keep our cars very clean."

So far, Bolan was impressed by this young woman. Her father had trained her well. "Did you plan to stop for the night here?" he asked.

"It would be best," she said. "We have a long way to go yet, and we need to eat and rest. We will leave before first light in the morning."

That was okay with him. Since they weren't racing the clock this time, it never hurt to keep rested until he had to go into action.

In keeping with their cover story, Yasmine booked two rooms for them in the town's best tourist hotel. Dinner was in the hotel restaurant, and the food was washed down with tea, not wine. After dinner, they retired to Bolan's room to go over the map of the route they would take the next day. Once that was settled, Yasmine made a quick cell-phone call to her father to keep him informed.

DEREK SANDERS WAS happy to see that his efforts to cover his backtrail had started to pay off. He had been notified the minute when the Mercedes with the man and the woman in it had left Mustapha's villa and crossed over to the Anatolian side of the Bosporus. The team that had been tailing them had screwed up, though, so all he really knew was that one man had taken all four of them down.

Whoever Mustapha had teamed up with this time was obviously a professional. Who he was and why he was on his trail, Sanders had no idea. But his best guess was that one of his contacts had leaked something about the warheads he was after. That information could have drawn the interest of any number of agencies from Interpol to the CIA. But the action this mystery agent had taken on the trail car indicated that he wasn't a part of anyone's officialdom. His reaction had been that of an assassin, not a cop, and that made him a little too much like the mystery man who had conducted his one-man war inside the Rainbow Dawn building to suit him.

Sanders briefly considered contacting Betancourt and reporting the incident, but decided not to. The industrialist was unhappy enough with him as it was, and he didn't want to add to it by getting paranoid. Plus, he had finally heard from his mole inside Mustapha's family and had learned that Gamal had been picked to lead the security screen that would be covering the smuggler's daughter and the mystery agent.

Had he known that earlier, he might have been able to arrange for the pair to have had a real accident on the highway. Something with more substance than four men obviously following them in a clapped-out Audi. But Gamal had also reported where the pair was spending the night, so it wasn't too late to get a team in to settle accounts with them for their actions that afternoon.

If it was at all possible, he wanted them to take the girl alive. He had an old account to settle with the bitch, and he was looking forward to doing it.

BOLAN'S HOTEL ROOM FACED onto the main street of the small town. Tall French doors opened onto a small wrought-iron-railed balcony big enough for only two people to stand. Yasmine was in the room next to his, and though the two rooms didn't have a connecting door, he was close enough to cover her, as well.

The night was cool enough that Bolan had left the doors to his balcony closed. Since they opened inward, he had taken the precaution of using one of the hard plastic wedges he carried in his kit bag to insure that they remained that way. He had done the same to her room and had given her another wedge to block her door to the hallway.

Since someone knew that they were on the road, Bolan slept in his clothes and his shoulder rig, with the sound suppressor screwed into the muzzle of his 93-R. That way he could take care of any business that showed up without rousing the rest of the hotel's guests. People on vacation hated to be awakened by the sound of gunfire.

Bolan had also placed an antiintrusion alarm on the door, but the sound of the lock being keyed wakened him before the silent alarm sounded. A quick glance at his watch showed that it was after two o'clock. It was a bit late for a social call but right on time for nefarious business.

Drawing his Beretta, he quietly rolled out of the bed, taking a position with it between him and the door.

With the curtain drawn, the room was pitch-black, but his eyes were adjusted enough for him to distinguish the three figures who silently entered the room and eased the door shut behind them. With the selector switch on his Beretta thumbed down to single fire so as not to blow out his sound suppressor, he targeted the intruder closest to the door first. He wanted the body to block the exit.

Even though it was silenced, the Beretta made an audible pop as he drilled the drag man in the head. The sound of the round punching through his skull was also hard to miss, as was the thud of his body hitting the floor.

In a panic, one of the intruders snapped on a small flashlight. Closing one eye to preserve his night vision, Bolan triggered two quick shots at him, and the flashlight fell to the floor before the body did.

While Bolan had been doing that, the third man had produced a pistol and fired a single shot at the pillows on the bed. Bolan zeroed in on the muzzle-flash and triggered two more shots. Another thud of a body hitting the floor told him he had been on target.

As Bolan got to his feet, he heard a faint knock on his door. The gunman had fired only one shot from a light-caliber pistol, and it hadn't been too loud. Nonetheless, he could take no chances. Holding his Beretta at the ready, he crossed the floor, cracked the door and saw Yasmine standing there with a Russian Makarov pistol in her hand.

When she recognized him, she slipped into the room and closed the door behind her. When Bolan snapped on the light, Yasmine wasn't put off by the bodies and pools of blood on the floor.

"Are you okay?" she asked.

"I'm fine," he said. "Do you recognize any of these guys?"

"No," she replied after she checked each body.

"Do you have another set of plates for the car?" he asked. Changing license plates often was almost mandatory for smugglers, and so far, he had found her to be well equipped.

"Yes. One set from Ankara and one from Izmir."

"We put on new plates," Bolan said, "and I'll drive from now on. Also, if we have to stop and stay overnight again, we will do it as man and wife. It's too late to change our identity documents, but staying together in one room will increase our security."

She knew that he was right, and there would be no loss of face since they were on a mission.

"Now," Bolan said. "Most importantly, who did you tell that we were staying here?"

"Only my father," she said.

"Who would he have told?"

"Only one of our security teams, our best one."

"You've got a leak in that team," he said. "Because someone knew exactly where we were."

"But that can't be," she said, her eyes troubled. "My cousin Gamal is in charge of that team."

"And you think that he wouldn't betray you because he's your cousin?"

"He's family…"

"But what?" Bolan caught her hesitation.

She looked at him, her eyes hard.

"But he could be compromised," she said. "He was once captured by one of our rivals and was released before we were able to pay the ransom. He said that they released him early because he was wounded and our enemy didn't want him to die in his custody. But the wound wasn't that serious, and I've always wondered."

"Is there any way that he could be tied in with Sanders?" Bolan asked.

"That I do not know," she replied. "But it is not completely impossible."

"Okay," Bolan said. "Here's what I'd like you to do. Get on the phone and tell your father that I've been badly wounded and that you need a security team to clean this up and help get me out of here. And—" he locked eyes with her "—make sure that Gamal is with them."

"I can do that."

NOW THAT ALL THE CATS were out of the bag, as it were, Aaron Kurtzman could stop looking over his shoulder to make sure that Price wasn't lurking around before he went to work. He could also now put the rest of his Computer Room staff to doing something useful.

"We've got a bit of a problem," Hunt Wethers announced. Having been coaxed from academia to work at the Farm, Wethers still retained the calm understatement of the full professor he had once been. In his lexicon, Custer's last stand and the attack on Pearl Harbor were both listed as "a bit of a problem."

Kurtzman wheeled around in his chair to take the bad news full in the face.

"Our K-12 suddenly went off-line last night."

"What happened?"

"It went into a standby mode," Wethers said, "and I can't reboot it. I've checked the initiation sequence, but it keeps kicking it back."

"That can't happen," Kurtzman protested. "We have the only data lines into it. The NRO's not working it now."

"I know," Wethers said calmly. "But it happened anyway."

"Dammit!" Kurtzman exploded. After all the years of having to beg, borrow or outright steal spy satellite time, having his own deep-space bird had been a dream come true. It couldn't be off-line already.

"Can you fix it?"

Wethers shook his head. "I tried to run a systems check, and it keeps kicking me out on that, too. Some kind of deep-level programming has been activated, and I can't even get a seeker probe in."

"Shit!"

Wethers knew that Kurtzman was worried about not being able to keep an eye on Hawkins, and he had already gone to Plan B to try to rectify the situation.

"I found an Air Force satellite," he said, "that had been tasked to DEA surveillance and nudged it over a bit to cover Costa Rica. I also put a course-correction block in it so no one can recorrect it until we're done with it. Let someone else have one of their satellites off-line for a while."

Kurtzman smiled.

"But," Wethers continued, "our bird was down for most of the night..."

Kurtzman's smile faded.

"...and I think we should have Phoenix make a drive-by recon just in case."

Kurtzman punched his intercom to Katz's line.

WHEN CALVIN JAMES piloted the small fishing boat around the southern end of the cove, the mercenary's camp appeared to be completely deserted. "Rafe," he called out, "come up and take a look at this."

Rafael Encizo came up from the engine room and joined his comrade on the boat's open bridge. "I think they've moved out," James said.

Picking up a battered but powerful set of binoculars, Encizo slowly scanned the camp from one end to the other but saw nothing. "It sure looks that way," he said. "Run in closer to the beach."

Retarding his throttle, James nosed the little boat

toward the shore while Encizo kept watch. "Still nothing," he said. "Pull up to the dock."

"You sure?"

"We have to."

When the boat's rail bumpers nudged the pier, Encizo jumped over the rail with the line in his hand to tie them up as James shut down the engine. Beyond the normal sights and sounds of a jungle beach, all was quiet. And this was one time when quiet wasn't good.

Unlocking a tackle box bolted to the port-side bulkhead, James took out a pair of M-16 rifles and two magazine carriers. Handing one to Encizo, the two Phoenix Force commandos stepped onto the dock.

"I don't like the looks of this at all," James commented as he scanned the empty camp from the end of the dock.

The sand leading up to the pier was well trampled, and there had been no rain for the past couple of days so the tracks were too intermixed to be read. There was, however, a fairly plain wide track laid over all the others showing that a large group of men had moved toward the dock as if marching in formation. That would be the case if they had gone aboard a ship in the night.

Keeping each other covered and on the alert for booby traps, the pair started their search with the closest building and found it completely bare. Every other building they searched had also been stripped, and not so much as a piece of paper had been left behind. A smoldering sanitary fill contained the ashes of everything the mercenaries hadn't taken with them. A forensics lab might have been able to make something of the burned debris, but any search they could make wouldn't find anything of value.

"This is getting us nowhere." Encizo shook his head. "Back to the boat."

James started the boat's motor and, cranking the wheel to the left, put it into reverse, swinging the stern out. As soon as he had maneuvering room, he snapped the wheel all the way over in the opposite direction and went into forward gear. As the boat pulled out to sea, Encizo kept watch from the stern with his M-16.

Once they were out of range of small-arms fire from the shoreline, he went down into the cabin to call in his report to McCarter.

"The entire place's cleaner than a baby's butt," Encizo reported. "They've moved out, and the only things they left behind are the bare buildings and the sand. Even the trash has been burned."

"Damn!" McCarter said. "Get back here as fast as you can. I'm calling the Farm, and I want us to be ready to move out if they any have idea where he went."

WHEN DAVID MCCARTER reported Encizo and James' findings to the Farm, the Annex almost exploded. Hunt Wethers and Akira Tokaido immediately started to search the shipping register to try to locate a ship in the area that could have made a midnight pickup at the dock of the Costa Rican camp.

Upon getting the report, Hal Brognola flew to the Farm immediately to confer with Price and Katz. One of the first things he did was to dispatch a DEA plane to Costa Rica to bring the remaining Phoenix Force members back to the Farm. He wanted them reoutfitted and standing by ready to be deployed as soon as this situation developed.

"Can I get Carl involved now?" Price asked Brognola. "I want them to start working on Betancourt."

"Do you have a target for them?"

She nodded. "A government warehouse leased through BII that might have the answers to some of the questions you've had about the mercenary units."

"Do it."

CHAPTER TEN

Turkey

Rather than risk a second firefight in the hotel, Bolan concocted a cover story to draw the enemy into the open. When Yasmine called her father, the conversation was in Turkish so he wasn't able to follow it, but he knew what was being said.

When she ended the call, her face was grim. "It is done," she said. "As you wanted, I told him that you were badly wounded and needed assistance. I told him that to keep away from the local police, I've taken you to a place of safety in the countryside. He is very concerned and said that he would send several men immediately by plane to do what was necessary here. And before I could even ask him to send Gamal to lead the team, he had said that he would be coming because he could be trusted."

"We'll see about that," Bolan said. "Now we need to take one of these bodies out to the car."

BOLAN AND YASMINE WERE at the meeting place early to set the stage. The site was well-known ancient ruins a few miles outside of the town. Turkey was dotted with the debris of several thousand years of history, and most of the ruins were seldom visited.

Bolan had parked the car in clear sight of the road with the passenger door open. The corpse from the hotel shootout was in the passenger seat, wearing Bolan's clothing and with his face half-covered with a bloodied bandage. From even a short distance, he made a fair imitation. If the meeting went down as planned, the cousin wouldn't see through the ruse until it was too late.

Yasmine got a cell-phone call when the small plane her father had dispatched touched down at the local airport. As she used her cell phone to guide the Mercedes carrying the rescuers to her, Bolan took up his position. The remnants of a stone wall with an olive tree growing through it gave him both cover and concealment.

The wait was short, and Bolan didn't need a score card to know which one of the four men who stepped from the car was the cousin, Gamal. The man looked like a cheap hood.

Bolan didn't need to know Turkish to follow the conversation. The cousin's tone of voice and the sneer on his face told it all. Yasmine was doing a fairly good imitation of a woman in distress, and he was obviously berating her. The three guys with him were looking bored now that there was nothing for them to do.

The soldier was caught off guard when the cousin reached down and ripped the bandage off the corpse's face. Even bloodied, it was obvious that the face wasn't that of an American.

The cousin screamed something in Turkish as he slammed the barrel of his pistol against Yasmine's head. She ducked, but still took a glancing blow. He caught her around the shoulders and, holding her close like a shield, drilled the muzzle of his pistol into her neck.

Bolan was lining up to fire when one of the other bodyguards shouted something to Gamal. He spun on the guard, turning Yasmine with him so that her body blocked Bolan's line of sight as he fired into the guard's head. Blood pumped in an arc from the guard's shattered skull for the instant before his heart stopped beating.

At the shot, the other two guards pulled their weapons, but they didn't train them on Gamal. Instead, they were trained on the woman, as well. That meant that the rot in Mustapha's organization was greater than Bolan had thought. Now he had three men to take out.

From where he was positioned, Bolan didn't have much of a target. Yasmine blocked most of Gamal's body. The cousin resumed his tirade at the woman, grabbing her hair and wrenching her head back. He slammed the gun against her head again, and she slumped to the ground.

When she was clear, Bolan got his sight picture

and tripped the trigger of the .44 Desert Eagle. The heavy slug tore through Gamal's chest, blowing out one lung and his heart before exiting through his spine.

With a shout of rage, one of the other gunmen turned to Yasmine, and Bolan drilled him next with a head shot. The third man was caught between the urge to run and the desire to avenge his boss. He died before he could make up his mind about which action to take.

Bolan didn't need to check the bodies of his kills, but went directly to Yasmine. She was sitting up with a dazed look on her face.

"Are you hurt?" he asked.

She touched her hand to the side of her head, but didn't see blood.

"You were right about Gamal." She shuddered. "He was a traitor. He said that he was going to turn me over to Sanders for money."

"Your father's an honorable man," Bolan said carefully, "but it's apparent that he needs to clean his house. And if you're going to continue with me, I'd prefer that you break communication with him. We were lucky this time, but I'm not sure we can afford another leak like this."

"You're right," she said.

In the South Atlantic

T. J. HAWKINS WASN'T averse to traveling by ship. In fact, he had always rather enjoyed it. Had he booked the trip, however, this aging tramp steamer wouldn't have been his vessel of choice. But, he had to admit, even though the beer was being rationed, the ship's larder had been well stocked for the cruise, so he wouldn't starve. By the size of the bow wake, it was also making pretty good time, which told him that the guts of this rust bucket were newer than the hull.

Back in Costa Rica when they had been told to pack, the cadre had only told them that they were moving out, and he had known better than to ask questions. The sun's position in the sky, however, told him that they were heading east across the South Atlantic. He didn't have to be a geography major to know that Africa was sitting directly in front of them. Their African destination, though, was completely unknown.

So, until the situation clarified itself, he could only do what the rest of the mercenaries were doing— eating, sleeping and passing the time before the next meal.

Turkey

MUSTAPHA THE BLACK was a troubled man. The call from his daughter the previous night was odd. Something had been going on beyond what she said, but he couldn't figure out what it was. She hadn't used any of the family code words that would have told him that she was under duress, but he had heard a strain in her voice that was unlike her.

He had trained her himself, and he trusted her skills and experience. But, even so, she was still only a woman and his daughter. He had seen the way she had looked at the blue-eyed Belasko, and he hoped that her heart hadn't run away with her common sense. If the American betrayed her and she came to any harm, his death would take many days. The Turks hadn't always been a civilized people, and he well remembered the old ways.

When he didn't hear back from Gamal and the team he had sent by late afternoon, he dispatched a second team, this time a dozen men.

DEREK SANDERS WASN'T surprised when he didn't hear back from the traitor Gamal. It could only mean that he had been killed, and he almost regretted having wasted him as he had. But, when this job was done, he doubted that he would ever return to Turkey again, so it was time that he forgot about Mustapha.

He couldn't, however, forget about the daughter and the mystery man riding with her. A report from another one of his spotters told him that they were still on his trail. Rather than let them follow him to Karim, he decided to stop and let them catch up with him. He had enough men with him that he was confident of the outcome.

There was a valley ahead with several caves in the surrounding foothills that was a traditional smuggler's meeting place. It was also a perfect place for an ambush.

WITH BOLAN DRIVING and Yasmine navigating, they made good time into the highlands of Anatolia. This was prime smuggling country, and several times Yasmine had him stop so she could talk to one of her father's contacts. From what they were hearing, it didn't appear that Sanders was even trying to cover his trail.

Sensing a trap, Bolan stopped every few miles at a high vantage point and scouted the area ahead of them with field glasses before driving through it. By midafternoon, they crested a ridge and stopped for a recon again. The road descended into a small valley a couple miles long before climbing out again. At the far end of the valley were the four Land Rovers that Sanders had been reported to be driving.

"I know this area," she said when he pointed out the vehicles. "And there is a place close by where we can hide the car and go on foot."

"Where?"

She pointed to the hills flanking the left side of the valley. "There's a big cave in that hill, and a trail behind the ridge leads to it. The smugglers hide in the cave when they don't want to be seen traveling on the road overnight."

Through the glasses, Bolan spotted the opening to the cave. If they could get in there without being seen, he could work his way in close on foot and have his back door covered.

"Let's try it," he said. "You drive."

SANDERS'S SCOUTS in the hills radioed their reports when the Mercedes appeared on the trail that led to the largest of the smuggler's caves. It was a good move for the mystery man to make, but Sanders was ready for him. As soon as the car was in the cave and the two set out on foot to investigate his camp at the other end of the valley, he'd swoop down on them. Cut off from their car, they'd have to surrender or die, and he really didn't care which.

"Keep watching them," he radioed back.

AS YASMINE HAD SAID, the track they were following led around the hill and right to the mouth of a large cave. The overhanging roof was tall enough that the car could get inside but cut off observation except at close range.

She drove in nose first, and he was surprised to see how spacious the cave was. After stopping, he got out and prepared his weapons.

"I'll be gone for at least an hour," he told her, "if not two. If I'm not back in three hours, wait till dark and get out of here. Call your father and tell him that you're coming back to Istanbul."

"But I thought that I would be..."

Bolan heard a groaning deep in the earth and felt the solid rock under his feet twist in impossible ways.

"It's an earthquake," Yasmine screamed. "Run!"

"No!" Bolan shouted as he reached out for her. "Get under the car!"

Grabbing the woman, he dived for the floor of the cave and tried to push Yasmine under the Mercedes. In her panic, she twisted free right as the roof came down. He was reaching to drag her back when everything went black.

IN THE VALLEY, Derek Sanders smiled as he picked himself up off the ground. Several of the Turks and Kurds were on their knees calling to God to keep the earth from opening up and swallowing them. Since they were all on flat ground, he thought they were being a bit hysterical. If a Turk wasn't used to earthquakes, who in the world was?

He didn't need his field glasses to see that the cave the Mercedes had driven into had collapsed. The cloud of dust roiling out from the fresh scar in the hillside where the cave had been told him everything he needed to know.

This was the perfect solution to the nagging problem that Mustapha's daughter and the mystery man had presented. They had both disappeared from the face of the Earth without a trace. The old smuggler would spend the rest of his life trying to find out what had happened to his darling Yasmine and would bother him no more.

Now he could link up with Karim, complete the transaction and call in the choppers to haul his cargo out.

BOLAN'S COUGHING BROUGHT him back to consciousness. The air was thick with rock dust, and it was completely dark. The first thing he needed to do was to get some light on the subject and see how bad the situation was.

Crawling out from under the Mercedes, he felt his way up to the driver's door and was able to get it open. Reaching in, he hit the headlight switch. Only one headlight came on, but even with all the dust in the air it was enough to show him what had happened.

The mouth of the cave and much of the roof had collapsed, burying the rear of the Mercedes in rubble. There was no way they would be digging that out. Seeing the bright colors of Yasmine's dress, Bolan hurried to her side.

The woman was breathing and her heartbeat was strong, but he wasn't able to wake her. After digging her legs out from the rubble, he carried her over to the front of the half-buried car to check her injuries in the light. Her legs were scratched and cut, but didn't seen to be broken. He was checking her arms when her eyes fluttered open.

"What happened?"

"We were caught in an earthquake."

She moaned and sat up.

"Are you hurt?"

"I don't think so." Her hand brushed through her hair. "Something hit my head."

"Let me see."

Turning her toward the light, Bolan checked both

of her eyes, which reacted normally. Parting her hair, he saw a small cut on her scalp and a slight swelling around it.

"You did take a hit," he said, "but it doesn't look serious. We'll have it checked out as soon as we get out of here."

For a moment, her eyes started to tear up as she looked at the back of the car crushed by the rocks. "What's going to happen to us?"

Rather than answer her question, Bolan asked one of his own. "Where's your cell phone?"

"I left it in the car," she replied. "In the door pouch on my side."

Bolan found the phone and brought it into the light. Holding the phone in the headlight beam, he checked the battery charge and saw that it was less than a quarter full. "Do you have a spare battery for this?" he asked.

"No."

"How about the battery-charging jack?"

"It should be in the glove compartment."

Bolan found it and plugged it into the car's cigarette lighter. When he plugged the other end into the phone and saw that it was charging properly, he cut the headlights.

"Why did you do that?" Yasmine called out in the dark.

"We need the battery to charge the phone because it's going to get us out of here."

"How is it going to do that?" she asked, sounding skeptical.

"We're going to start digging, but we're not going to try to dig out through the entrance. it's much too deep. We're going to try to dig up through the roof or find a way out the back. If I can make even a hole, we can call for help."

"But we can't see to dig."

"We won't need to," he said. "But first, is there a jack and tire tools in the trunk?"

"I think so."

"They'd better be there, since they're our ticket out of here."

CHAPTER ELEVEN

Bakersfield, California

Carl "Ironman" Lyons had known better than to expect that this gig would turn out to be easy. Trying to do this kind of thing without leaving traces was never simple. But, as his nickname implied, he wasn't the kind of man who allowed much to get in his way. And certainly not something as inconsequential as a solid steel security door with a state-of-the-art electronic lock and alarm system attached.

He and the other men of Able Team were getting into the game late this time. But, even starting well behind the power curve wasn't going to keep them from doing their part. He hated it when he wasn't brought in at the beginning of a mission and had to play catch-up. Yakov Katzenelenbogen had tried to explain what had gone down at the Farm, but that had only made it worse. Brognola should known better than to try to keep them safe when the others were putting it on the line.

He intended to take a major strip off the big Fed's

ass for that the first chance he got. But right now he had a job to do, and he had the means with which to do it.

"Blow it," he told Gadgets Schwarz.

"That's going to set off the alarm," Schwarz reminded him, "and there's no way to shut it off. It's got a battery backup and a power-off response mode."

"Just blow the damned thing and to hell with the alarm," Lyons snapped. "We'll be out of here long before anyone can respond to it."

Schwarz shrugged. "You got it, Ironman."

Taking a pair of mini-RDX charges from his bag, he placed them against the hinges of the steel door. Usually, he would blow the lock plate, but this one looked as if it could take the blast of a full pound of plastique and still hold. The hinges were supposed to be the strongest part of a door like this, but that was only if you didn't know how to undo them. In fact, hinges were one of his specialties.

After placing the charges against the hinge pins, he backed them up with quarter-pound Kevlar bags full of lead dust to tamp the charges. The bags had a strong adhesive backing that would hold them in place long enough to direct the force of the explosive charges against the hinges. He and Cowboy Kissinger had come up with that idea during one of their all-night beer-and-bullshit sessions at the Farm, and this would be their first field test of their invention.

After arming the charges, Schwarz backed off to

the side a few feet and turned his head away. "Fire in the hole," he said as he keyed the detonator.

The minicharges worked as advertised. With a muted thud, the hardened-steel hinges parted company with the steel door frame. Before the smoke had even cleared, Lyons had a crowbar between the door and the frame and was prying it open.

After all that work, though, the inside of the warehouse didn't hold what they had expected to find. A few long tables parked up against one wall, scattered packing material and some empty forklift pallets were visible beyond the steel security door.

But the absence of evidence could of itself be evidence. Particularly when there was supposed to have been a complete palletized load-out kit for a light infantry battalion stored in this warehouse. That kit included everything the battalion would need for a thirty-day operation except for the required number of naked infantrymen. Everything from clothing and field gear to weapons, rations, medical supplies, communications gear, CP furniture and all the rest of the items that were required to conduct modern warfare.

That much matériel could also outfit a rather sizable mercenary force and keep it in the field for a long time.

Taking a camera out of his goodie bag, Schwarz snapped a series of photos that would show the empty floor.

"Okay," he said as he stowed the camera. "We're out of here."

On their way out, the two Able Team commandos didn't bother to try to put the door back in place. The alarm would bring someone to investigate shortly, or the next time the place was inventoried, the break-in would be discovered. Either way, it didn't really matter because there was no way that they could put the door back together well enough to hide their intrusion.

They had just cleared the building when Schwarz stopped in a deep shadow and put out a hand to halt Lyons. "The rent-a-cops are here," he said.

Lyons had his .357 Colt Python in his hand with the hammer back before Schwarz finished speaking.

"Wait, Ironman," Schwarz cautioned. "These poor bastards aren't part of the problem here."

Lyons relaxed the Python's hammer. "Have you got any flash-bangs?"

"That's what I was thinking."

When Lyons held out his hand, Schwarz dropped a flash-bang grenade into it. "Go for the five-second delay."

After keying the fuse for five seconds, Lyons reared back and lobbed the baseball-sized grenade over the roof of the warehouse.

The flash of the detonation was hidden from them, but the sound rattled the building. Excited shouts told them that the security guards were scrambling for cover. That should keep them busy looking in another direction long enough for Lyons and Schwarz to make their break.

"Let's go."

The two men sprinted across the sand for the chain-link fence fifty yards away.

ROSARIO BLANCANALES, the third man of the Able Team trio, had stayed with the team's Bronco to monitor the action over their open com links. As Lyons and Schwarz had made their entry on the back side of the fence because it was closest to their target, he hadn't been able to see the security force arrive through the front gate.

Since they'd been blown, there was no point in lingering, nor in being subtle any longer. It was time to go into rock-and-roll mode.

Taking up the electric chain saw that had been converted to a cyclone-fence cutter, he stepped out of the cab and walked up to the fence. He switched on the saw, and its tungsten blade zipped through the steel links as if they were pasta, creating a man-size hole in a few seconds.

"It's clear here," he sent over the team com link. "And the gate's open."

A few seconds later, Schwarz was through the hole with Lyons close behind.

"Get us out of here," Lyons growled as they scrambled into the vehicle.

Blancanales dropped the clutch.

Behind them, the security guards were still cowering under cover.

HAL BROGNOLA WASN'T surprised to get Carl Lyons's report. Yakov Katzenelenbogen had picked Able Team's target because the long-term storage compound was leased to the federal government by one of Betancourt's BII subsidiary companies. That was the biggest advantage of running a conglomerate—it gave the CEO a chance to have his fingers in more than one pie at a time. If Betancourt was outfitting mercenary units as he was thought to be, he would need to get their gear from somewhere, and it was too easy to get it from one of his own properties. It also didn't leave a paper trail that way.

Once more, Katz's hunch had been right on.

"What's our next target?" Lyons asked over the phone.

That question gave Brognola pause. He didn't have a follow-up for them at the time. "I don't have anything right now," he answered. "But why don't you get with Katz and see if he has any ideas."

"Patch me into him."

"THERE ARE SEVERAL WAYS we can go about this," Katzenelenbogen said to Carl Lyons.

"Just cut to the chase," Lyons growled. "I want the most active option you've got. We've screwed around with that Betancourt asshole for far too long, and I don't care if he's God's best friend. I want a piece of his action, and I want it right now."

"How well are you equipped?"

"We're minutes away from one of Cowboy's

stashes, so we can handle damned near everything short of a major war.''

Since moving weapons and hardware on short notice could get dicy, the Farm's armorer, Cowboy Kissinger, had several caches of his most requested ordnance items spread throughout the country. These prestocked armories had come in handy more than once.

"Okay," Katz said, clicking on his overlay that showed Betancourt's holdings in the United States. "Since you insist, let's go for it. How about starting out with the destruction of his satcom facility?"

"Where is it?"

"Not too far out of Phoenix."

"We're on it," Lyons said. "Send the layout."

"It's on the way. And," Katz added, "when you're done with that, get back in touch with Akira. He'll have a list of options for you."

"I want a target list, not options."

"Coming up."

Arizona

EVEN AT NIGHT, the towering dish antennae of Zip Com Inc.'s satellite communications facility were visible from several miles away. The red anticollision lights on the dishes insured that they couldn't be missed, which was the reason they were there. It also helped that the antennae were on the top of a small hill out in the middle of nowhere with nothing but open desert for miles around.

"It's nice of them to light up the targets for us," Gadgets Schwarz said when they spotted the lights.

"We're going to light those puppies up, all right." Carl Lyons affectionately patted the three-foot-long metal tube with the sight and firing grip resting across his knees.

One of the nice things about working for the Farm was that Cowboy Kissinger had sources that few armorers in the world could match. For this job, he'd had the perfect weapons stashed away in the prestock cache they'd tapped, a pair of 90 mm M-67 Recoilless Rifles. In a day when shoulder-fired, laser-guided, antitank missiles dominated the mechanized battlefield, the World War II technology of recoilless rifles didn't seem to be very modern. But that didn't mean that they did not still have their uses.

When the M-67s had been updated back in the sixties for jungle fighting in Vietnam, someone had come up with the ultimate ammunition loads for them. As with the artillery's Beehive rounds, smaller fléchette rounds had been produced for the recoilless rifles to be used in the last-ditch defense of firebases. The HEAT warheads on the 90 mm ammunition had been replaced with canisters loaded with more than a thousand two-inch-long, finned-steel darts. When the canister left the muzzle of the recoilless rifle, a secondary bursting charge sent the fléchettes spraying out like a thousand 12-gauge shotguns going off all at once.

Not only would the two-inch, hardened-steel flé-chettes tear up the dish antennae quite nicely, but also any of them that lodged in something solid instead of passing through would completely screw up any attempts to transmit signals. When Able Team was done with this gig, the facility should be off-line for at least a week, if not more, while the big antennae were repaired or replaced.

Leaving their rented Hummer parked five hundred yards from the objective, Able Team made its way up the slope to the perimeter fence surrounding the antenna farm. Lyons and Blancanales each carried an M-67 and three fléchette rounds while Schwarz packed his M-16 and three extra rounds for the portable cannons. According to Tokaido's report on the target, there should be only a small staff on duty and no armed security guards, but it never hurt to be prepared.

Five of the dish antennae were set up in a hundred-yard circle around a sixth antenna in the center. Since they were on the high ground in the area, they would have to shoot uphill. But the M-67 had an effective range of four hundred yards, so that shouldn't be a problem.

What would be a problem, though, was that as with all recoilless weapons, the M-67 had a back blast that could be seen for miles at night. Anyone in the area would be able to see it and would come running. To counter that drawback, they would make sure they didn't linger in the area after they took out the targets.

Schwarz served as loader for the two M-67 gunners. As Lyons knelt with the weapon on his shoulder, Schwarz opened the breech, slid a fléchette canister round into the firing chamber and locked the breech.

"Up!" he said as he patted the Lyons on the shoulder to signal that he was loaded and ready to fire.

When he had loaded Blancanales, as well, Schwarz stood between the two gunners to stay well clear of the back blast. "Acquire your targets," he told them.

"Up," Lyons replied.

"I'm on," Blancanales said.

"Fire!"

Both men fired, and the night was lit by the fiery blast of propellant gas jetting out the backs of the tubes. A few yards out of the muzzles, the two Beehive canisters detonated, sending their deadly steel darts on their way at the speed of machine-gun bullets.

The targets, the two closest dishes, sparkled as several thousand fléchettes tore through them. At that distance, the spread was so good that most of the red marker lights on top were shot out, as well.

Once the rounds were on their way, Schwarz sprang into action. Cracking the breech of Lyons's M-67 ejected the smoking case of the spent round, then he shoved a fresh one into the firing chamber.

"Up!" he said before turning to load Blancanales.

The second two shots were also on target, and so far there had been no response to the shelling. The on-duty crew would have had to be deaf not to have heard the M-67s going off.

After firing the third volley, they were six for six and still had three canisters of fléchettes left.

"Try for the power line," Schwarz suggested.

"Load me," Lyons said.

The sight optics showed that the power pole with the transformers was at a range of 380 meters. That was getting close to the maximum effective for the weapon, but Lyons applied a little Kentucky windage and fired.

This time, not only did the sparkles of the steel fléchettes striking tell him that he was on target, but the transformers blew up, as well. The coolant oil they contained burst into flame and washed down over the pole, igniting it, too.

Blancanales still had a live round in his tube, so he zeroed in on the base of the central dish and fired. This time the steel darts punched through the transformers and electrical boxes at the base, trashing them.

"Give me the last one," Lyons said.

Schwarz quickly loaded it into the tube and tapped Lyons on the shoulder.

The Able Team leader aimed the tube at the two vehicles they could see sticking out behind around the curve of the hill. Again the M-67 roared, and the fléchettes sparked as they peppered the bodywork of the two pickups.

The tube was smoking when Lyons brought it down from his shoulder. "Let's get out of here."

"You want me to collect the empties?" Blancanales asked about the ammunition cases.

"Leave them," Lyons said. "I want the bastard to know what hit him."

BLANCANALES KEPT the Hummer on the back roads all the way back to the outskirts of Phoenix. At one point, they saw a small convoy of police cars, gumballs flashing, roaring toward the satcom facility. A few minutes later, a pair of fire trucks raced after them.

"I wonder who they're after?" Schwarz asked innocently. "It can't be us. We were just out for a scenic drive in the desert at night, Officer. What are those? Well, Officer, we thought that we might run into drug-crazed bikers or—"

"Can it, Gadgets," Lyons said.

Blancanales laughed. It was good to be busy again.

CHAPTER TWELVE

Phoenix, Arizona

If Grant Betancourt had had any lingering doubts about his being under attack, they were gone now. Launching a military attack with antitank weapons against his satcom facility amounted to an open declaration of war. The question still was, though, who was attacking him?

The news accounts of the attack were labeling it as a postmillennium event. To back that up, a previously unknown group calling itself the Earth Angels was claiming responsibility for the raid. According to the manifesto that had been e-mailed to local media, the antennae had been polluting the desert with secret rays that were causing cancer in lizards and desert mice.

The story was being taken seriously this time. There was something about a group armed with antitank weapons that struck a note with the public. Fanatics who were willing to take a recoilless rifle to the focus of their objections showed nerve. The fringe-oriented talk shows were being flooded with calls from people asking how they could join the Earth Angels. Equal numbers wanted to know how they, too, could get their hands on a recoilless rifle.

Betancourt was no novice when it came to understanding tactical operations. He had studied the classics of the art of war and routinely used military tactics against his business opponents. That knowledge told him that whoever was waging war on him had the advantage, for now at least. He knew that there was no way to stop a small, determined group from carrying out attacks against him almost at will. A decade of ecoterrorism against any number of industries and logging facilities had proved that point. But that didn't mean that he was helpless against them.

He would, of course, take all the usual precautions against these terrorist incidents and boost his security. He would also do what the owners of a logging mill or a mink farm couldn't—call on the Feds to help. And his line of communication to the government was to the biggest Fed of all, his old college roommate.

Stony Man Farm, Virginia

AKIRA TOKAIDO WAS really getting off on his new assignment. As the junior member of the Computer Room crew, he rarely got a chance to let it all hang out as he was doing now. Not that he didn't always make his contributions to the mission at hand, but he'd never had a chance to run an operation himself. With Katz and Kurtzman tied up covering Bolan and trying to find Hawkins, he had been given the task of coordinating Able Team's rampage, and he was loving every minute of it.

He was the one who had come up with the Earth Angels name, and he had also penned their so-called manifesto for the media. He was also hacking into major regional newspapers and planting notes from the group's leader, Captain Freddie, to increase the disinformation campaign. He had also logged on to several environmentalist Web site message boards and was spreading the gospel on them, as well. As with so much else, if it was on the Internet, it was taken seriously.

The best part of all, though, was working with Carl Lyons to plan the strikes. As Katzenelenbogen had briefed him, these needed to be nuisance attacks in the grand tradition of guerrilla warfare. The object wasn't to kill Betancourt's minions, but to destroy valuable resources and force him to spend his time defending his business empire. The industrialist could shrug off the costs of repairing the damage, but he couldn't ignore what the attacks were doing to his reputation. Allowing something like that to happen made him look weak, and men like him who looked weak became prey.

Betancourt's corporate headquarters in Phoenix looked like an armed camp. Concrete-filled barrels rerouted vehicular traffic so no one could get a car bomb in close enough to take it out. Armed, black-uniformed guards from Security Plus walked the grounds of almost all of his facilities. He was bolstering his defenses, but as he was about to find out, it wasn't going to be enough. In fact, as in any guerrilla war, it could never be enough because the advantage always lay with the attacker.

When the industrialist did figure it out, he would come to the conclusion that his best defense would be to call upon the power of the United States government to protect him and his facilities. He was the nation's largest defense contractor, and he was being attacked by domestic terrorists. Anything that adversely affected him would adversely affect American combat readiness.

When it got to that point, Able Team would have to back off. They weren't going to start shooting at U.S. agents. But until such time as federal marshals or National Guard troops started to stand guard on Betancourt's properties, it was going to be open season on him. And on anything that belonged to him.

GRANT BETANCOURT'S air fleet was large enough that he had his own hangars and maintenance facility on the general aviation side of Sky Harbor Airport in Phoenix, Arizona. Dozens of business jets and cargo haulers resplendent in the BII black-and-gold livery lined the ramps and filled the three large hangars.

"That's quite a fancy private air force," Schwarz said when he pulled his Buick rental sedan into the slot labeled Reserved For CEO BII in the maintenance office parking lot.

"I must admit that it is," Blancanales replied. "Let's see how long it stays that way."

Schwarz laughed as he got out of the car.

Blancanales looked every inch a Fed when he walked into the office of the BII maintenance facility. From his highly shined, plain black shoes, to the dark suit with the white shirt and dark tie and ending with the close-cropped haircut and dark sunglasses, he looked like a Secret Service extra in a Tom Clancy terrorist movie.

Schwarz wasn't as well decked out, but he was playing the tech weenie on this gig, so he didn't need to have the complete Fed kit. He was, though, wearing a dark blue nylon windbreaker with the letters FAA on the back in bright yellow. Those three little letters had the power to make the blood of any pilot or aircraft mechanic run cold.

"Are you the man in charge here?" Blancanales asked the man behind the counter.

"Who are you?" the man asked.

"I'm Special Agent Joe Black of the FAA," Blancanales said, flipping open his badge case.

The man carefully read the ID card before looking up. "What do you want?"

Blancanales knew how to deal with an uncooperative employee. His sunglasses glinted as he focused in on the man.

"If your boss isn't standing in front of me in zero

five," he said quite unemotionally, "I'm shutting this place down. Got that?"

Schwarz could see the man start to puff up. "You'd better do what he says, mister," he said. "He's the guy who put the hammer to ValuJet. Remember them? Half of their management and most of their maintenance employees went to jail."

"Ah, shit. I'll get him."

A minute later, an older man in a button-down shirt and chinos came out of his office. "What is this crap?" he asked. "You guys inspected my operation not three months ago, and we got a clean bill."

"Was I here?" Blancanales asked calmly.

"No, but—"

"And you are...?" Blancanales asked.

"I'm Ralph Fisher," the manager said. "I run this place."

"Very good, Mr. Fisher. I'm Special Agent Joe Black, and this is my chief technician, Alf Price. If you will show us to your facility, we'll get to work."

"Wait a minute. Just what do you think you're going to be doing here?"

Blancanales didn't smile. "You didn't get the maintenance alert?"

"What alert?"

Blancanales turned to Schwarz. "Make a note of that if you will, Alf. They claim not to have received the maintenance-alert notice."

"Yes, sir." Schwarz flipped open his aluminum clipboard and started to write.

He looked over at the manager. "What was that name again?"

The manager exploded. "It's Fisher, dammit."

"I'm calling my corporate headquarters." Fisher reached for the phone.

"Make a single call without my permission," Blancanales said calmly, "and I'll close this place for a full investigation. I have a DEA team on standby, and I can have them here in five minutes, and the immigration team will take ten. The IRS people won't be able to make it until sometime tomorrow, but you know how they are. They come late, work long hours and leave late."

Fisher pulled his hand back. "Okay, what do you want?"

"What is this inspection, Alf?" Blancanales turned to Schwarz.

"It's for the Delta 5 Model automatic-landing sequencing modules, sir," Schwarz said.

"But none of my aircraft have anything like that," Fisher said. "And I've never heard of them."

"They don't?" Schwarz checked his list. "I could have sworn that you were on the list for an inspection. Well—" he shrugged "—I guess that means that we'll have to check the onboard fire-suppression systems, then. They're the alternate item on the alert."

"This is harassment."

"Feel free to fill out a complaint form after our inspection tour is completed," Blancanales said smoothly. "I can give you the form or you can do it on-line. You do have Internet access, don't you?"

"Okay, guys," Fisher said, giving up. "Do what you have to do and get the hell out of here."

Blancanales turned back to Schwarz. "Make a note of Mr. Fisher's use of profanity to federal agents. That's the second time he's done that today, and you know what the director thinks about such talk."

Schwarz's clipboard snapped open again. "Yes, sir."

"Oh, Christ," Fisher said.

CARL LYONS WAS in a white van parked outside the airport fence, monitoring the office conversations through the open com links. If anything went wrong, he'd crash the party and pull out his teammates one way or the other. So far, though, Blancanales was doing his thing and didn't need any help. When it came to jacking people around, no one was better at it than Blancanales. He was always at his best when he was playing the tight-assed, nit-picking federal agent. He played that role to perfection.

He could tell when Blancanales and Schwarz got to the hangar by the change in the background noises he could pick up on the com link. He heard Schwarz tell one of the mechanics to open a plane so they could check the onboard fire-suppression equipment. The man had to have tried to go into the plane with them, because Blancanales told him to wait outside.

A few minutes later, they asked to get into another one of the planes.

The inspection took most of an hour, and fifteen minutes after it was over, Lyons pulled his van alongside the Buick in a department store parking lot. Schwarz and Blancanales transferred to the van, and Lyons took off again.

A short time later, he pulled into the public park on Camelback Ridge. As the highest ground in Phoenix, it gave them a clear view back to the airport, a couple of miles away. Lyons pulled out a pair of field glasses and focused on the BII facility.

"Everything looks normal down there," he said.

"For now." Schwarz grinned as he flipped the arming switch on his multiple-channel radio detonator. "Ready to go?" he asked Lyons.

"Do it."

Schwarz selected autosequence fire and pressed the button. Down on the airfield, a series of explosions sounded in the BII hangars. Black smoke billowed out the open doors, and the occasional window blew out.

When the last charge had detonated, the BII facility looked like Pearl Harbor after the Japanese left. A fire had broken out, and the airport fire unit was racing to the scene. Since BII was well away from the other hangars, there was little danger of the fire spreading.

"I think I pretty well know what the lead story for

the six-o'clock news in the Greater Phoenix area is going to be tonight," Schwarz said with a grin.

"Don't forget our next stop," Lyons said.

"That'll have to be the film-at-eleven piece."

Lyons laughed.

THE SECURITY PLUS corporate headquarters was in a newly developed suburban area north of Phoenix's city center. Though this company didn't proudly display the BII logo, it too was an essential part of Betancourt's empire. In fact, it was the action arm of his enterprises. His industrial-espionage campaign and dirty tricks were run from there, and when he needed shock troops as he had at the Rainbow Dawn building, they were supplied from Security Plus.

For this hit, the Able Team trio waited until dark before driving to the target. Parking their van a block away, the three commandos walked across an empty lot, stopping a hundred yards from the rear of the building.

For this outing, the M-67s were loaded with high-explosive plastic rounds. Where and how Cowboy Kissinger had been able to score these rounds was even more of a marvel than the M-67s themselves.

A HEP round was a thin-walled shell filled with C-4 plastic explosive and fitted with a base detonating fuse. They had been designed to spall off armor on the reverse side by the pressure wave created by the explosive. When the round hit, the plastic spread out like a handful of mud thrown against the wall before it went off. The effect was to form a crater inside a tank's armor, and the metal that was displaced destroyed the turret and anyone caught inside. From the outside, however, all one saw was a big dent in the steel, not a penetration.

The Security Plus building was pseudo-Spanish stucco over concrete, perfect material for HEP rounds. The plastic explosive would spall off six-foot-diameter craters on the interior walls with ease. Only the naked rebar would be left.

Since they expected the response time to be swift this time, the attack would be two rounds from each tube before they bugged out. Two rounds would go into the upper floor and two in the lower.

Again, Schwarz was playing the ammo humper, and he quickly loaded the weapons of the kneeling gunners.

"Fire," he commanded.

The night lit up with the fiery back blast as the two HEP rounds streaked for the fake Spanish portico on the second floor. One of the rounds hit one of the pillars and detonated. It took out a large section of the railing but failed to damage the wall behind it. The second round hit the wall by a door, taking out the door and twelve feet of the stucco wall next to it.

The second pair of rounds were aimed at the flat expanse of real wall on the first floor. Again the recoilless rifles thundered as their HEP rounds were sent on their way. This time, they both slammed into the wall twenty feet apart halfway between the ground and the roofline. When the smoke and dust cleared, as if by magic, two huge holes had been blasted through the walls.

"That should take care of that urban-renewal job," Schwarz quipped.

"Load me again," Lyons said.

Schwarz had brought one extra round in case of a misfire in the aging ammunition. Cracking the breech, he cleared the spend case and rammed in the fresh one. "Up!"

"Okay," Lyons said. "Let's go."

"Aren't you going to fire that thing?"

"Not yet."

They were halfway across the open field to their van when they heard shouts from the ruined building and Lyons spun, swinging the M-67 onto his shoulder.

With a roar and a flash of back blast, the last shot went into the lower part of the second story, showering chunks of concrete on whoever it was who had been making all the noise.

"Now run!"

CHAPTER THIRTEEN

Stony Man Farm, Virginia

David McCarter stormed around the Annex like a maddened bull. "Goddammit!" he said to no one in particular. "I thought this fancy-ass setup was supposed to give you people everything you needed to keep track of the entire world, and you can't even find one bloody boat for me."

"I've got thousands of boats under surveillance," Aaron Kurtzman shot back. "And, if you know how to tell which one Hawkins is sailing on, if in fact he is on a boat at all, I'm willing to listen to it. If not, kindly get the hell out of here and let me get back to work."

"I'm still running the owners on those ships," Hunt Wethers broke in, "and the owners of the owners, but it's slow going. Some of those ships are covered by so many cutouts that it's almost impossible to find who's really running them. For all I know, Betancourt could own half the shipping in the world, but I'd have to break into damned near every bank database in the Western World to find which ones were his.''

Seeing that he was getting nowhere fast, McCarter headed back to the farmhouse. If these guys couldn't help him, maybe he could badger Brognola for a while.

AKIRA TOKAIDO HAD his disinformation campaign running at full tilt. No sooner had the last explosion gone off in the BII hangars in Phoenix than the Earth Angels were posting their latest communiqué in cyberspace. This time, their explanation for the attack was that BII was using an experimental fuel in the aircraft that caused warts on desert frogs. Further use of this fuel, they said, would result in more attacks.

The press release ended with what had become the Earth Angels' motto No Creature Too Small To Be Important, No Risk Too Great To Save Them. Tokaido had even created a composite photo of Captain Freddie, the leader of the Earth Angels, from mug shots of famous politicians.

The Earth Angels' Web site was also up now, and every time someone from a government agency clicked on to it, it transmitted a cyber worm that sent the EA manifesto to every address in that computer's e-mail file. The best part was that the manifesto carried the return address of Betancourt's BII headquarters.

HAL BROGNOLA DIDN'T LOOK happy when he stepped off the chopper. In fact, he started to dig in his pocket for the antacid tabs before he even cleared the still spinning rotor disk.

Barbara Price had seen that look before and knew what it meant. "What's the bad news?" she asked.

"Well," he said, "the President has tasked us with finding, and stopping, whoever is behind the Earth Angels and their attacks on BII immediately."

"That's easy enough to do." She grinned. "We can disappear any time we want."

"It may not be that easy," he replied. "He sees the attacks as being a serious domestic terrorist threat, and he's not kidding around. He's got the FBI and NSA in on it, as well."

"Aaron says that we're bulletproof on this one," she said, trying to reassure him. "The cyber messages are being sent out of the EPA's main office or the EPA headquarters, so that's as far as anyone will be able to track them."

"But he expects us to track this thing down and he's serious. Apparently, Betancourt gave him a big song and dance about national security and how this is affecting his defense industries. With BII being a major contributor to space station Freedom, the Man is worried about his 'legacy.'"

Brognola grimaced. "Betancourt really knows which of the Man's buttons to push."

"We haven't hit any of Betancourt's defense-industry or space-related facilities," Price pointed out. "We've just been targeting his personal assets."

"I know, but since the Man doesn't know that we're doing it, that's not the way he sees it."

"Let's get Aaron and Katz in on this," she suggested. "I know we can get around this."

"I hope so."

GRANT BETANCOURT couldn't keep the smile off his face as he flew back to Phoenix. His meeting with his old college friend had been their usual laid-back, informal affair. They'd had a casual private dinner followed by cigars and a few drinks in the President's private office. Betancourt had been able to lay out his case in such a way that he'd gotten everything he'd wanted. It was so easy for him to maneuver the most powerful man in the world.

He'd also gotten an unexpected bonus. Thinking out loud, the President had promised that he'd have "the Farm" look into the attacks. No sooner were the words out of his mouth than he had asked Betancourt to forget what he'd just heard. 'It's national security, Grant," he had said, "I'm sure you understand."

Betancourt had assured his old friend that he was good at keeping national secrets, reminding him of the secret missile fire-control module one of his companies was designing for space station Freedom. Though the new space station was to be a symbol of peace and international cooperation, Betancourt had been able to convince the President that it needed to be able to defend itself in the name of national security. His plans to take over the space station were still far in the future, so his need to find out what this "Farm" was all about took immediate priority.

Betancourt had eyes and ears in almost every level of government, but he had never heard of this place. Back during the early days of the cold war, there had been a horse breeding ranch outside of Arlington that had been called the Farm. The OSS had started it during World War II, and it had been taken over by the CIA to train operatives destined to work inside the iron curtain. Jimmy Carter had shut it down and transferred the personnel to the CIA facilities at Langley and Quantico, and the place had gone back to being a real horse ranch.

If a new Farm had been established, he hadn't heard anything about it. Yet. As soon as he got back to Phoenix, though, he'd soon find out. On something this important, he couldn't even trust the security of his own plane's communications systems. He was well aware that NSA ran a series of Comint satellites that could pick up more than cell-phone calls. They could read the EMP of almost any phone line transmission, as well. To avoid detection by these spy birds, one had to use shielded land lines or a state-of-the-art encryption system. Since he supplied such systems to the NSA, he knew how to keep someone from eavesdropping on him.

If this Farm was what he thought it was, some kind of supersecret dirty-tricks establishment, it might be the answer to what had gone wrong both in L.A. and with his plans for Jerusalem, Mecca and the Vatican.

Stony Man Farm, Virginia

BUCK GREENE HAD KNOWN for some time now that something was going down. Even though he was the Farm's security chief, his duties usually didn't extend beyond securing the boundaries of the Farm itself. That didn't mean, though, that he didn't have a pretty good idea of what was going down when the action teams were in the field. Because of that, he wasn't surprised when he got a summons from Barbara Price to report to the War Room.

"You wanted to see me ma'am?" he asked when he stopped at the open door.

"Come on in, Buck," Price said. Yakov Katzenelenbogen was also at his usual place, so Greene knew this was to be an ops briefing.

Right after Greene took his seat, Hal Brognola walked in and took his place at the head of the table. "Chief," he said, nodding at Greene.

"Here's the score." Katz got right to the point. "As I'm sure you know, Striker's in Turkey. Hawkins is currently places unknown, and Lyons and his guys have been harassing Grant Betancourt, the guy we think was behind the recent aborted attacks against religious centers. While it may not look like it, these efforts are actually connected and they come together in Betancourt. And with the exception of temporarily losing track of Hawkins, we've been making good progress."

"Now, however," Brognola said, "the President has ordered us to find out who has been harassing Grant Betancourt and put an end to it."

"I take it that we've been working off the book lately," Greene observed.

"You might could say that, Buck. I like to think that we've just been researching a potential threat to national security."

"In the guise of 'domestic terrorist' attacks?"

Brognola shot him a fox-in-the-henhouse kind of look. "The Man sees it that way," he said. "And he's pulling out all the stops. We're not the only agency involved this time."

Knowing what that could mean to the Farm, Greene saw his part in this. "Do you want us to go into an Alamo preparation?" he asked.

"Not yet," Katz said. The Alamo Protocol was the code name for a physical defense of the Farm against all comers. "And while I hope it doesn't come to that, I want the blacksuit shift leaders to review that plan just in case."

"No problem."

"What I'd like you to do, though," Katz said, "is to go to full-spectrum active monitoring. I expect a

Comint effort to be made against us, and all our communication has to be encrypted or shielded."

"We're doing that right now at level six," Greene said.

"I want it taken up to nine," Katz replied. "We have to expect that Betancourt will have access to the full array of NSA Comint feed."

"We can do that," Greene said, quickly running the Comint security protocol through his mind.

"And," Brognola added, "I also want your people to keep a sharp eye out for anyone attempting any kind of ground recon against us. Strangers asking questions in town, unexpected deliveries, telephone line workers, the whole bag. Anyone who shows up gets looked at."

"Can do."

"I don't think that the President's going to shop us," Brognola clarified to calm fears. "But our target's too tight with the Oval Office, and I'm afraid that we might get mentioned in passing or something like that."

"And, Buck," Price said. "Should it come to an Alamo situation, more than likely our opposition will be federal agents. So I want a no-fire order in effect until Hal or I say otherwise. I know it's risky, but it has to be that way."

Greene nodded. "I understand." And he did.

While the U.S. government wasn't their enemy, the more than top secret nature of the Farm meant that they were an unknown group. Under these conditions, they could easily become persons of interest.

Turkey

BOLAN DISCOVERED that the rock chimney at the back of the cave had apparently at one time been larger; earlier earthquakes had narrowed the passage. But there was a good chance that he'd be able to widen the shaft enough for what he planned. One end of the car's jack handle was flattened to pop off hubcaps, and it made a perfect tool to wedge into the cracks in the rocks to use as a pry bar. Working without light, there was the all too real danger of his prying on the wrong rock and bringing down the whole mountain on top of them. But the only option was a slow death from thirst and starvation.

After several hours of carefully prying rocks loose from the base of the shaft, Bolan felt that he was making progress. The chimney had been formed over thousands of years by the same water that had carved the cave out of the limestone. The rocks blocking it had fallen from the walls during earthquakes and had gotten locked in place. The trick was to feel around each rock he planned to take out and make sure that a one-ton boulder wasn't resting on top of it.

Since there was no food, and water was what they could lap from a damp spot at the base of one wall, Bolan worked steadily until he had to stop and rest. On what he thought was the third day, he was jamming the jack handle up against the rock above his head when he felt it break through. A sudden gush of fresh air brought him the smells of the world aboveground. Looking up through the small hole, he first saw black, but as soon as his eyes adjusted, he saw stars. The hole was small, but it would serve his purposes.

Climbing back down, he went to Yasmine. "I've made a hole to the outside," he told her. "It isn't big, but it will give us some fresh air."

"Do you really think that you can open it enough for us to get out?" she asked listlessly.

For most of the time that Bolan had been laboring, Yasmine had slept. He didn't know if it was because of the blow to the head she had taken, or if it was more of a psychological thing. She had shown herself to be brave enough aboveground, but being buried alive was another matter.

"I don't think I'll need to," he explained. "If I can enlarge it enough to get my head through, I can make a call with your phone and get help to us."

CHAPTER FOURTEEN

Turkey

It took Bolan another complete cycle of work and sleep to open the hole in the limestone roof of the cave wide enough to get his head through. More importantly, he could do it with the cell phone held to his ear and the antenna completely clear of the rocks. Climbing back down, he found Yasmine asleep again. So, without waking her, he made his way back to the half-buried Mercedes to put his plan in action.

After being in the dark for so long, the glow of the car's dash lights were glaring to Bolan's eyes. Squinting, he saw that the cell phone's battery was registering a full charge again. Grabbing the map, he found their general location and got the cardinal directions from it. If he'd been able to get to his compass in the rock-crushed trunk, he could have shot a back azimuth and been able to pinpoint himself within a few yards. As it was, the rescuers would have to look for him and try to zero in on the cell phone.

According to his watch, the comsat should be well within range now, so it was time to see about getting out of their predicament.

Snapping off the dash light, he waited until his eyes readjusted to the darkness before making his way to the chimney at the rear of the cave. He automatically stopped to check on Yasmine and, finding her still asleep, decided to wake her only if he was successful. If this didn't work, he'd have all the time in the world to tell her he'd failed. An eternity, to be exact.

Wiggling up through the narrow passage, he got his right arm and head through the hole he had opened onto the outer world. He first punched in the number of Aaron Kurtzman's personal line and, after hearing the clicks and buzzes of the satellite link up, got the warbling tone that told him that the line was operating in secure mode. When he tried Barbara Price's office number next, he got the same thing.

Apparently, the Farm was locked down. Rather than go through the memorized Stony Man phone list one by one and run down the battery in hopes of finding an open line, he punched in the emergency contact number. This time he got a ring.

Stony Man Farm, Virginia

WITH THE FARM LOCKED down for Comint security, communications with the teams in the field became difficult. But, as always, the emergency number was kept clear. When it rang on Kurtzman's console, he punched the line open.

"If you're not too busy, Bear," he heard Bolan's voice say, "I could sure use a hand over here. I've got a problem."

"Where the hell are you, Striker?" Kurtzman had to keep himself from shouting.

The pause before the answer told Kurtzman that the call was being routed through a deep-space satellite. "I'm in southern Turkey under several tons of rock. We got caught in a cave during an earthquake, and the roof fell in."

"Are you okay?"

"I'm fine. And so is my partner, but we need rescuing. We can't dig our way out by ourselves."

"Give me coordinates."

"I can't do that. But I can give you the geographical references."

"Send it."

"I can't stay on the line much longer," Bolan said after giving the map references. "I don't want to use up this cell phone's battery."

"Phoenix is here right now, and I'll get them in the air to you as soon as humanly possible."

"Have them bring a cell phone, too, because I'm going to have to talk them in to my location." Bolan gave him the number. "Starting eighteen hours from now, I'll turn the cell phone on for ten minutes every hour on the hour. Once we're in contact, I can vector them in."

"That should work."

"Also," Bolan added, "have them load up with extra ammunition, because we're going to war as soon as I get out of here."

"Hang in there, Striker. I'll have them on the ground in Turkey in less than twenty-four hours."

"Make it less if you can," Bolan said. "We've been here a couple of days with no food and very little water."

"I'll sure as hell try."

Kurtzman punched in Barbara Price's phone number to give her the good news. His second phone call would be to Hal Brognola.

DAVID MCCARTER and his teammates were waiting in the War Room when Hal Brognola walked in. Hawkins was still missing, but if Bolan needed them, they were his.

"Since we're still working off the book," Brognola stated, "you'll be going in as DEA agents on special assignment to do a recon into Kurdish territory. I've got clearance for your mission load, and you're manifested on a C-141 out of Andrews as soon as you can get there. The C-141 will pick up a KC-10 over Spain for a refuel, and your scheduled ETA at the air base at Incirlik, Turkey, will be 1100 local tomorrow."

"How about ground transportation once we're there?" McCarter asked.

"Your C-141 will be carrying two fully outfitted

Hummers with gun mounts in the back. Katz will cover that in the tactical plan.''

Katz stood to deliver his part of the briefing. ''Right after you get into Incirlik, your vehicles and equipment will be loaded into a Herky transport for the final hop to your target area.''

''Is there any chance that we can get an AC Herky to cover us in case we need some fire support on the way in?'' McCarter asked.

''Sorry, David,'' Katz said, shaking his head. ''That's a no go. The Air Force thinks it's supporting a DEA operation, and they'd have to clear any shooting with their higher command, which would give us away. The same goes for using a Sky Hook extract. After you recover Striker, you're going to have to drive out.''

McCarter wasn't worried about that part of the operation. As soon as they linked up with Striker, there were a dozen ways they could to get back to safe ground.

''Once you've penetrated the general area,'' Katz continued, ''he'll be waiting for a cell-phone call for ten minutes at every top of the hour, so you'll try to get through to him and he'll vector you in. He says that he's okay for now, but speed is clearly of the essence here.''

''Lastly, David,'' Katz said, grinning, ''pick up my and Jack's move-out kits from Cowboy and add them to the mission load. We're going with you.''

Brognola looked up from his briefing notes. ''It

would have been nice if you'd have run that past me first, Katz.''

"It has to be done that way, Hal," Katz stated flatly. "And I need Jack with us in case we have to borrow a plane. Remember, the opposition is picking up nukes, and they're going to have a quick way to get them to wherever they're going to be rigged for the attacks. We're going to have to stay loose and be ready to react to the situation. That means having a pilot and the ability to break up into smaller teams."

"Okay, okay," Brognola said, giving in. "Just get it on the road."

"We're on the way."

BEFORE HE LEFT for Washington, Hal Brognola put an end to Akira Tokaido's stint as Able Team's outlaw operations officer. It had been fun while it lasted, but with the pressure on the Farm now, they couldn't afford to get distracted.

CARL LYONS WENT ballistic when he called in and was told that Able Team was to stand down for the moment. "Let me talk to Hal," he said.

"He went back to D.C. a couple of hours ago," Tokaido said.

"Patch me through to Barbara."

"Carl," Price said, coming on the line, "I take it Akira told you that Hal wants you to back off tormenting Betancourt for a while."

"Dammit, Barb, we've got a real program going.

We're hitting him where he lives, and if he's worried about us, he can't concentrate on whatever other nastiness he's up to.''

"I know,'' she said, "but Hal's in a spot. In fact we all are. The President's pushing for us to put an end to the attacks on Betancourt and bring the terrorists to justice.''

"Right,'' Lyons growled. "That's what we get for getting mixed up with politics. We're trying to take out a whacko who's a real danger to this country, and we get tagged as being the terrorists.''

"Carl, that doesn't mean that I don't have a mission for you. I need you to be our early-warning system. Hal isn't the only high-ranking Fed who's been called in to protect Betancourt. The Man's called for a full-court press on this, and that means everyone from the Fish and Game Department to the Federal Reserve Board has been alerted to be on the lookout for the terrorists.''

"Christ!'' Lyons spit.

"Hal wants you and your men to activate your Justice Department special agent IDs and start canvasing the other agencies to find out what they're picking up. He also wouldn't mind your working a misinformation campaign into it.''

"I'll put Pol on that,'' Lyons said.

"Aaron thinks that it might be a good idea to start in the Phoenix area and see if you can find out what, if anything, Betancourt has learned so far.''

"We can be there in a couple of hours."

"Good."

GADGETS SCHWARZ WAS disappointed that the fun and games had been put on hold. Blowing things up was his favorite pastime. Rosario Blancanales, however, was up to the challenge of their new assignment. Working against the opposition from within was his second-favorite thing to do. As for Carl Lyons, he would stay in the background again to support his teammates' efforts and hope that an opening presented itself for him to get a chance to bust someone's skull.

The trio quickly got into their Fed kits and drove to Scottsdale where they booked a room in the Embassy Suites. Since they were playing Feds on a government expense account, it didn't look odd for them to be staying in an upscale hotel.

After checking into their room, their first stop was to make contact at the Phoenix office of the FBI, specifically with the domestic terrorist unit. In Phoenix this unit turned out to be one agent, Jason Bridges, and a GS-3 secretary.

After they introduced themselves and explained their business, Agent Bridges was more than willing to share what his unit had discovered about the mysterious terrorists who had struck the BII facilities. "The DTAU is of the opinion—"

"DTAU?" Blancanales interrupted.

"The Domestic Terrorist Analysis Unit," the agent explained. "In D.C."

Blancanales nodded.

"Anyway, they think that the Earth Angels are a classic example of a Type Three PM threat."

When Blancanales looked blank, the agent explained again. "The DTAU has developed a six-tiered classification system for domestic terrorists."

"What's a Type Three PM threat?" Schwarz couldn't keep himself from asking.

"That's a Post-Millennial Type Three group. They're characterized by a deep-seated disappointment with the lack of Y2K destruction. They see their mission as doing what should have been down back then, destroy the status quo so as to bring on the new times."

"I see."

"But," the agent continued, "I happen to think that there's a strong Type Two B carryover and maybe even a little Type Four D admixture."

He leaned forward, his eyes glittering, as he got deep into his rap. "When you're trying to run the parameters on something this far-reaching, the inclination is to short stroke the indicators and bypass some of the fourth-level material. But I think that when they complete the analysis of the Earth Angel manifesto, they're going to find that there's a lot of long-term commitment on the part of at least the first- and second-tier personnel. True, there may be a large admixture of the all too common angst displacement types who see the organization as a surrogate group-therapy unit. But I think that the age-displacement-per-hierarchy level won't turn out to be more than maybe 4.89 and that's almost too close to call it a mentor-mode organization. In fact, it's more of the sibling—"

"That's certainly very interesting," Blancanales said, keeping a straight face after having absorbed that barrage of double talk, "but have you developed any leads on who these people are yet?"

"Oh, no." The agent acted surprised at being asked such a mundane question. "We have to finish the analysis first and then start fielding some probe teams, you know, interdiction units, and they take at least four weeks per hierarchical level before they can start building the profile of what we like to call the zero member. After that, it takes—"

"Thank you, Agent Bridges." Blancanales stood. He had heard about all of this psychobabble he could take. If this guy was an example of what the FBI was doing, it was no wonder that they couldn't find their domestic terrorist ass with both analytical hands. "We'll be in touch."

"Oh," Schwarz said, "one more thing, if you don't mind. I'm curious. What kind of background do you have to get into this kind of work?"

"I did my graduate work in psychology with a stats minor," the agent said proudly.

"Fascinating."

When they got back to their rented Buick sedan, Carl Lyons was still shaking his head. "I've never heard such pure, unadulterated bullshit in my entire life.''

"Be glad that they've got their heads so far up their asses,'' Blancanales said. "Remember, we're the 'terrorists' they're looking for.''

"I still can't believe it.''

"I want to check in with the Arizona State Patrol next,'' Blancanales said. "They may be trying to crack this case the old-fashioned way. And, if they're making any progress, we need to know about it.''

"Whatever they're doing, it has to make more sense than that fool.''

Stony Man Farm, Virginia

WITH THE FULL WEIGHT of the federal government breathing down their necks, Aaron Kurtzman had handed over all of the mission-support activities he had been working on to Hunt Wethers. To do what he needed to do, he had to have his board clear.

Great advances had been made recently in antiviral cyber security, particularly in preparation for the Y2K festivities. Effective virus hunter-killer programs were now as common as dirt, and almost every computer owner had a good working knowledge of what to be on the lookout for. That didn't mean, however, that the danger of cyber viruses had ended. All it meant was that the amateurish attempts of would-be cyber anarchists and bored teenage hackers to create chaos in cyberspace had been blunted. It didn't mean that a professionally designed computer virus couldn't get past the security firewalls. The key word here was *professional,* and few were as professional at what they did as Aaron Kurtzman.

This time he would be going up against one of the best computer security systems he had ever encountered. Betancourt's people weren't slouches when it came to weaving bytes into cyber armor. That was why he decided to use the U.S. government to carry his virus to Betancourt. He had a long established satcom back channel into several government computer networks with prepared pathways through the firewalls.

The cyber weapon he chose to use this time was a worm that would burrow into the e-mail systems he invaded. It would remain dormant until messages with Betancourt's name or the name of his company were either received or composed. The worm would then hatch a one-time virus that would ride the message to its recipients and transfer the worm to their computers, as well.

The other thing the worm would do was encrypt the contents of the message in a code that only he could read. His personal code was based on the ancient Hittite language matrixed with the ancient Babylonian base-six numerical system and cross-indexed with the third sentence of each chapter of the first U.S. edition of *Winnie the Pooh.* It had taken him years to build the code, and he was confident that no one could bust it. At least not before Betancourt was cold in his grave.

CHAPTER FIFTEEN

Incirlik, Turkey

After touching down on the U.S. side of the air base at Incirlik, the C-141 carrying Phoenix Force taxied into a hangar for immediate off-loading. While their Hummers and gear were being taken from the Starlifter's cargo hold, Yakov Katzenelenbogen played the role of the DEA agent in charge of the operation and briefed the two Air Force officers who would be taking them to their final destination.

A special-ops C-130 Hercules turboprop transport had been chosen to fly them. The aircraft's pilot looked over the maps and recon photos Katz had brought.

"There's not all that much out there," he said. "We overfly that area a lot, keeping an eye on the Kurdish rebels for our Turkish allies."

"That's why I want to go in there," Katz said. "I don't want anyone to see us off-loading."

"I sure as hell wouldn't want to be stuck on the

ground anywhere around there," the copilot said. "That's some nasty country."

"We can come in from east to west," the pilot said, "and touch down on that dirt road." His gloved finger stabbed onto the photo. "We'll do the turn-around here." His finger tapped again. "Drop the ramp and put you out. That'll give us the downhill slope to take off with."

"Sounds good to me," Katz replied. "I'll have my men position the vehicles nose out, so we can be out of your plane and off the road in about six zero."

"You've done this before." The pilot grinned.

Katz kept his face straight. "You might say that."

"That's good, because I'm supposed to be a Spectre gunship driver, and I get a little weak-kneed when I'm driving a trash hauler and don't have anything to shoot back with."

"This is supposed to be a green LZ all the way."

The pilot looked a bit skeptical. He'd heard that line several times before and usually it was pure bull. To him, every LZ was hot until proved otherwise. "When do you want to leave?"

"Immediately."

The pilot raised one eyebrow. "We'd better get our act together, then."

"What can we do to help?"

"Just stand out of the way and let the ground crew do what they do."

"No sweat."

Once empty, the C-141 Starlifter was towed out of

the hangar and a charcoal-gray special-ops C-130 with its rear ramp down was towed into its place. Within a few minutes, they were airborne again.

THE C-130 BANKED up on one wing to give Katz and McCarter a good look at their Landing Zone. "You're right about this place being deserted," the pilot called back to Katz on the intercom. "There isn't even a goat in sight."

"Roger," Katz replied. "Put us down."

Phoenix Force took a cinch in their seat belts as the pilot brought the aircraft down in a steep, banked dive, leveling out at the last minute. The situation didn't call for the extreme acrobatics, but it was hard for a gunship pilot-to break his old, hard-earned habits. The instant the wheels touched down, he threw all four Allison T-56-A turboprops into reverse pitch and stood on the brakes.

Right before the aircraft shuddered to a stop, the pilot kicked in full left rudder, pushed the starboard prop controls into full forward pitch and nailed the portside brakes. The ship tried to spin on its own axis like a tank in neutral steer. The ramp started coming down before the turn was even completed, and the crew chief was standing by the Hummers' quick-release tie-downs.

The pilot called back, "Go! Go! Go!" and Phoenix Force leaped for their vehicles as the crew chief hit the releases on the tie-downs.

Jack Grimaldi was in the first Hummer and had it

down the ramp in a flash with Gary Manning hot behind him in the second vehicle. The other men grabbed the loaded duffel bags and ran down the ramp.

"We're clear," Katz shouted to the crew chief as he threw him a thumbs-up signal.

The Phoenix Force commandos turned their backs to the dust storm kicked up when the pilot revved his turbines and pulled full pitch to the prop blades. Seconds later, he came off the brakes and the aircraft was accelerating down the dirt road.

As the aircraft banked away to the north, the pilot wagged his wings in farewell.

Even though they hadn't seen anyone in the area on their approach, the Phoenix Force commandos quickly mounted up. Katz rode shotgun, with Grimaldi driving and Calvin James on the M-60. McCarter rode in Manning's Hummer, with Rafael Encizo on the machine gun. The location Bolan had given them was an hour and a half away, and they would be on full alert for every mile of the trip.

THE TWENTY MEN with Karim were the Kurdish leader's most trusted guardsmen, his blood brothers as he called them. Even so, it still took special men to guard nuclear weapons. Nuclear warheads represented real wealth and power. Even one of them could make a man wealthy beyond his wildest dreams.

Even though he had three such weapons, Karim

didn't have those dreams. His dream was to become the king of the Kurds. Not their elected president nor their prime minister, but their king. He wanted to leave his son something really worth having, a Kurdish kingdom.

His payment for these warheads wouldn't be mere money. That he could get by buying and selling almost anything. For this sale, he would be paid in goods that simply weren't obtainable in his part of the world. And with the goods would come the men to teach his people how to use them. Some of these goods would be weapons, granted. Any king had to defend what was his. But most of the rest would be things he would need to build the Kurds into a strong people.

In the long list of things he expected to receive were three complete hospitals, including the medicine that would be needed. All he would have to do would be to put the equipment in a building, staff it and be able to start caring for his people. Backing up the medical care would be water-purifying and well-digging equipment. Books and computers for schools were also high on his list. Agricultural equipment and supplies followed close behind on that list.

The Kurdish people were at best nomads and small farmers, living a lifestyle millennia old. That life had been disrupted when both the Iraqis and the Turks had started their programs of denying Kurdish statehood. The wars were on hold for now, but so was international aid to his people when the West allowed itself to become distracted. What little aid that did come in was for immediate survival needs, not what was needed to build a country. If the Kurds were to become a strong and independent people, they would have to do it for themselves, as he was now trying to do.

Karim knew what the outside world thought of those who trafficked in nuclear weapons, but he didn't care. It was no concern of his if the Arabs and Jews blew each other to oblivion just as long as it didn't affect the Kurds. He also had no great love for the Americans or the Russians. The U.S. had stepped in to protect them against Saddam Hussein, but that hadn't been from love for the Kurds. When he and other Kurdish leaders had tried to get U.S. approval for a Kurdish homeland, it had been denied. American aid had also vanished quickly, proving that they were of little importance to U.S. policy.

The Kurd warlord knew that the man he was selling the warheads to was as treacherous as a viper. Had he not been so useful, Derek Sanders would have been killed long ago as a warning to others who made their living by exploiting people in need. Karim himself would take great pleasure in ridding the world of him if Sanders were not the key to the betterment of his people.

Because of that, he had to host him for now. But after this deal was completed, if he ever saw Sanders again, he would kill him on sight.

WHEN DEREK SANDERS arrived at the Kurds' camp, he got right down to business. "The first ship is in Beirut," he said, "and the cargo has already been turned over to your people there."

"When are the other ships due to come in?" Karim asked.

Three shiploads of nonmilitary goods formed the core of the deal for the warheads. Since the Kurdish homeland had no access to the seas, Karim had been forced to use middlemen to pass the shipments on. Sanders was covering the costs of the bribes as part of the payment, but some of Karim's most trusted men were accompanying the goods.

"They'll arrive within the week," Sanders replied.

"And the weapons?"

"As we discussed, they're coming overland and should start arriving any time now."

"Good."

"Where are the warheads?" Sanders asked. "I need to make my arrangements for them to be picked up."

Karim smiled. "They will be here at the proper time. You can have your helicopters pick them up here. And to give you more security—" he pointed to a group of four men "—I have brought Stinger missiles to make sure that no one interrupts your plans."

Sanders looked and saw that each of the Kurds had a U.S.-made Stinger antiaircraft missile carrying case slung over his shoulder. It had been stupid for the

Americans to have handed those damned things out like cheap hot dogs during the Afghan war. The give-away had come back to haunt more than one man who tried to do business in the region. The presence of the missiles meant that Sanders would have to modify his plans.

"I understand," Sanders said. "I'll make sure to tell the pilots not to make any threatening moves when they approach this area."

"Also, tell your people not to come here in gun-ships. We Kurds have much experience with helicop-ter gunships, and we do not like to see them. If one should fly over, I might not be able to keep my men from shooting it down with their missiles."

"I'll tell them."

IT TOOK the full hour and a half for Phoenix Force to reach the center of the area they would search for Bolan. He had told them to come in from the east rather than risk being spotted on the road he and Yas-mine had traveled. Even though they had a full map and recon pack, the aerial recon photos didn't show how rough the terrain was, nor how barren.

"Time to make a call," Katz said when he checked his watch. He wished that Bolan had a radio with him, but the cell phone was better than nothing.

"About time you guys showed up," Bolan said, answering on the second ring. "Where are you?"

"We're on a flat to the west of a small ridgeline," Katz replied. "Right in the middle of the area you gave Kurtzman. One of the hills to the east looks like it's been through a landslide recently.''

"That should be the one we're under. There used to be a cave opening on the west side. Approach it from behind and you should find a small opening in the ground with a cell phone sticking out of it.''

"We're on the way.''

As Bolan had said, halfway up the reverse slope of the hill was a small opening in the ground. A brightly colored scarf was waving from it like a flag, and when Katz put his field glasses on it, he recognized Bolan.

"I've got you,'' he said over the phone.

"You're just in time.''

"Are you okay?'' Katz asked as he jumped out of his Hummer and rushed up to Bolan.

"We're fine,'' the soldier replied. "But how about passing down a couple of canteens?''

Katz handed him the one on his assault harness, and Bolan disappeared back into the cave with it.

He found Yasmine awake, but not sure of the voices she had heard. "What is happening?'' she asked.

"My friends have come to get us out of here,'' he said. Finding her hand in the dark, he gave her the canteen. "Here's water, but you have to drink it slowly.''

"I know,'' she said.

"I'm going to turn on the car's lights, too. Now

that they're here, it doesn't matter if I run the battery down.''

She squinted against the light, and Bolan could see that her face was drawn. "You stay here and drink the water," he told her. "I'm going back to help them widen the hole so we can get out."

"I'm sorry," she said.

"For what?"

"For not trusting you. I was afraid that we were going to die in here and I hate caves."

"It's okay now. We'll be out of here soon."

WHEN BOLAN GOT BACK to the opening he had made, he found Manning and Katz discussing a demolition solution. "I can quickly enlarge that hole with a couple of charges," Manning suggested. "Is there someplace you can take cover while I blast?"

"Don't do anything too vigorous," Bolan cautioned. "I don't trust the remaining rock ceiling. If any more of it comes down, we'll never get out."

"I'll just use a couple of RDX minicharges in the cracks and try to just flake some rock off, not blast it. Limestone breaks pretty clean."

"Go ahead," Bolan said. "But give me a com link so I can follow the countdown. We'll have take cover under the car again before you blast."

BACK IN THE CAVE, Bolan saw that Yasmine was looking better already. Water worked quickly on dehydration. "We need to take cover under the car again," he explained. "My friends are going to use explosive charges to enlarge that hole so we can get out."

When he saw her eyes flick to the roof of the cave, he said. "It's okay, they know what they're doing."

Once they were safe under the car, Bolan keyed the com link. "We're under cover."

"Roger. Fire in the hole."

When the smoke and dust cleared, Bolan went to the base of the chimney and saw that a six-foot-wide hole had been blasted out of the top and it was showing blue sky.

"Striker?" Manning yelled down into the dust.

"We're okay," Bolan called back over the com link. "Stand by to help my partner out of here first."

Now that their rescue was at hand, Yasmine seemed to have come out of her near coma. Bolan helped her to her feet and guided her over the rocks to the bottom of the chimney.

"I could use a rope down here," he called out over the com link.

"On the way."

When the rope slithered down from above, Bolan tied a rescue loop and slipped it over the woman's shoulders. "They'll pull you up slowly," he told her. "Just use your feet to keep yourself from slamming into the wall."

THE APPEARANCE of Yasmine as Bolan's partner brought a few grins from Phoenix Force. It wasn't written in stone anywhere that you had to spend all of your time in the field with a guy.

When the rope was thrown back down. Bolan came up hand over hand. The greetings were enthusiastic when he appeared and was unhurt.

"That's the first time I think I've seen you trapped in a cave," McCarter said, grinning.

"And the last as far as I'm concerned," Bolan stated, dusting off his clothing. "I don't recommend the accommodations."

CHAPTER SIXTEEN

Sudan

Even from a mile out, T. J. Hawkins could smell the camp their French Super Frelon helicopter was headed for. The stench of unwashed humanity and open latrines lay in the air like a thick, overpowering fog. The almost bare plain they had been flying over was one of the most desolate places on earth he had ever seen. It was little more than sunbaked red dirt broken only by stunted trees and the occasional mud hut. He had seen no animals and few humans. In fact, beyond the scrub brush, abandoned vehicles, most of them ex-military, were the most prominent landscape feature of the region.

His tramp steamer had made good time cross the Atlantic and had docked in some tiny Third World harbor whose identity he didn't have a chance to learn. The mercs hadn't been allowed off the ship until a flight of Super Frelon choppers had appeared. Though the aircraft had been built in France, the hel-

icopters were used all over Africa as civilian cargo
haulers and military troop transports.

One at a time, the choppers were loaded with men
and equipment from the ship and took off, continuing
eastward. They had landed once for refueling at another no-name place, but now Hawkins had a sinking
feeling that they were heading for their final destination.

The chopper full of mercenaries flew to a small
compound on the edge of the sprawling larger camp.
Ringed by barbed wire and sandbagged fighting positions, this was more what Hawkins had expected to
find at a mercenary camp. As the Frelon flared out
for a landing in the middle of the compound, he spotted a similar barbed-wire-ringed enclosure a half mile
away on the opposite side of the main camp. The two
fortified camps looked almost identical, and he had
to wonder who was occupying the other one.

After dropping their personal gear in the already
erected squad tents, the mercenaries spent the rest of
the day off-loading and positioning supplies from the
arriving choppers. By nightfall, Hawkins felt as if he
were back in the waiting days before the Gulf War
got started for real. Mercenaries usually weren't
worked like common laborers, but since their comfort
was in the offing, they didn't complain too much.

Dinner that night was Meals Ready to Eat—
MREs—as the mess hall hadn't been set up yet, but
their paymaster had seen fit to provide a three-can-
per-man beer ration. It was a nice gesture, but the

men were edgy that night and a couple of cans of beer weren't going to mellow them out. Only information would do that.

At formation the next morning, an older man with close-cropped hair, spit-shined boots, starched desert fatigues and a green beret walked out in front of them and called for them to stand at ease.

"I'm Major Bernard Hart, late of the South African Rifles. I don't have to be a bloody mind reader to know that you men want to know 'what in the hell is going on,' as I believe you Yanks like to say."

That brought a couple of laughs. Whoever this Hart guy was, he was an experienced officer who knew how to talk to men who weren't terribly happy.

"To start off," Hart said, "your mess hall and shower facilities will be up and running by tomorrow noon. Secondly, we will start the final phase of your training schedule the day after."

"What are we training for?" someone in the rear ranks called out.

Hart knew what the real question was and stated it. "You mean 'what is the mission and when do we kick off,' don't you?"

That got a few cheers, but Hawkins kept his mouth shut.

"I can tell you that your target is in a built-up area," Hart continued. "As far as the mission goes, you will go in wearing UN blue berets and armbands, and your transportation will carry UN markings. The plan is for you to be flown in, take vehicles to the target area, deposit an explosive device and withdraw. As the exercise is planned, you should be on the ground no more than an hour."

"What's our opposition?" one man in the group couldn't resist asking.

"Most of your opposition will be national police, but your UN markings will protect you from them. At the actual target site, there may be paramilitary resistance, but the numbers will be small."

Hawkins had enough experience with small-unit raids to smell a rat here. The size of the urban area they would be attacking hadn't been mentioned. But the size of the unit, sixty men, indicated that it wouldn't be some small desert town. Further, placing an explosive device and withdrawing wasn't how one properly employed a mercenary strike force. Unless, of course, and Hawkins felt his blood go cold at the thought, that device was nuclear. If that was the case, he was certain that he knew the identity of the target.

One of the few places in the Middle East where wearing UN uniforms and markings would protect them was Jerusalem. The UN contingent that had been sent to Jerusalem during the last attempt to destroy the city hadn't been withdrawn yet. If they went head to head with the UN troops, once the initial confusion cleared, it wouldn't go well for them. If the Irish Rifle Regiment was still there, it wouldn't go well at all. Those people were real pros.

"...day after tomorrow," Hart said. "We will air-lift you to the training area, and you'll start walking through the assault phase. Security on this has to remain tight, I'm sure you understand, so I ask you not to waste too much time speculating on the target. Just get the attack sequence down cold, and there should be no problems. It'll be a 'piece of cake,' as we used to say in the regiment.''

When the briefing broke up, Hawkins was surprised to see how few of the men showed any interest in what the mysterious target would turn out to be. As one of the mercenaries stated, "I don't give a shit where it is as long as I get to grease me some ragheads.''

That attitude concerned Hawkins. He was aware that the troops in this unit had been chosen from the religiously motivated, but he had expected a more professional caliber of men. More and more this was beginning to take on the aspect of a crusade, and everyone knew how those usually turned out. A burning religious zeal to kill the unbelievers, whoever they might be, was no substitute for hard-core military experience. And, while Hawkins had learned that there were quite a few peacetime-service veterans in the group, there weren't many actual combat veterans.

The mercenaries' lack of buckle in the dirt, bullet time combined with a burning desire to kill those who didn't think the way they did wasn't a formula for battlefield success. The peacetime U.S. military did a pretty good job training a man to shoot and to work as part of a team. But, when it came to combat, that which was untested, remained unknown.

If his hunch was right and Jerusalem was the target, these mercenaries could get off on killing Arabs and Jews, but they would also be going up against battle-hardened Israelis, as well U.N. troops. Anyone who took on the Israelis on their home turf knew there were easier ways to commit suicide.

And, speaking of suicide, if the explosive device Hart had mentioned was a nuke, as he feared, it would be a suicide mission. The only problem was that those who would be doing the dying hadn't been let in on the joke.

Hawkins decided to wait until they started the final training before he tried to bail out and contact Stony Man. The more he could report, the more helpful it would be to get to the bottom of just what was going on.

The barren landscape he had seen on the flight in indicated that he was right in the middle of miles and miles of miles and miles, as they said at home. The only way he'd be getting out of the area was by driving. That meant that he had to start scouting out a vehicle. It would also help if he knew where in the hell he was. From as far as they'd flown and the nature of the terrain, his top picks were Somalia, Ethiopia or maybe even Sudan. They all had high desert plateaus like this and were known for their sprawling refugee camps.

He'd keep an eye out for a map and try to learn at

least what country he was in. That would make a big difference when he did finally split. Until then, though, he had a soldier's job to do, and he could soldier with the best.

Turkey

"WHO'S YOUR FRIEND?" Katz nodded toward the young woman who had been offered an MRE. She was hungry enough that she had accepted it and was wolfing it down as if it tasted good.

"She goes by Yasmine," Bolan replied, "and she's the daughter of Derek Sanders's worst enemy in the region, a smuggler named Mustapha the Black. Sanders kidnapped her for ransom when she was younger, and neither father nor daughter have forgotten the incident."

"'The enemy of my enemy is my friend,'" Katz recited, the number-one rule of conducting business, any kind of business, in the Middle East.

"That's about it," Bolan replied. "Plus, her father runs one of the biggest smuggling networks in the region. I wouldn't have been able to stay on Sanders's trail if it wasn't for him and Yasmine. They have eyes in damned near every village in the area."

"That's the way things usually work around here," Katz acknowledged. "His spies are probably the members of an extended family group."

"Striker," James called over the com link from his observation post on top of the ridge, "we have a small convoy of black Mercedes sedans heading our way fast.''

"Wait one, I'm coming up."

"Yasmine," Bolan said, turning to the girl, "your father might be coming. My friends spotted a convoy of cars approaching."

As soon as she had been pulled out of the cave, Bolan had let her call her father to let him know that she was safe. In her exhaustion, she hadn't thought to let him know that Mustapha was already in the area looking for her. Since he knew the smuggler's cave well, he had made good time.

Bolan took Yasmine to the vantage point and loaned her his field glasses. "Those are our cars," she said, nodding. "I will go down and meet them so there is no misunderstanding."

"I need to have my people surround the meeting place," Bolan said. "And until we can talk things out, I'll need to disarm them. I can't take chances on a distraught father."

Yasmine took a deep breath. Whoever this Belasko man was, he was a true warrior and he had saved her life, so she owed him. "I will see that a fight does not start."

"That will be best for all of us."

"I KNEW YOU were a soldier," Mustapha the Black said bitterly as he watched his men being disarmed under the muzzles of Phoenix Force's Hummer-mounted M-60 machine guns. Katz had positioned the commandos along an L-shaped ridgeline in a classic ambush layout while Bolan and Yasmine waited in the open below so they couldn't be missed. Mustapha had been so overjoyed to see his daughter safe that he had completely missed seeing her new bodyguards.

When all the Turks were out of their cars and focused on the reunion of father and daughter, the Phoenix Force warriors came down. There had been no chance for them to resist.

"I didn't lie to you," Bolan said. "We're not American soldiers, and, while we sometimes work for the U.S. government, this time we're working on our own."

"But you have—"

"Like I told you," Bolan said, "we're here to put an end to Derek Sanders and to keep those warheads out of his hands, nothing else. If we get the chance, though, we're going to take out Karim and his organization at the same time so this can't happen again."

"What are you going to do with me and my men?"

"As soon as you're no longer a danger to us, you're free to go."

"Just like that?"

"Why not?" Bolan answered. "I appreciate all the help you've given to put me on the right path to catch up with Sanders. But from now on it's going to get serious, and you don't need to be involved."

"He is not the enemy, Father." Yasmine spoke up

in English so the Westerners would understand what she was saying. "He uncovered the traitor within our family, and he saved my life in the cave. We owe him and his men."

"For saving you from a danger he himself put you in?"

"No—" she met her father's eyes squarely "—for being an honorable man."

Mustapha shook his head. "Are you sure that you weren't hurt in the earthquake, daughter? This man came into my house as a guest and he—"

"He did what he had to do so that he could get on the trail of a man who has once again proved to be a danger to us. He did not abuse your hospitality, and, in fact, I think the family is indebted to him for exposing Gamal. That I was at risk was my own choice, and if you are not going to help him, I will go alone."

"Daughter—" Mustapha started to say in Turkish.

"Don't 'daughter' me," she snapped back in English. "Since I am over eighteen, under the enlightened laws of the modern Turkish republic, I am my own woman. I will go with these men wherever I want to avenge my family's honor."

"Yasmine," Bolan said, "maybe it would be better if..."

She spun on him, her green eyes flashing. "Are you telling me that you do not want me to help you, Mr. Belasko? Do you also think that I am merely a woman, an 'ill favored' woman if I remember what you said about me correctly."

McCarter and Katz exchanged glances, and the Israeli intervened. "Striker," he said, "I think we can use her. For a start, she knows more about the target than we do. Secondly, I barely have enough Turkish to order a beer. We may need someone who understands what's being said."

When Bolan nodded his assent, Katz turned back to the Turk. "Mustapha," he said, "when I look at you, I see an honorable man who has a dilemma. On the one hand, I see a father who is trying to protect his daughter. And, I must admit that if I had a daughter who was such a rare beauty, I would protect her with my last drop of blood. I also see a man who has raised this rare flower to uphold the honor of her family. She feels that she has been wronged, and she wants vengeance.

"We—" Katz swept his arm out to encompass Phoenix Force "—aren't men who are accustomed to losing the battles we fight. We also know, though, that any man or woman can die, and I cannot promise that all of us will come out of this alive. I can, however, promise you that as long as even one of us is on his feet, he will be at your daughter's side protecting her."

"Now you shame me," Mustapha said to Katz. "You foreigners pledge to protect her while I only want her to go home and be safe. You are a wise man, but you are also a very devious man. I do not think that I would like to gamble with you. I would lose my teeth."

"Only your back ones." Katz smiled. "I always leave a man his front teeth."

"Okay," the Turk said, "if you give us back our guns, we will go with you. What will happen—" he shrugged "—will be in the hands of God."

The mood lightened when Mustapha's men got their weapons back.

WITH MUSTAPHA'S dozen men reinforcing Phoenix Force, Katz had a strike force large enough to take on whatever they might find when they caught up with Derek Sanders. After a short conversation with Bolan and McCarter, the consensus was to go for it and finish the job.

"What do you think we can expect to find when we catch up with this Sanders?" Katz asked the Turk.

"My information is that he's meeting with a man named Karim," Mustapha replied. "Even for a bastard Kurd, he's a bad one. He deals with anyone who will pay him for his goods or services, and he's worked with both terrorists and government agencies alike. If he is selling missile warheads this time, he will have a large bodyguard with him. Maybe twenty to thirty men, and they will be well armed."

"How about heavy weapons?" McCarter asked.

"Maybe a machine gun and certainly a couple of RPGs."

McCarter and Katz exchanged glances. That was a little heavier force than they had expected to have to deal with, but it had to be done.

"Don't forget that Sanders has a dozen men with him, as well," Yasmine added. No one had noticed her walk up to the council of war, but when Bolan nodded, McCarter and Katz accepted her input. "They are believed to be men for hire, but that does not make then any less dangerous."

Breaking out a map, McCarter laid it on the hood of one of the Hummers. "Okay," he said. "That makes us outnumbered by only two to one. Let's recon this thing and get it on the road."

CHAPTER SEVENTEEN

Stony Man Farm, Virginia

The news that Bolan had been rescued flashed through Stony Man Farm like a lightning strike. Barbara Price knew that the soldier had more lives than a bag full of cats, but he had sure used up one of them this time. An earthquake wasn't something that skill and determination could automatically conquer. Surviving an earthquake required an element of luck, as well, and once more the big guy's legendary luck had held.

As happy as Price was to have Bolan accounted for, it reminded her that Hawkins was still missing, and she had to turn her attention to finding him. At the time she had sent him undercover, it had made good tactical sense. But, as the situation had developed, it turned out to have been a bad move. Part of the problem was that Stony Man had too many pots on the fire and too few people to watch them all. Making it worse was the fact that she couldn't openly call upon the resources of the United States government to help out.

Damn Betancourt anyway! She had to resist the urge to ask Lyons to make a serious attempt against the man, but he was too well guarded. If there were any way to get to him, she would have no compunctions against taking him out, sanctioned or not. He had crossed the line and was living on borrowed time, but he was still in a position to be able to cause untold damage before he was finally taken down.

Even though Brognola had told her to have Able Team back off, she wasn't willing to play turtle and pull everything inside the shell of the Farm. Betancourt needed watching, and there were still things Able Team could do that shouldn't set off any alarm bells in the Oval Office.

Turkey

WHEN THE STONY MAN team and its new allies moved out again, Mustapha's four black Mercedes sedans led the column. Katzenelenbogen rode with the Turk in the lead car, and Yasmine took her place in the lead Hummer with Bolan. The M-60s on the Hummers were manned again as they carefully moved up into the mountains. Mustapha had said that they wouldn't be able to get closer than a mile to Karim's camp in the vehicles, but they would run the trails and back roads as long as they could.

It HAD TAKEN several cell-phone calls before Karim was satisfied that Derek Sanders had fulfilled his end of the bargain. When the Kurd gave the word that the deal was on, Sanders only had to make one call to have the transport on the way. In ten minutes, three desert-camouflaged Russian-built Mi-8 Hip helicopters appeared over the Kurdish camp.

These machines were the Russian equivalent of the American UH-1 Hueys, and they were the most common chopper throughout the Middle East and Eastern Europe. As he had instructed the pilots, they flew in high and slow so as not to spook the Kurds. On a radio command, they dropped down to land at the makeshift chopper pad in the middle of the valley. Sanders had the pilots keep the turbines burning and the rotors turning. It wouldn't take long for the warheads to be loaded on, but he didn't want to waste any more time here than he had to. The Hips were larger than Hueys, so they could carry cargo, as well as troops. One warhead would be loaded into each of the aircraft and Sanders's bodyguards would split up to accompany them.

As soon as the choppers landed, the Kurd produced the warheads as if by magic. They had been on-site all along. Sanders checked each of the stainless-steel transport cases and found them to be intact with all of their monitoring and triggering devices present. There was nothing more useless than a nuke weapon without its trigger.

After the last warhead was securely strapped down,

Sanders turned to Karim. "Maybe I will see you again someday," he said as he stuck his hand out.

Karim took the American's hand. It wasn't out of friendship, but it signaled the conclusion of the deal. "As God wills it." The Kurd wasn't willing to commit himself any further than that.

Sanders smiled as he swung himself into the lead chopper. Karim was soon going to learn that God played games with those who depended on him too much. Giving the pilot a thumbs-up, he said. "Let's get out of here."

The pilot twisted his throttle, pulled pitch on the collective and the helicopter rose off the ground. Looking out the side window, Sanders saw the other two choppers following behind and relaxed. He had pulled it off, and now it was time for the insurance shot.

"Come and get them," he transmitted over the radio.

PHOENIX FORCE HAD halted its vehicles a mile short of Karim's camp and went the rest of the way on foot. Surprisingly, they spotted few outposts in the hills around the little valley. For a transfer of nuclear weapons, they had expected better security. When they finally reached a vantage point above the valley, they saw why the security had been pulled in. The goods had already been transferred and the Kurds were packing up their camp.

"Damn!" David McCarter said when he saw the

three Hips lift off and turn to the southwest. "We're too late."

"Not too late to deal with that scum." Mustapha nodded toward the Kurd's camp below.

"That's not what we're here for," Katz said as he studied the valley camp through his binoculars. "But..."

Even though the helicopters had cleared the area, the sounds of chopper rotors suddenly returned and the smugglers looked to the sky in alarm. A couple of the Kurds unslung the Stinger missile launchers from their backs and readied them for firing.

"They've got company," McCarter said, spotting the intruders. "Take cover."

Looking like flying dragons, the unmistakable shapes of two Russian Mi-24 Hind gunships rose over the top of the ridgeline. In the realm of rotary-winged warfare, the heavily armed, and armored, Hind was king and every Kurd alive knew it.

These two aerial killers mounted a full load of ordnance under their stub wings, four 57 mm rocket pods each containing thirty-two ground-attack rockets, and a pair of Swatter antitank missiles. Their nose turrets contained a four-barrel 12.7 mm heavy machine gun, and they had come to kill.

Rather than working as a pair, the two Hinds split up and flew into the small valley from opposite directions in a figure eight orbit. As they started their initial runs, both gunships started to fire flares to counter heat-seeking missiles.

The Hind working from the west was pulling out of its run when the first Stinger was fired. Someone in the Hind had to have caught the Stinger's launch flare because the decoy flares started to fire again. The Stinger locked on to the first flare that crossed its path and vectored into it to detonate harmlessly.

The second Hind was covering the first and saw the launch flare, as well. With a twitch of its tail, it was on the cluster of Stinger gunners in a flash, all four 57 mm rocket pods blazing.

For a relatively small ground-attack weapon, the Russian 57 mms weren't to be scoffed at, particularly when they could be salvoed by the dozens. A couple dozen of the rockets tore into the Kurds, shredding them and everything around them for a fifty-yard radius.

Since the Kurds had now proved themselves to be a serious threat, the Hinds got serious.

"We got suckered big time," McCarter said as he watched the Hinds work out. Since the Russian gunships were armored to withstand 20 mm cannon fire, there was nothing Phoenix Force could do but duck and cover and hope they weren't spotted.

"How about those poor bastards down there?" James asked.

"Screw them," he snapped. "They're just getting what they deserve. They should have known that trafficking in nukes could be hazardous to their health."

As soon as the Hind gunships had cleared the area, Katz sent Mustapha's men into the Kurd's camp, with

Phoenix Force following in the Hummers. He didn't think that the surviving Kurds would be up to much of a fight, but he would take no chances with them. If they hadn't had enough, he was ready to give them more of the same.

Mustapha's men started to round up the survivors of Karim's bandit band. The Kurd leader himself was among the dead, having gotten in the way of a hail of 12.7 mm machine-gun rounds. Being the equivalent of the U.S. .50-caliber round, they had left barely enough of him to identify.

With Karim dead, the others had lost all their fight. All they wanted to do was to return to the Kurdish heartland and their families. Once more, a Kurdish leader had shown himself to be less than wise in the ways of the rest of the world. Now that Karim was dead, they would sign on with the next candidate for the job who looked to have the ability to bring his people out of the situation they were in.

The Kurds openly told Mustapha everything they knew about the transaction their late leader had made. The problem was that they didn't know anything. They knew Sanders's name, the nature of the cargo they had loaded into the three choppers, but that was it. They had no idea where the choppers were to deliver their cargo.

"Get Kurtzman on the horn," Katz told Manning. "I need to talk to him."

Phoenix, Arizona

GRANT BETANCOURT SMILED when he got the report from Sanders. The warheads were now en route to their final destinations. Once they were in the hands of the mercenary units, the final phase of the training could start. Since he wasn't working against a rigid deadline this time, he could have the men rehearse the attacks over and over until every last detail had been worked out to his satisfaction. And he wouldn't launch until they were.

Nothing less than the future of humankind was at stake here, and he wouldn't allow himself to fail a second time. Now that the new millennia had started, the sooner that the age-old religious hatreds and superstitions were eradicated, the sooner that humanity could finally start working to reach its full potential.

His BII companies were poised and ready to help the people of the Middle East, in particular, to make the difficult transition from their backward Bronze Age cultures to the bright world of modern science and technology. The transition would be easier in the Western European Christian countries because they had been forced to modernize somewhat in the past century. The Eastern Europeans of the old Soviet Bloc, though, had been cursed by both the church and Marxism and would need almost as much help as the Muslim nations. In any case, once the priests, under whatever name they operated, lost their power structure, he was ready to bring these people into the modern world.

BII had everything from modular hospitals and schools to agricultural advisory teams ready to kick start an industrial revolution in these regions. He was aware that it would take a few years for all this to get into full operation, but it would be worth the wait. Children who now could only look forward to a life of abject poverty living in shacks and herding goats would now be able to become engineers, technicians, medical doctors, architects and teachers instead.

His name would never be associated with this revolution, but he would die knowing that he had given humankind the greatest gift since the invention of the wheel. The wheel had freed men's backs; he would free their minds.

With that part of his plan well in hand now, Betancourt could refocus on his domestic enemies, the elusive Farm the President had accidentally mentioned. So far, he hadn't found anyone who would admit to knowing of it. A few of the older men remembered the cold war CIA Farm outside of Arlington, but they knew that it had been closed a long time ago.

Everyone had also heard unsubstantiated stories, modern myths more than anything else, about a group of commandos who worked completely off the books to handle critical jobs that couldn't be allowed to see the light of day. Everyone had his favorite version of the story, a fertilizer factory in the Libyan desert destroyed, a chemical-warfare stockpile in Iran blasted, a terrorist gang hunted down and killed, the list went on. In each case, though, there was just enough substance to the stories that he had come to realize that this was what he was looking for.

Modern international politics didn't lend itself to swift, effective action against any danger. How many times had Saddam Hussein been warned to stop doing something, or else? The problem was that the threat of "or else" was never carried out, so the threats to take action were more than empty; they were a joke. If these stories he had heard over drinks in private offices and exclusive clubs had any basis in truth, however, someone was making good on the threats. In fact, there was a finely tuned weapon in existence that was being freely, albeit secretly, employed.

He understood the principle involved and wholeheartedly approved of it. He, too, believed in direct action rather than endless blustering and blathering. If he could get his hands on a spare nuke, he'd probably take out the UN building when the delegates were in session. That, too, would improve the condition of humankind. But, as much as he approved of this clandestine action group, it was being targeted against him instead of against the real threats in the world and he had to put a stop to that.

Stony Man Farm, Virginia

THE JUBILATION that had come with Bolan's rescue quickly faded when Katzenelenbogen reported that

Derek Sanders had gotten away with the warheads.

"Now what?" Hal Brognola asked.

"I'll be damned if I know. None of the surviving Kurds know anything about where the nukes are going."

"What do you want to do now?"

"I'm thinking about taking us down to Adana," Katz replied. "It's the fourth-largest Turkish city and has an international airport and a port in nearby Mersin. We can base out of there and see what we can develop."

"If I remember correctly," Brognola said, "there's a DEA office there that's keeping an eye on Syrian and Kurdish smuggling, so you can continue to use your cover story. I can tell them to expect your arrival and to put their resources at your disposal."

"Don't tell them we're actually coming," Katz cautioned. "Just put them on alert in case we need them. I'd like to play this one as close to our vests as we can."

"I understand," Brognola said, and he did. Involving other federal agencies always carried a risk, and this time it could be downright dangerous. He'd be glad to get back to the status they had enjoyed before the Betancourt affair started. If, that was, they survived this.

THE GODS OF WAR WERE a fickle bunch, and few men knew that as well as Yakov Katzenelenbogen. They had cost him one of his arms and his beloved son. He knew war cold, and he had created Phoenix Force to be the finest strike force on the planet. But even the best couldn't win all of the time. The gods didn't allow it.

Phoenix Force had lost this one. Three Russian missile warheads were in the wind, and there was no telling where they would turn up next. He had a good idea though; Mecca, Jerusalem and the Vatican. Phoenix Force and Able Team had turned back one attack against those three most sacred sites, but a man didn't get to where Grant Betancourt was without being able to accept setbacks, reload and try again.

The simple solution to ending this threat would be to take out Betancourt. That was usually the most effective action to take in these circumstances, but it was the one that was the most rarely used. In the muddy world of politics, where clear thinking was against the law, killing the viper was never seen as the sure cure for snakebite. In the name of pious ideals and misplaced humanity, everyone always wanted to somehow magically turn the poisonous snake into a harmless bunny.

Historians had written volumes on what history would have been had Hitler been assassinated before his rise to power. If Stony Man couldn't pull this off, they would do the same about Grant Betancourt.

With Betancourt off limits, Katz had to go back to basics and run a search-and-destroy mission. But locating the enemy was always where those operations fell short. Destroying the bastards was never much of a problem—finding them was.

Also, in the rush to rescue Bolan and the attempt to capture the warheads, the fact that T. J. Hawkins had disappeared had taken a back seat. Katz was sure that Hawkins would understand, but now that the Farm was back in a searching mode, it wouldn't hurt to look for him while they were at it. When he had mentioned his concern about Hawkins to Barbara Price, he'd been happy to hear that her mind was working on the same track. He wanted the Southerner back safely within the fold.

[faded text from previous page bleeding through]

CHAPTER EIGHTEEN

Sudan

Hawkins's first day of training in the new location had gone well. They had been flown to a training site, disembarked and formed into an assault team and a security team. Then they had practiced moving through a replica of a built-up area marked out by engineer tape tied on stakes. The final objective had been a square building inside of a larger rectangular enclosure. He didn't have to be a map maker or an archaeologist to recognize it as the area around the Dome of the Rock in Jerusalem.

So far, his hunch had been right on, and if a nuclear weapon showed up in the next couple of days, he wouldn't be at all surprised. This obsession with blowing up major religious centers was starting to get real old. Hawkins didn't consider himself to be a religious man, but he knew that many people defined themselves by the religion they followed. He'd killed more than his share of his fellow man, but to kill and destroy based on religion had always struck him as being the most monstrous of crimes.

It had been, however, one of the most constant stories of the past two thousand years. And it didn't look as if it was going to be ending any time soon.

"YOU KNOW," one of the mercs in Hawkins's tent said that evening, "there's something real fishy going on around this place."

"What do you mean?" Hawkins asked.

"Well—" the man winked "—I kind of stepped out last night looking for a little poontang, you know. And I ended up on the other side of this shithole and you can't guess what I found there."

"What was that?"

"Well, I found out that there's another camp exactly like this a quarter mile or so from here, but it's filled with Arabs."

That got Hawkins's immediate attention. "How do you know that?"

The soldier shrugged. "You know, they're wearing tablecloths on their heads like those goddamned Palestinian terrorists," he said, "and they're armed, too, but with AKs and RPGs."

Hawkins's group was equipped with U.S. weapons, M-16 rifles, M-60 machine guns and M-203 grenade launchers. For a mercenary force of Americans, it made sense to give them weapons they were likely to be familiar with. It made equal sense to equip an Arab unit with the Russian-designed weapons they knew so well.

"Shit, man," the mercenary said. "If I didn't know any better, I'd say that they're PLO or maybe even Iraqis."

"How do you know they're not?"

"Well, I saw that major who comes here talking to what looked like their officers. What in the hell would a guy like him be doing with Arabs?"

"Maybe they're white guys just wearing the head-dress like we're going to wear UN berets."

"Nope, they're some kind of Arabs. I saw enough of the bastards in the Gulf to know what they look like."

"Did you find that tail you were looking for?" one of the other men asked with a big grin.

"No. When I saw those bastards, it kind of ruined the mood, if you know what I mean, and I just came back."

"I don't know what to tell you," Hawkins said. "This is kind of a strange setup any way you look at it."

"It beats the hell out of me," the soldier said. "But I can tell you that I don't like being around those bastards. I've got no fucking use for them."

That didn't surprise Hawkins; most of the men in the unit had expressed strong feelings about both Muslims and Jews, and they hadn't been positive views. He remembered that he had been asked what he thought of Arabs and Jews when he had been interviewed in the States to join the unit. His response had been guardedly neutral, but apparently it had been right enough for him to be selected.

This did, however, add a piece to the puzzle. Kurtzman's initial information had indicated that three mercenary groups were being recruited. If his American unit was being targeted against Jerusalem, the Arab unit would certainly be targeted against the Vatican. The Arabs hadn't forgotten the Crusades and still had a hard-on against Christianity for the two-hundred-year bloodbath that had been conducted in the name of the Prince of Peace.

His theory left Mecca still to be accounted for. And, for that target, he was certain that the unit would be made up of radical Jews. He hadn't seen a third camp on the flight in, so this hypothetical third merc group was probably stashed away somewhere else.

He now had enough information to make it worth his while to try to escape. He still hadn't, however, learned where he was, nor had he located a vehicle. Both of those things needed to be done before he would plan his exit.

Since the mercenary hadn't had much trouble getting out of the camp at night, Hawkins decided to try it himself. If he got caught, he could always say that he had heard that there were native women for hire. That he was trying to get laid was a story anyone would believe of a bored mercenary.

ALTHOUGH SENTRIES were guarding the merc camp, it was no trick for Hawkins to talk his way out of the front gate. He had decided not to go out armed, but he did tuck the sheath of his fighting knife into the back of his belt under his fatigue jacket. If he ran into any situation that he couldn't take care of with cold steel, he'd get the hell out of the area.

The mercenaries' camp had a cleared zone of one hundred yards all the way around it marked with razor wire to insure that the locals left them alone. As beaten down as these people were, however, it was probably a waste of good wire. From what he had seen, the refugees weren't about to mess with well-fed men with guns.

There were no streets through the camp, but Hawkins had his bearings and made his way more or less in the direction of the other armed compound. With crude brush huts and plastic-tarp tents scattered haphazardly, making a beeline for his destination was impossible. The camp should have been featured on one of those celebrity sponsored telethons. But the place was so far away from anything that there was no easy way for the TV cameras to get in. These people were slowly starving to death, but since they were doing it off camera, no one cared.

When Hawkins reached the center of the camp, he came upon a large tent that was showing lights. Since the only way to get light was a portable generator, this was worth detouring to take a look at.

A dusty Toyota pickup truck was parked in front of the tent. In the light spilling from the open tent flap, he made out the words Sudan Relief Agency hand-painted on the door. Bingo, that answered his biggest question. Now he knew that he was in one of the worst hellholes on earth. Nearly anywhere else in the world would have been better than being in the Sudan.

One of the worst things about the Sudan was that it was a big country, and he had no idea what part of it he was in. The second thing was that the entire country had been embroiled in an utterly vicious religious civil war for decades now. Even for Africa, the Sudan had never really been a part of the modern world and now it could barely even be called primitive. The idea of finding a train or even a long-haul trucker to get him to the border was completely out of the question.

That left his feet. Or a Toyota pickup belonging to the Sudan Relief Agency.

The truck was the first vehicle he had seen in the camp, but he had no idea if it was stationed here or just visiting. Making a snap decision, he headed in closer to check out what he hoped was going to be his ride.

Just as he was stepping into the light from the tent, he caught voices and saw a man step out. Ducking back into the shadows, Hawkins waited to see how this would shake out. When the man got into the driver's side of the truck, he saw his way out. He'd hitch a ride to wherever this guy was going and make his way out from there.

He was just about to go into his carjacking mode when another man stepped out of the tent, and this one was packing an AK held at the ready. With nothing but his fighting knife to back his play, the assault rifle was a trump card. Keeping in the dark, he watched the truck drive away.

He'd missed this chance, but maybe the truck would come again and he could make his move then.

Rather than press on to the Arab compound, he returned to his own camp.

"Hey, Dub," one of the sentries called out to him from the camp gate. "You'd better get your ass back in here, man. They're having a formation in fifteen minutes and they sound pissed."

"Thanks, buddy," Hawkins said, sketching a salute.

Turkey

WHEN MUSTAPHA HEARD that Bolan and Phoenix Force were planning to stay over in Adana, he arranged for them to have the use of a safehouse in the city complete with cook and security guards. Since Yasmine insisted on going with the Westerners, that was the least he could do. He had also arranged for their heavy hardware to be secreted into the town so Phoenix Force wouldn't have to run the risk of being caught with it in their vehicles. Since they were coming out of Kurdish territory, there was always the chance of their running into a police counterterrorist checkpoint.

"Your father's people are efficient," Bolan told Yasmine when he found their machine guns and rocket launchers waiting for them when they arrived at the villa in Adana.

She smiled. "We have been successful in this business for a long time now, so we have had to be good."

Waiting also at the house was a room full of cosmetics and clothing for her. After her ordeal in the cave, she couldn't wait to get cleaned up.

AFTER FLYING the warheads to the Turkish side of the divided island of Cyprus, Derek Sanders remained behind when the choppers were refueled and took off again. As Betancourt's offshore-operations officer, he would oversee the attacks from a fortified villa on the island. His European mercs and their two dozen men would provide his security and be on standby as an additional mobile strike force.

On Sanders's second day on the island, he got a report from his agent in what was left of Karim's Kurdish war band. To keep from wasting another valuable contact, he'd made sure that the man hadn't been in the camp when the Hinds had sanitized the place after the warheads had been delivered.

According to the report, Mustapha's daughter and the mystery man traveling with her had somehow been rescued from the cave-in. Then, along with other soldiers believed to be Americans and accompanied by Mustapha's house troops, they had swooped down on what was left of Karim's camp to interrogate the surviving Kurds. Reportedly, the sole topic of the interrogation had been the missile warheads and where Sanders was planning to take them.

That much was to be expected from this mystery force. The big surprise, though, was that after the questioning, the men had moved into one of Mustapha's safehouses in Adana. Sanders had no idea why these Americans—and that tentative identification made sense to him—were staying there. There was no way that they could know where the warheads had been taken. Nonetheless, their continued presence in Turkey was a threat to his operation, and he didn't like threats.

Betancourt had chosen to run his enterprises from Turkish Cyprus for several reasons. One was simply its geographical location with easy connections to Syria, Lebanon and Israel by sea and the rest of the Middle East by air. Secondly, the divisive politics and depressed economys of the divided island made it a perfect breeding ground for the kind of men he hired to do his dirty work. And, when he needed trained specialists instead of thugs, Cyprus was also a major overseas R and R camp for a dozen terrorist groups.

It took no time at all for him to find out that there was a large Islamic Brotherhood action team that was resting and refitting on the island. If he could hire them, it was a fast ferry ride to Mersin, the port near

Adana, and a shorter drive into the city itself. The Brotherhood didn't come cheaply, but Betancourt had given him a generous operating budget and he had the funds to buy a little of their time.

EVEN THOUGH Katzenelenbogen didn't know of any active opposition against them now, he wasn't about to let his guard down. Adana wasn't Beirut, but it wasn't Disneyland, either. Even without an active war going on in it, there was no place in the Middle East that could really be called safe. The region had been a virtual war zone for so many decades that peace was a stranger.

Mustapha's villa was walled, and the Turk had placed a dozen of his men at his daughter's disposal. She had put them to work guarding the villa. Even though he was a guest, Katz carefully inspected the villa's defenses. He found few flaws in either the physical layout or the men, but that didn't let him relax his guard. All it did was make him remind Phoenix Force not to let their weapons get too far away from their hands.

THE DOZEN-MAN Islamic Brotherhood strike force waited in a van parked in the shadows at the edge of a wealthy residential district in Adana. They were waiting for the return of their scout from the final recon of their target. When a man wearing Turkish clothing walked up to the van, the rear door opened and he entered the vehicle.

The report was as the strike force leader had expected. The villa was at the end of a narrow street, but the road was wide enough to get their van though. The entrance gate in the villa's walls was directly in line with that street, making it perfect for one of the Brotherhood's signature car-bomb attacks. As had been seen earlier, there were two Turkish guards on the gate and four more stationed around the walls.

As the scout changed into a night-black combat suit, the other men in the van made a last check of their weapons. When the leader nodded, six men paired in two-man teams left the van and started toward the target. They would go over the walls after the bomb went off.

The leader and four of the remaining men waited out the time for the first teams to reach their targets before they exited the van. They were the main assault team and would follow the van.

One of the remaining men was considerably younger than the other holy warriors, and he burned with the desire to remove a stain on his family's name. A few years earlier his older sister had gone to France to study medicine, but had fallen in love and married a Christian. When his older brother, a member of the Brotherhood, had gone to Paris to kill his sister for disgracing the family, he had been captured by the French antiterrorist police. Immediately after his arrest, several Brotherhood cells in France had been raided. It was believed that he had broken his vows and had talked under interrogation.

In order to regain God's grace for his family, the young man had volunteered to drive the van laden with explosives into the villa compound and detonate it.

"Go with God." The leader reached through the open window of the driver's door and patted the young man on the shoulder.

"As God wills it," the young man answered firmly as he started the van's engine and slipped the gearshift lever into first.

"Put your lights on," the leader reminded him. "You're supposed to be lost and you stop to ask for directions."

"*Allah ahkbar,*" the driver proclaimed as he switched on the lights.

"*Allah ahkbar.*"

CHAPTER NINETEEN

Adana

The guards Mustapha had assigned to protect the Adana villa were some of his most trusted men. After the Gamal incident, he wasn't taking chances with his daughter's safety again. Nor was he taking any chances on firepower; all of his troops were packing either 9 mm Beretta Model 12 submachine guns or 5.56 mm H&K G-33 assault rifles. Six guards were on duty at a time, and at least three of the off-duty crew were always on the premises as their backup. Combined with the firepower of Phoenix Force, both Katzenelenbogen and Mustapha felt that they were well covered.

The firepower, though, hadn't made the Turkish guards overly confident. The events of the past several days had shown them that they were facing a resourceful, dangerous enemy. Also, with their boss's daughter in-house, they knew better than to allow any harm to come to her. Mustapha was a fair man, but he was also a father.

Both guards at the gate instantly reacted when they saw the headlights of the Fiat van come out of the side street and turn toward them. Taking cover, they trained their assault rifles on it and waited. Since the vehicle was coming on slowly, they didn't panic, but neither were they going to ignore it.

The driver braked the vehicle to a stop in front of the gate and leaned out of his open window. "Hey!" he asked in lightly accented Turkish. "I am lost. How do I get on the road for Mersin? I'm late for a delivery."

"Do you have a map?" one of the guards asked.

"Yes." The driver reached across and waved a piece of paper. "But it doesn't make sense to me."

"They never do." The guard laughed.

"But where is the road?" the driver asked when he saw that he wasn't going to be able to suck one of the guards out from behind the gate.

"Just go back the way you came until you reach the highway," the other guard offered. "Then turn to your left and follow the signs."

"Thanks," the driver said, pretending to ignore the rifles trained on him.

Slipping the van into first gear, he cranked the wheel to turn. When the rear of the van was directly in front of the gate, he shouted, *"Allah Ahkbar!"* and pressed the button on the detonator.

The two hundred pounds of RDX lit up the neighborhood like the world's largest bolt of lightning.

THE SHOCK WAVE from the courtyard below threw Bolan out of bed. He was groping for his weapons when he heard the rattle of AK fire outside, followed by the screams of dying men. Clipping on his com link, he heard Katzenelenbogen calling for Phoenix Force to check in.

Bolan slipped into his boots and was halfway down the dark stairs when a satchel charge blew in the thick wooden doors, catching one of the Turks in the blast. The man's shattered body was thrown across the marble floor like a rag doll.

"Stay back!" Bolan yelled when he saw Yasmine come out of one of the first-floor rooms, an H&K in her hands.

A long burst of autofire came through the now open door, followed by a pair of black-clad gunmen with AKs in their hands.

Crouching against the inside wall of the stairwell, Bolan locked the lead gunman in the sights of his Desert Eagle. The .44 Magnum pistol roared, catching the gunman high on the left side of his chest and slamming him off his feet.

When the second gunman spun to face Bolan, a long burst of autofire from Jasmine's H&K almost cut him in two.

"Pull back," Bolan yelled, motioning her back into the hallway.

If they could defend the front door and keep the gunmen outside, the battle was more than halfway won.

DAVID MCCARTER and Rafael Encizo had been sharing one room on the lower floor while Calvin James and Gary Manning had another. The car-bomb blast had served as their wake-up call, as well. With Katz's voice in their com link earphones, they raced out the back door to join up with Mustapha's guards.

Even with the initial casualties of the surprise attack, the Stony Man team and the surviving Turks quickly got the upper hand of the wild firefight. With Bolan and Yasmine holding the front of the villa, the others fanned out from the rear of the grounds and started working their way forward.

The Brotherhood fighters had intended to storm the villa and kill the inhabitants, but finding their way blocked didn't slow them. They had come to Adana to kill or die.

On the north side of the house, one of the terrorists knelt and raised a RPG-7 antitank rocket launcher to his shoulder.

James spotted the movement. "I've got him," he yelled to Encizo, and swung to target him.

But before he could fire, the rocket jetted from the launcher with a whoosh. The villa's walls were thick, but the 85 mm antitank projectile blasted a ten-foot hole in the masonry.

The smoke and dust were still billowing from the broken stone when another gunman jumped up and raced for the hole in the wall, his AK blazing on full automatic. The roar of a .44 Magnum pistol from inside the house stopped him in his tracks and threw him backward.

The snarl of an H&K on full-auto resulted in another terrorist being drilled with holes while trying to lob a grenade from the prone position. The armed bomb rolled from his nerveless hand and detonated a few feet from his head.

The terrorists had lost over half their force, and hadn't even gained a foothold inside the villa. But withdrawal wasn't an option. Instead they tried a different tactic.

On the opposite side of the house, the Brotherhood fighters laid down a withering base of fire. One of Mustapha's Turks took a round in the chest, and the rest of the defenders could only hug dirt.

Two gunmen jumped out of the dark and raced for the side of the villa, clutching what looked like canvas bags to their chests.

"Cut them down!" Katz shouted. "They've got satchel charges!"

Like the rest of the defenders, Manning had his belly in the dirt. Rolling up on one hip, he triggered the grenade launcher on his M-203. The 40 mm round barely had time to arm itself before it detonated between the feet of the leading suicide bomber.

The grenade's explosion sent concussion and shrapnel into the chest pack of the terrorist. The overly sensitive RDX detonated, and the larger explosion set off the other satchel charge. The night sky rained blood and chunks of what had been men.

In the stunned silence that followed, Katz bellowed, "Finish them off!"

It was the terrorists' turn this time to face a barrage of full-auto fire. True to their creed of victory or death, they tried to charge, but were mercilessly cut down.

On the other side of the villa, Encizo, James and the Turks had also made short work of the remaining Brotherhood fighters. When the firing cut off abruptly, the defenders spread out to recover their wounded and to look for stragglers.

No one saw the lone black-clad figure slip over the wall and disappear into the night.

Sudan

THE MERCENARIES' late-night formation at the Sudan camp was to announce a change in the training schedule. They were to form up at 0400 hours and provide security for a helicopter that would be landing in the dark. It was also announced that the mercenaries were restricted to their own camp until further notice and that any infractions would be dealt with severely.

Back in his barracks tent, several of Hawkins's tent mates wanted to stay up and talk, but he was too experienced not to sleep when he could.

The wake-up call at 0330 disoriented him for a moment, but he slipped into his boots, grabbed his rifle and went out into the dark. Half of the men were sent to the perimeter to reinforce the guard while the other half laid out a strobe-light marker for the in-coming bird, then formed a cordon around the landing pad.

The early-morning visitor turned out to be a Russian Mi-8 Hip helicopter this time instead of a Super Frelon. But they, too, were as common as flies in Africa. After the ship touched down, four of the cadre opened the side door and went in to unstrap a large stainless-steel carrying case. The interior lights in the cabin were on and, while they were dim, the object was plainly visible.

Hawkins didn't have to be a Russian linguist to read the Cyrillic writing on the carrying case to know what it held. The yellow-and-black international radiation warning label said it all in any language. His hunch had been right on. He finally had hard information and there was nothing he could do about it.

Turkey

EARLY THAT MORNING, Mustapha flew to Adana himself to survey the wreckage of his villa. It had been one of his favorite houses, and his public concern for his property served to mask his real concern for his daughter. Ever since this American Belasko had arrived, all of their lives had been turned upside down. But he had to admit that Belasko had awakened him to a danger he had thought was over.

When he had received the initial call from Yasmine the night before, he had immediately contacted a friend in the national police intelligence office in Istanbul. When he told the officer that the attackers were Islamic terrorists, no questions were asked about why Mustapha had had a private arsenal ready to defend himself.

When Mustapha arrived in Adana, he wasn't surprised to find that Belasko and his friends were all packed up and ready to move on. It was rather apparent that they had outstayed their welcome in Turkey. When Islamic strike forces came calling in the middle of the night, it was time to move to somewhere that was a little less obvious.

"Where are you going?" Mustapha asked.

"Someone here doesn't like us," Bolan replied, "and I think they want us to go back to America. But we have some unfinished business to take care of first."

"It is my business, too," Mustapha said seriously. "And now more than ever. My house was attacked while you were staying here as my guests, and some of my men were killed. If I allow this outrage to pass unanswered, I am not a man."

"It goes beyond that," Bolan said. "This is more important than just another vendetta. More than likely, this was Sanders's work again. But how he knew that we were staying here is the big question. It's obvious that the man has an extensive network, and we need to go somewhere to escape observation for a while."

"I can help you do that," Mustapha offered. "I

have a fast boat you can use. It is large enough to sleep all your men and it has a helipad on the rear deck."

"That sounds like quite a boat."

"Oh," the Turk added, "I also need to tell you that it has full radar, both sea and air, a communications suite and the ability to defend itself. I sometimes go up into the Black Sea, and one has to be careful trading up there."

"I'm impressed," Bolan said.

Mustapha shrugged. "The Greeks aren't the only ones who can appreciate a fine ship."

"We'll accept your generous offer. Now all we need is to find out where Sanders is staying."

"I am working on that, too."

DEREK SANDERS HADN'T reported the abortive raid on the Adana villa to Grant Betancourt. That had been strictly between him and the mystery soldier. Once more, though, the man had proved to be invincible. The Brotherhood team he had hired was one of the most experienced in the organization, and only one man had survived and he had been wounded. The mystery man was either the luckiest man alive or something else was going on that was beyond his comprehension.

Either way, Sanders had no more time to devote to him now. With the nuclear warheads in the hands of the three action groups, it was time for him to go into the final preparation phase for the attacks. Betancourt himself would be on hand when the teams launched, and nothing could be left to chance.

Stony Man Farm, Virginia

THE ADANA ATTACK and Bolan's decision to relocate Phoenix Force to Mustapha's boat brought Brognola down from Washington again for a briefing.

"This is turning into a plot for a thriller movie," Hal Brognola grumbled after Barbara Price outlined the incident in Turkey for him. "About the only thing we haven't had yet is a helicopter-chase scene, and we still don't know where those damned warheads are."

"It's not over yet," Price reminded him. "But putting Striker and Phoenix Force on that boat will solve a lot of our immediate problems. Keeping them out of the line of fire while we work on our leads has to be to our advantage."

Working without the sanction of the Oval Office had severely limited the number of safe havens the Stony Man team could call upon.

"It should," Brognola admitted.

"What's the latest from Lyons?" he asked, changing topics.

"They're still going from door to door with the state and federal agencies," she said. "But, fortunately for us, they're not coming up with much. As always, we've covered our tracks pretty well."

"As soon as you think they've canvased enough, you can pull them off that and let them stand down."

"I'm expecting a call from Carl later and I'll see how it's going then."

Brognola glanced at his watch and Price knew he had to go again. "Can I have the cook make you a sandwich for the flight back?"

"How about a refill on the Maalox?"

ABLE TEAM HAD JUST about run out their welcome at the state and federal agencies they had been repeatedly checking. So far, though, no one had developed anything concrete that pointed to them having been the terrorists everyone in the federal government was looking for.

The best forensic evidence, the empty recoilless rifle cases and the fragments of the timing devices found in the rubble of the BII hangars, had proved to be untraceable. The M-67 ammunition was from lots that had been taken off the books decades before. One FBI forensics report said that the timing devices looked like standard CIA-issue time pencils. The spy agency, however, had been quick to deny that they had been involved in any way.

"We're still clean," Lyons reported to Price. "But I think we need to back off of making the rounds of the agencies for a while. It's starting to look a little obvious, and we don't want anyone trying to run our rap sheets and coming up with zilch."

"You've got a point," she said. "Why don't you

come back here and link up with Buck Greene so you can help him work the local area?''

''That sounds good,'' Lyons said. ''I'm ready for a little home cooking anyway.''

''I'll have the kitchen stand by.''

''I think a thick steak would be in order.''

Turkey

MUSTAPHA'S BOAT TURNED out to be everything he had promised and more. The gleaming white hull had originally been built as a Soviet navy Osa-class Fast Attack Boat. The ugly, angular armored bridge and the missile mounts had all been scragged and replaced with a graceful superstructure, and gold letters in the bow and stern proclaimed her now to be the *Roxalana*. At 128 feet, she was big enough to accommodate twenty people in comfort, as well as the chopper on the rear deck.

''You were too modest when you talked about your ship,'' Katzenelenbogen said in open admiration. ''That thing's a floating palace.''

''I picked it up from a former Ukrainian naval officer,'' Mustapha said proudly. ''He had the papers for it, and I had the goods he wanted in quantity. It was a fair exchange.''

Katz didn't want to ask what the medium of exchange had been, but drugs, gold or gems readily came to mind. This wasn't the first time that Stony Man had teamed up with someone who lived on the verge of the law. As before, the circumstances made the alliance. If the circumstances changed someday, they might have to take on Mustapha for his other activities. But that was in the unforeseeable future. Right now, they needed him and his boat.

As soon as everyone was on board, Mustapha had his crew cast off and ordered the captain to set sail for the clear blue waters of the eastern Mediterranean. If the Stony Man Farm team had to hide out for a while, there were far worse places to do it.

CHAPTER TWENTY

Phoenix, Arizona

Despite his attention being focused on the delivery of the Russian warheads to his action units, Grant Betancourt hadn't been idle on his other priority project, finding the elusive Farm. He couldn't allow them to stay in business because they knew too much about him.

After canvasing his contact people in the various federal agencies, he had come up with only one agency that might be running an off-the-books operation. And he had been surprised when it had turned out to be the Justice Department. His money had been on the FBI or the ATF as being the culprits, but they had turned out to be clean. After the Waco fiasco, they had been forced to clean their house from top to bottom and were under constant Congressional oversight now.

The person-of-interest he had uncovered was a high-level Justice Department official. On the surface, this man had a real position in the government; he was listed as a special liaison officer to the White House. But, when he had looked closer at this man, few of his contacts knew him or what he did to earn his federal paycheck.

He had no idea why the Justice Department would be running a renegade dirty-tricks operation. But the fact that this Hal Brognola had stayed in his position through all of the recent administrations meant he had some kind of protected, special status. Each incoming President traditionally cleaned out the upper levels at Justice in order to install his own people as part of paying his campaign debts. Being "tough on crime" had become the universal campaign promise, and to make good on the promise meant that the last batch of political appointees who hadn't been tough enough on crime had to go.

For Brognola to have been able to hang on for that long meant that he was something special. But, apparently, he also lived openly in D.C. so there should be no trouble keeping him under close surveillance. And that was where the assets of Security Plus would come in handy again. He immediately called and ordered two three-man surveillance teams dispatched to Washington with instructions to learn everything there was to know about Brognola and what he did.

Once his routine was known, Betancourt would decide what to do with him. But a snatch and a lengthy interrogation seemed to be the best way to get to the bottom of this. And, if it was revealed that his old roommate was running this outlaw organization, having that information could be better than having his own key to the Oval Office.

Turkey

MUSTAPHA'S INTELLIGENCE network was like a spiderweb spread over the eastern Mediterranean, and it didn't take long for him to get a line on the elusive Derek Sanders. By the second day at sea, he had a report for Bolan and Katzenelenbogen.

"I had to beg for favors that I will be paying off for the rest of my life," the Turk explained, "but I have located the viper Sanders. He is in a villa on Turkish Cyprus."

"If there were any out-of-pocket expenses involved," Katz offered, "we can—"

"No, no." Mustapha waved his hands. "This was, how do you say it, my treat? The man has darkened my days for the final time. The next time I see him, he will die."

"Where is this villa?" Bolan asked.

Mustapha produced a map of the divided island. "Here," he said, stabbing his finger on a cove on the southern coast, close to the Green Line separating the two parts of the island. "You can see his boat mooring here and the house is on the hill above it."

The map was detailed enough that Bolan could see that the villa sat on the best defensive position in the entire neighborhood. It was perched on top of a rugged hill, and the map indicated that it had a wall all the way around it and a cliff protecting the side facing the sea.

"Is the place walled like it shows here?" Bolan asked.

"Yes, it is," Mustapha replied.

Not only did walls defend, but they also concentrated the opposition in one place so they could be killed easier.

"How many men does he have up there?"

"I have been told maybe two dozen," the Turk answered. "They will not be as good as your men, but I think it is not going to be easy to attack that place."

Katz looked out at the Bell JetRanger lashed down to the chopper pad on the rear deck of the boat. "It will be a lot easier if you can loan us that." He nodded toward the chopper. "We have an experienced pilot with us."

"The helicopter?" the Turk said. "Certainly. Anything I have is yours."

"With that and the loan of a dozen of your men," Katz said, "we should be able to finish Mr. Sanders once and for all."

"You will have a dozen of my best," Mustapha replied, "and I will lead them myself."

"Welcome to the party." The Israeli smiled.

BOLAN WAS GLAD to be able to take the war to the enemy for a change. Ever since he'd arrived in Turkey, he'd been on the receiving end of someone else's moves, and he was tired of having to react to them. He was overdue for proacting and making a few moves of his own. He had missed recovering the warheads in Turkey, but he could insure that the man who knew where they were didn't run free.

McCarter's Phoenix Force was also ready to go to war. They'd pulled off the rescue they'd been sent to accomplish, but like Bolan, they were tired of being someone's target. They were supposed to be dishing it out, not taking it, and not even a free Mediterranean cruise could change that.

Jack Grimaldi was also happy that Phoenix Force was on the offensive and that he would have a role to play in it. Driving a Hummer or just standing around wasn't his idea of a great time. The Bell JetRanger Mustapha had loaned the team wasn't exactly a dedicated gunship, but he had flown worse into combat before.

Converting the JetRanger to a makeshift gunship turned out to be easier than he had thought it would be. Mustapha hadn't been joking when he'd said that his ship was able to defend itself. Except for missiles, it had been fully armed when he had bought it, and not all of the weaponry had been sold on the black market. Concealed compartments in the ship's double hull contained an arsenal, and the Turk had given the pilot carte blanche to help himself to anything he needed.

The first thing Grimaldi sought out was a searchlight, and he found it on the ship's bridge. It wasn't a Nightsun, but it would do and it mounted easily under the ship's nose. Phoenix Force had it's own M-60 machine guns with them, but no mounts. Digging into the ship's armory, he found a pair of armored car-style fixed mounts for the Russian 12.7 mm guns with their feed trays and the electric solenoid firing devices. The M-60s easily fitted into the mounts, and the combined units bolted to the front of the skids with little fuss.

To keep from attracting attention to themselves in the busy shipping lanes off Cyprus, he couldn't afford to test fire the jury-rigged guns when he was done. The firing circuits and the solenoid triggers for them had checked out, though, and Manning had bore sighted the M-60s to converge at two hundred yards, so he could live with that.

Looking over his handiwork, the pilot smiled. Life was beautiful. He had a gunship again.

WHEN THE SUN WENT down that night, the mixed force of the Stony Man team and Mustapha's Turks formed on the rear deck of the *Roxalana*. Bolan wasn't surprised to see that Yasmine had suited up for war, as well. He would have preferred that she sit this one out, but she had fought well enough at the villa and he didn't have the time to try to convince her to stay behind.

"She wants to go with us." Mustapha shrugged

when he saw Bolan glance at his daughter. "And I did not have the heart to tell her that she could not come."

Running with his lights completely blacked out, the captain of the *Roxalana* brought the ship to within a half a mile of the docks below Sanders's hilltop fortress. Mustapha had two Zodiac inflatable boats in his ship stores, and they were slid off the diving platform on the stern into the water. Along with two Phoenix Force warriors and fourteen Turks, the rubber boats were loaded past capacity, but the surf wasn't high and they made it to the dock without capsizing.

"The pier is clear," Calvin James radioed to Katz. "We're landing and will head for the cliffs."

"Roger," Katz replied. "We're taking off now, too."

Grimaldi punched the turbine's starter button, and the JetRanger's rotor started to turn.

CALVIN JAMES WAS a bit winded from the climb when he reached the top of the cliff face. The half-dozen Turks with him were all experienced mountain men, but they were breathing hard, as well. Yasmine, though, looked as if she were out for a midnight stroll. Someday he might catch that woman at a disadvantage, but not this night.

Snapping down his night-vision goggles, James scanned the section of the wall some fifty yards in front of him. When he could see no guards, he clicked in his com link. "I'm clear here," he whispered to Manning.

Manning, Mustapha and the other half of the Turks had climbed the cliff a hundred yards farther to the right. They had farther to go to reach the base of the wall, but the approach was flatter. "We're moving out now," Manning sent back.

WHEN GRIMALDI GOT the call from James and Manning, he clicked on the intercom back to Bolan, Katzenelenbogen and Encizo. "They're in place. You guys ready back there?"

"Do it," Bolan radioed back.

Breaking out of his high orbit, the pilot swooped down on Sanders's stronghold. As expected, the sound of the approaching rotors drew the attention of the guards on the villa's grounds. When Grimaldi saw that he had drawn a small crowd, he flipped up his NVGs and switched on the spotlight.

The men caught in the cone of light had apparently never been under aerial fire before, and they froze like deer caught in the headlights of an oncoming car. Holding a steady aim with his makeshift gunsight, Grimaldi flicked on the gun switch and the twin M-60s started blazing fire.

With the machine guns aimed to converge their fire at two hundred yards, it was almost like having a minigun mounted on the chopper. With a combined fire rate of 1100 rounds per minute, nothing could live in that cone of fire.

The initial barrage cut down a handful of the guards and sent the survivors scrambling for cover as fast as they could run. Since the guns were fixed to the mounts, Grimaldi had to kick the tail around with the rudder pedals to bring them to bear on his fleeing targets. Fishtailing through the night sky like a crazed goldfish, he rapped out long bursts of 7.62 mm rounds at anything that moved and most of what didn't. Half of the value of a gunship attack was the chaos it created on the ground, and Grimaldi was big on chaos.

With everyone scrambling to take cover from the gunship's fire, the two ground-assault teams hit the villa wall at the same time. Grimaldi's attack had emptied the top of the wall, and in a flash, they were up and over and onto the grounds inside the compound. With James and Manning's Turks inside the wall, Grimaldi backed off on the M-60s. But that was a mixed blessing for the guards. Now they were being hunted up close and personal.

Stomping down on his right pedal, Grimaldi snapped the chopper's tail around to set up for a landing on the villa roof. Just as he was flaring out, he spotted a pair of guards caught in the cone of light. Dropping the chopper's nose again, he tripped the firing trigger to his M-60s.

The short burst cleared the landing zone, and no sooner were the skids down than Bolan, Katz and Encizo jumped down onto the rooftop. Pulling pitch, Grimaldi took the JetRanger back up into the air.

Katz covered Bolan and Encizo from the roof

while they rappelled onto the patio outside of the back door.

THE GUNSHIP ATTACK was a surprise, but Derek Sanders knew what was coming and he was enough of a realist to know that he'd screwed up big time. He had underestimated the mystery soldier, and it was going to cost him his life—or at least his freedom. Since death was the lesser of the two penalties to him, he sprinted back into the villa. If he was going to hell, he wanted company on the trip. He also needed to get to the computers and set their self-destructs. He had a family, and he didn't want Betancourt taking vengeance on them just because he failed in his duties.

THE FIGHT WAS OVER before it had even had a chance to get started. The combination of the chopper's aerial gunfire and the grim determination of the ground-assault teams created an instant rout. Sanders's hired villa guards weren't made of the same stuff the Brotherhood gunmen had been. They owed little more than their time to their paymaster and certainly not their lives. The ones who couldn't find a chance to run dropped their weapons and fell to their knees with their arms in the air.

As the Turks were rounding up the guards and collecting their weapons, Bolan and Encizo completed their sweep of the villa itself. Unexpectedly, they found it empty.

"Has anyone seen Sanders?" Bolan called over the com link.

James and Manning were helping Mustapha check their prisoners and the bodies outside, but so far none of them were the elusive Derek Sanders. "Not yet," Manning reported.

"I don't have Sanders," McCarter's voice came over the com link, "but I've got a live one who looks like he's a European."

"Where is he?" Bolan sent back. If the man was one of Sanders's lieutenants, Katz might be able to get the information they so desperately needed out of him.

"We found him on the grounds," the Briton responded. "He took a grazing shot to the head and was knocked out."

"Bring him inside," Katz cut in.

The prisoner was obviously a northern European. Katz pegged him as German and, in that language, asked him if he spoke English.

"Of course," the man replied as if he had been insulted.

"We don't know who you are," Katz continued, "and we don't care. Our only interest is Derek Sanders and the Russian warheads he got from the Kurds. If you help us find them, you can go free."

The man laughed. "I can only help you with half of that. Sanders is probably in his command post in the basement, but I do not know where the warheads went."

"Show me," Bolan said.

The man shrugged and pointed to a wood-paneled wall. "The stairs are over there."

THE CAMOUFLAGED DOOR opened to reveal steep stone stairs leading to a lower level. They were only wide enough for one person, so Bolan let the mercenary take the point, with Yasmine bringing up the rear. With the Desert Eagle in his hand, he didn't have to tell the man what would happen if he tried to betray him.

At the bottom of the stairs, the man turned back and placed his finger to his lips as he reached out to activate the lock. It clicked, and a shotgun cartridge fired directly into his face. The booby trap had almost decapitated the prisoner, but Bolan saw that it was a one-shot device.

"Stay here," he told Yasmine as he stepped over the body and booted the wooden door.

The door slammed open on a small, windowless room with whitewashed walls. Along the far well, a man was typing furiously on a computer keyboard.

"It's over, Sanders!" Bolan shouted.

The mercenary grabbed for his Beretta subgun without even looking up.

"He's mine, Belasko!" Yasmine shouted as she pushed past him into the room.

The sound of the woman's voice made Sanders turn his head just in time to see her right arm snap down and a flash of bright steel leave her hand.

The throwing knife embedded itself in the hollow of Sanders's throat. His eyes went wide, and his hands flew up to claw at the hilt of the blade in his neck. With blood pouring into his lungs, he could only choke, but Bolan read the question in his eyes. Who?

Derek Sanders died without getting an answer.

CHAPTER TWENTY-ONE

Cyprus

Bolan turned to Yasmine, his voice cold. "We needed him alive."

"I needed him dead," she snapped, her green eyes flashing.

That was the biggest problem of working with people who lived by the ancient code of vendetta. A death trumped an interrogation every time.

But this might not be the end of the trail to the warheads. Hopefully, Sanders hadn't had enough time to wipe his computers' hard drives. If they were still intact, Kurtzman could mine them for the information he needed.

MUSTAPHA WORE a big grin when Bolan told him of Sanders's death. "You did well here, my friend," the Turk said. "That snake Sanders will bother us no more. And the men who were killed at Adana have been avenged."

"How soon will it be before the police come to investigate the gunfire?" Bolan asked.

"You should have at least another hour," Mustapha replied. "I paid them very well to take their time responding. I told them that this was a vendetta between that foreign dog and I. Since they have worked for me in the past, I think they will stay bribed."

"Maybe so, but you and your men should leave now. When we're done here, Jack will fly us out and we'll meet you at sea."

"We will go," the Turk agreed. "And I will drop Yasmine off at the airport on the way out."

"That may be best," Bolan said carefully. "She is a formidable woman, and you should be very proud of her. She has been a great help to us, but it might be safer for her to go back to Istanbul and stay. Sanders is dead, but this isn't the end of it for us, and from now on, it's going to be even more dangerous."

Mustapha knew the truth of Bolan's words and turned serious. "As you know, I hate the weapons that Sanders bought, and I, too, fear what he plans to do with them. So, I will continue helping you and your men if there is anything I can do to help you stop them from being used."

"I appreciate the offer," Bolan said, "but at this point, beyond hosting us on your ship, I don't know of anything you can do right now."

"If there is anything you can think of at all," the Turk said, "do not hesitate to ask. And, as for the

Roxalana, you can stay on board as long as you want.''

Sudan

NOW THAT the nuclear bomb had arrived at the mercenaries' camp, the pace of the training had accelerated. They weren't practicing with the actual thing, but a weighted container shaped like the warhead's carrying case was getting a real workout. Their training area had been moved to an abandoned village that had been remade to resemble their objective. Some of the huts and houses had been demolished or moved into different places to create the proper ground plan with approximately realistic distances between the buildings.

They were also training under live fire with four of the cadre officers and NCOs acting as the defenders. No one had been hit yet by their carefully aimed fire, but it added a distinct aura of realism to the exercise. The mercenaries weren't allowed to fire live ammunition back, but they were quick to concentrate their blank fire on their attackers.

As much as Hawkins hated to admit it, this group was coming together quite nicely. There had been some reshuffling of men in the squads and appointments of others to leadership positions.

"Burton," their sergeant called out to Hawkins one afternoon.

"Yo, Sarge."

"You're the new squad leader for your people," the mercenary said. "I'll post it in the morning."

"Thanks, Sarge."

"You earned it," the mercenary replied. "And you'll earn it again at the target."

"Rank hath its privileges." Hawkins grinned.

"One of those privileges is to keep on top of your people. We'll be moving out before too much longer, and I need everyone to stay sharp."

"You got it, Sarge."

THE PROMOTION to squad leader didn't sit well with Hawkins. He had tried his best not to stand out in this crowd, but he was a soldier and it was hard not to do what came naturally to him. This meant that had lost the last vestige of anonymity he'd had in the unit. There would be no more sneaking away at night for him now. Not when the sergeant might come looking for him at any time to discuss the training schedule or some other necessary military detail.

But, as far as he could tell, there was nothing for him to sneak away for. On every training flight out and back, he had scanned the refugee camp below, but he hadn't seen that pickup he had spotted again, or any other vehicle for that matter.

He had climbed onto the back of the dragon of the apocalypse and, like it or not, he was along for the ride. Where it would end, he had no idea. But the shadow of a mushroom cloud loomed large in his thoughts.

Arizona

THE REPORT of the destruction of the Cyprus villa and Derek Sanders's death hit Grant Betancourt hard. Sanders had been a critical operative in the plan. He was needed to coordinate the attacks and to provide the necessary air support for the strike forces. With him dead, Betancourt would have to seriously reconsider the scope of the operation, in particular the attack on the Vatican. That one was to have been staged out of the Cyprus location and it would be difficult, if not impossible, now to do it that way.

He could still, however, go ahead with the Jerusalem and Mecca operations as planned, particularly the Jerusalem mission. The American mercenary unit in the Sudan was more than ready. to be deployed. The Israeli contingent in Uganda was also primed to go. Both units had their necessary air assets with them and only needed to be given the go. That was something he would give them himself.

With the Cyprus command post gone, he would go to the mine in Uganda and control the operation from there. The mining engineers of Wagner Metals loved all of the modern conveniences in their headquarters. Most of it they didn't use, but it hadn't been installed by mistake. He had enough communication, command and control assets there to conduct a war.

Before he left his Arizona headquarters, though, he would put the plan in operation to eliminate the mystery organization that had dogged him for so long. It had been learned that Brognola routinely flew out of D.C. to an unknown location. His next step was to have his operatives find out where he went and kidnap him as soon as possible. Once in their hands, he would be put through chemical interrogation.

The information recovered from that would be privately passed on to his good friend at 1600 Pennsylvania Avenue for action. End of problem.

Stony Man Farm, Virginia

ALL OF Aaron Kurtzman's hard work trying to break Betancourt's cyber codes had finally paid off. When the contents of Sanders's computers were downloaded to him, he was able to read the data with no problem. As expected, he found that it contained the entire plan and timetable for three attacks that were a repeat of the three that Stony Man had foiled before. The targets were the same—Mecca, Jerusalem and the Vatican. But, this time there was no finesse to the attacks as there had been before. There was also no provision to even try to preserve anything of the sacred sites for future generations of humankind.

Betancourt's new plan called for each site to be taken out with a 2.8 kiloton nuclear weapon. While that wasn't all that large as far as nuclear weapons went, the detonations would be powerful enough to destroy the targets, as well as a sizable chunk of the surrounding areas. Jerusalem and Mecca would cease to exist, and the core of Rome would become smoking, radioactive rubble.

As he opened each file and saw the amount of detail that had gone into the planning, Kurtzman grew even more angry. He was no stranger to evil schemes emanating from the mad and the power hungry; it had been his stock in trade for a long time now. This, though, was unemotionally calculated, which made it even more loathsome. This was the product of a mind that was so far outside the perimeters of human behavior it could hardly even be called human.

For the first time in quite a while, Kurtzman acutely felt the restrictions that had come with the bullet he had taken in the back. Most of the time, he barely thought of the fact that he lived in a wheelchair; it was something that was a part of his life. But, this time, he burned to have his legs back. He wanted them so they could get him within arm's reach of Betancourt. Then he wanted to kill the inhuman bastard with his bare hands.

But, since that wasn't to be, he would have to let someone else take care of it for him. And, to insure that vengeance would visit that evil man, he would work from his chair as he always did. And, this time, no cyber code and no computer trick was going to keep him from tracking down the man.

AARON KURTZMAN'S CALL about his findings had put Hal Brognola in the air to the Farm again. A few days earlier, he had joked with Barbara Price about the frequent-flyer points he was racking up, but it wasn't funny anymore.

The chopper was only halfway to the Farm when the pilot glanced down at his threat radar. "We may have a problem, sir," he told Brognola.

"What do you mean?"

"Well, I think we've picked up a hitchhiker. When we left out of D.C. another plane left right behind us on our same flight path. It happens all the time, and I didn't think much about it. I did, though, bookmark his tail number and he's still back there."

When Brognola tried to turn to see if he could spot the plane, the pilot tapped his radar screen. "He's right here," he said. "Charlie three-niner-five. He reads out as a Piper Apache flying three thousand feet above us and about five miles back. But he's got us on visual."

"Can we get away from him?"

"We can't run away from him," the pilot replied. "He's going to be at least a hundred miles per hour faster than we are. If you want to shake him, all I can do is to go into some fancy chopper stuff and try for a low-level evasion."

"Do the turn to set up for the southern approach to the Farm," Brognola ordered. To keep from setting up too much of a routine on his visits to the Farm, Brognola's pilot used four different flight paths to approach the chopper pad and varied it with almost every flight.

Right after the pilot fed in a little tail rotor to turn

to the east, the mystery plane made the same turn. Brognola got on the radio to Stony Man Farm.

BUCK GREENE RESPONDED to the "Balaclava" alert immediately by racing for the new blacksuit security operations center in the Annex.

"What do you have?" he asked the blacksuit on radar duty.

The new air-defense setup in the surface building of the Annex included a military air-traffic-control radar unit. Since the dish had been set up on a neighboring hill, they could see for several hundred miles in all directions. The airspace over the Farm was marked restricted for low-flying, nonmilitary aircraft. But several times a year, a pilot who couldn't read his charts strayed into the restricted area. Usually, all it took was an official-sounding voice on the radio to get the pilot to quickly change his flight path.

After checking the radar plots of the two aircraft, though, Greene decided to take another tack with this potential intruder.

"I've got your tail on the screen", Green radioed to Brognola. "And your pilot's right. He's been following you since you took off."

"I think if we get down on the deck, we can shake him," Brognola sent back.

"You know," Greene said, "if you go into some fancy dancy maneuvering to try to lose them, you're just telling them you know you're being followed. Why don't you divert to Richmond instead and take the backup car. Lyons and his guys are here and, if they follow you on the ground, I can have them set up a reception committee along the route."

"Good idea," Brognola said. "Tell Barbara what we're doing."

"Will do."

"Also," Greene added, "I want you to put on one of the Kevlar vests that're stored in the chopper before you get out, Hal. And I'm not kidding."

"I will," Brognola promised.

"I'll kick your ass if you don't," Greene growled.

WHEN BROGNOLA RADIOED from Richmond that he had a tail, Buck Greene sent Carl Lyons and his team on the way. Lyons drove the first of the two cars, a Pontiac Turbo Firebird, and one of the Farm's blacksuits was riding as his shotgun. Gadgets Schwarz and Rosario Blancanales were in a one-ton Dodge Ram pickup, following a mile of so behind him. All four men were armed to the teeth and were wearing Kevlar body armor.

"I just passed Skyline," Hal Brognola called from his rental sedan, "and I still have the tail hanging on about a mile back."

"Roger," Lyons said. "We're ten miles ahead of you on 28, and I've found a good spot for the takedown. When we make our move, just keep on driving so you're out of the line of fire."

"Will do."

WHEN BROGNOLA'S TAIL breezed past Lyons's Firebird on the side of the road, he saw that the vehicle was a new Chrysler 300 four-door with two men inside. It was fast, but had no chance of getting away from him.

"I'm behind him," Lyons radioed Brognola when he pulled out onto the road.

"I'm overhead now," Brognola's chopper pilot radioed in. "I'm at four thousand about five miles to the north."

After a quick refueling in Richmond, the pilot had taken off again and had been vectored in to be their air cover.

"Roger," Lyons replied. "Maintain station."

"I'm good for a couple of hours."

"This'll be done a lot sooner than that."

SCHWARZ AND Blancanales waited until Brognola's sedan passed them before pulling their big Dodge onto the highway. With the bend in the road in front of them, Brognola's pursuers wouldn't be able to spot the pickup until they were right on top of it. Lyons had booted the Firebird's turbo and was now only 150 yards behind their target. They had him sandwiched.

When the driver of the Chrysler rounded the bend, all he could see was the massive chrome bumper and grille of the Dodge Ram charging down the center lane of the narrow country road right at him.

Rather than take on the big Dodge nose to nose, the Chrysler's driver headed for the right-hand ditch. Even though he was driving a big car, the ditch was deep enough to cause it to bottom out and slow down fast. With the left front wheel dropped into a hole, the car came to an abrupt stop.

The Chrysler had barely stopped moving when Lyons's Firebird slid in behind, blocking it. Lyons and the blacksuit were out of the car in a flash, their weapons ready.

The Chrysler's driver seemed to have been stunned by the impact and was slumped over the wheel. The passenger sprang out of the car, digging at the back of his belt for a pistol.

Almost too fast for the eye to track, Lyons had his .357 Python out of his shoulder rig and the hammer thumbed back for that smooth first shot. ''Freeze!'' he bellowed.

When the gunman cleared leather and tried to bring his semiauto pistol to bear, Lyons fired the Python. The heavy slug took the gunman high in the left chest, blowing his heart to shreds. He was dead before his brain could even register the fact.

In the split second that it took for Lyons to draw and fire, Schwarz had driven his pickup in front of the Chrysler to completely box it in. He had the driver's door open and the dazed man behind the wheel face first on the ground in a flash. After a thorough pat-down, the driver was cuffed and blindfolded.

Just as fast, the body of the passenger was stripped of his ID and loaded into the trunk of the Chrysler. Lyons kicked dirt over the blood on the ground.

CHAPTER TWENTY-TWO

In the Valley

Carl Lyons had Brognola's chopper pilot touch down in a nearby clearing long enough to load Gadgets Schwarz and the prisoner on board for a quick trip back to the Farm and a wringing out under the needle.

As soon as they were airborne, Rosario Blancanales used the Dodge Ram to pull the Chrysler out of the ditch. "How's that left front rim?" Lyons asked, seeing a dent in the front of the fender well.

"Looks okay," Blancanales said, "but I wouldn't drive too fast without a wheel alignment."

Lyons turned to his blacksuit shotgun rider. "Take this car back to Richmond," he said, "and leave it in the middle of the airport parking lot. Hal's pilot will pick you up at our chopper pad and bring you back."

"Yes, sir."

"And make sure you wipe it for prints before you leave."

"Will do," the blacksuit said as he pulled a pair of thin leather gloves from his jacket pocket.

Stony Man Farm, Virginia

GADGETS SCHWARZ WASN'T smiling when he reported the results of his chemical interrogation of their prisoner. "He doesn't really know much that we can use, Hal," he said. "He and his partner were simply told to shadow you and find out where you were going. Obviously, whoever sent him was looking for this place. He didn't have any kidnapping orders, but I think we have to consider that would have been next."

Brognola's face grew hard. "He works for Betancourt's Security Plus operation out of Phoenix, right?"

Schwarz nodded. "That's what his ID says. But he doesn't know anything about Betancourt's connection with the company. He says he was given his orders by a Ralph Blackwell, one of the firm's operations officers. And, by the way, there's another surveillance team out there, too, but he doesn't know where they are right now."

That wasn't what Brognola had wanted to hear. If someone was following him, he wanted to know the details. Particularly if they were setting him up for a kidnapping "Do you think there's any more you can get out of him?"

"Not really," Schwarz replied. "I had him wired

up while I fed him the scope, and he's telling us everything that he knows. I prompted him on Betancourt several different ways while he was under, and I really don't think that he's ever even heard of the man.''

Brognola made his decision in a snap. ''Tell Buck to give this guy the full 'material witness to a federal investigation' rap and put him in isolation. I don't want him back on the street until this is over. I'll worry about the legalities of it later.''

''No problem. Buck's got a room waiting.''

THIS WASN'T the first time that Hal Brognola had been targeted by the opposition. Even though he ran the Sensitive Operations Group from inside the deepest cover possible, nothing remained a secret forever. In the past, though, the opposition targeting him hadn't been the best friend of the President and a frequent guest at the White House. That relationship had played large in his thinking, and for the first time since Grant Betancourt had been identified as the source of this continuing problem, he finally saw his way clear.

He now realized that he had approached this thing completely wrong. He had tried containment, but no matter how many of Betancourt's mad schemes Stony Man was able to foil, the man would simply come up with another one. As long as he was alive, the welfare of humanity as a whole was threatened. The Sensitive Operations Group had been formed to protect the interests of the United States first and foremost, but Stony Man had gone to war for other nations, as well. The time had long passed when Americans could turn a blind eye to the evil taking place anywhere in the world, inside or outside of her borders.

Since Betancourt was a proved threat to the world at large, he had to be eliminated once and for all. It was as simple as that. It no longer mattered who Betancourt's friends were or where he dined, and it never should have figured into the equation in the first place.

Brognola was determined to let nothing stand in the way of his completing the mission as he saw it. And, when this was all said and done, Brognola would present a package to the Man that would detail everything the Farm had gathered on the late Grant Betancourt and his plots. Along with that package would be his prepared, and signed, resignation as the head of SOG. That way, if there was any fallout, it would all land on him.

Before that could be done, though, he had to give the orders that would put the phrase "the late" in front of Betancourt's name.

Reaching out, he punched a button on his intercom.

"Price," Barbara answered.

"We need to talk about Betancourt," he said. "We have to put an end to this now."

"About time," she replied. "Your place or mine?"

ALL THE STONY MAN players were present in the War Room for the briefing, either in person or via cyberspace. Wethers, Kurtzman, Price, Greene and Able Team were seated around the big table. Katzenelenbogen, Bolan and McCarter were on-screen.

Kurtzman led the briefing. "First off," he said, "Striker, you got to the computers just in time. The data dump program was short-stopped and I was able to recover almost all of the data."

No one said anything about Phoenix Force not having been able to take Derek Sanders alive.

"According to what we got from Sanders's computer," Kurtzman said as he flashed a map up on the briefing screen, "Betancourt has three mercenary units training in Africa right now, which confirms our earlier information. Two of these units are in separate compounds outside a large refugee camp in the Sudan, and the third is guarding a mining operation in Uganda. More than likely, each of these units has been issued one of those Russian warheads that got away from Phoenix. We have evidence that the targets for these weapons are the same as they were the last time we were dealing with this guy—the Vatican, Mecca and Jerusalem."

"The mission is this," Brognola said. "Find Grant Betancourt's operations wherever they are and shut them down. Then—" he paused to phrase it exactly the way he wanted it to show up on the tape he was making of this War Room session "—considering the unique circumstances surrounding Mr. Betancourt's activities, I have concluded that the only way I can insure that he will no longer present a threat is to have him terminated with extreme prejudice.''

He paused for a beat. ''Prior signed and filed executive order applies.''

The formal phrasing of this order didn't surprise anyone. When a person was targeting the President's best friend, he or she wanted to have all the bases well covered.

''But,'' Brognola continued, ''any of Betancourt's operatives who are willing to surrender should be allowed to do so. That doesn't, however, mean that I want you to take any risks with prisoners. Completing the mission must take full precedence at all times.''

Again, everyone was familiar with the legal boilerplate Brognola was spouting, and they weren't surprised. In Stony Man operations, the mission always came first.

''What's the time line on this?'' Katzenelenbogen asked.

''There is none,'' Brognola replied. ''It'll be over when it's over.''

''I mean did you come up with any indication of when he intends to attack his targets?''

''No, we didn't find a timetable,'' Kurtzman answered. ''We have to assume that the attacks will be initiated on his command.''

''What's the mission priority,'' Katz asked, ''Betancourt or the warheads?''

That gave Brognola pause. His hatred for Betancourt was overpowering, but killing the man needed to take a back seat to stopping the attacks again. "As I said, his operations must be shut down and the prevention of the loss of innocent lives must always take precedence. If, however, you feel that killing him first will short-stop the attacks, you may do it that way."

"I have an idea," Katz offered. "Why don't you give an anonymous 'heads up' to the Arabs, the Vatican and the Israelis? They will probably ignore it, but if Betancourt has the contacts in those governments that you think he has, they might report the warning to him. That may cause him to hold back for a while until things calm down again."

Brognola chuckled. "You've got more angles than a protractor, Katz."

"I just don't want him to slip those things past us while we're working up our attack plan."

"We'll do it."

"Hal?" Kurtzman spoke up. "I've got a mission-support request I need to run by you."

"What's that?"

"The field teams are going to need a lot of satellite support to pull this off—full-spectra recon, Comint, real-time retrans, the whole package. I'm going to have to divert a couple of dedicated U.S. birds for a while to give them the support they need."

"And?"

"And I just wanted to let you know."

Brognola smiled. "When stacked up against everything else we're doing this time, it don't think that hijacking a few satellites is going to matter very much.''

That got a round of unspoken agreement. Stopping nuclear terrorism required an all-out effort.

"Did you find anything on T.J.?'' McCarter asked.

"Not yet,'' Kurtzman replied. "My assumption is that he's still with the American mercenary unit in Africa.''

"He'd better be,'' the ex-SAS man said.

"If there's nothing else,'' Brognola said, "everyone knows what to do.''

CARL LYONS WAS more than happy to have been given the first shot at punching Grant Betancourt's ticket. He'd killed far better men for much less. Before he could plan the hit, though, he had to get as much information on the man's hideaways as he could. Since Betancourt seemed to spend most of his time at his BII headquarters, that would be their starting point.

Kurtzman had been able to find a blueprint of the BII headquarters complex in the Phoenix city records, but there were a couple of problems with it. For one thing, it didn't show any security features, not even the electronically controlled doors the building was known to have. More importantly, it didn't indicate where Betancourt's private office was located. Since that would be the most likely place they would find him, they needed that information before they started to plan.

"Wasn't he interviewed for *Forbes* not too long ago?" Hunt Wethers asked.

"Damned if I know," Kurtzman said, shrugging. "I've never read the rag."

"I'll try there and take a run through *AD* while I'm at it."

"*Architectural Digest,*" Wethers added when he saw the blank look on Kurtzman's face. "Guys like Betancourt love getting their private digs featured in *AD*. It means that they've made the A-list."

"Whatever," Kurtzman said. "Just come up with something we can use."

Wethers was back in a few moments with a printout in his hand. "Bingo!" he said with a grin as he laid down a full-page color shot from the *Forbes* article showing the man at his desk. "This says that his office is on the eighth floor, and from the view through that window behind him, we should be able to locate where it was taken from."

"Okay," Kurtzman replied, flashing the blueprint of the building onto one of the big-screen monitors, "let's start working the background."

WHILE WETHERS and Kurtzman were working up a detailed plan of the BII headquarters, Gadgets Schwarz was working with Akira Tokaido to refine their communications intercept program. Kurtzman had been able to break down most of the BII codes, but some of their scrambled communications were still holding their secrets. Most of what they could read was junk, but Tokaido hit a nugget in all the dross.

"Look at this," he said as he read through a list of decoded BII landline messages coming out of the printer. "I've got an intercept from Betancourt's headquarters to his flight-operations office to prepare his personal aircraft for immediate takeoff, and it's dated yesterday."

"He's gone?" Lyons was outraged.

"Yeah."

"Dammit!"

HAVING BETANCOURT slip out of the States didn't faze Brognola at all. This was total war, and there was no place on the planet the man could hide without being tracked down and made to pay for his crimes. As long as a single Stony Man warrior was still on his feet, he would be going after Betancourt's blood.

In the com center, he phoned up Katzenelenbogen. "I'm sending the Ironman and his boys over to give you a hand," he said. "The way this is shaping up, you're going to be a little thin on the ground."

Katz chuckled. "That's a little like saying water is wet, Hal. It's a big world out here."

"Not big enough for him to hide."

Katz was glad to finally have a shoot-on-sight mission, but Brognola was getting a bit obsessive. Running Betancourt down was going to take a lot of luck, as well as skill and manpower, but having Lyons and his team on hand was a big plus.

KATZENELENBOGEN, Bolan and Phoenix Force should have been lounging on the deck of the *Roxalana,* taking in the sun and enjoying their luxurious cruise. Mustapha kept playing the perfect host, tempting his guests with fine food and expensive drink, but, for the most part, the commandos stayed focused.

Bolan, McCarter and Katz spent most of their time in the ship's com room keeping touch with the Farm. The Computer Room staff faxed every new satellite-recon shot the moment it came in, and the intelligence updates were flying. Grimaldi and Phoenix Force passed their time cleaning weapons and preparing for the next phase of the operation. Sooner or later, they were going to have to get their buckles in the dirt again, and they would be ready for it.

As they approached Egypt, Mustapha again loaned his helicopter to the Americans. With the guns and searchlight removed, it was once more just another rich man's aerial toy flitting around the blue skies of the Mediterranean. Since the Turk had extensive business connections in Egypt, he had the necessary paperwork that Grimaldi would need to land in Cairo without ending up in jail.

CHAPTER TWENTY-THREE

Cairo, Egypt

When Jack Grimaldi climbed out of the cockpit of the JetRanger at the general-aviation side of Cairo's international airport, he was the picture of a rich man's private pilot. He had the standard navy blue pants and white shirt, epaulets on the shoulders and the ship's name embroidered on the left pocket. The outfit was topped off with a jaunty captain's cap, complete with gold braid on the bill.

"Nice getup," Gadgets Schwarz commented when he saw the pilot.

"Isn't it, though?" Grimaldi said with a grin. "Wait till you see our boat. It beats the hell out of the Princess cruise lines. We're up to our armpits in gourmet food and fine wine, but Katz nixed the dancing girls."

"No silken sheets?"

"Those, too."

"I can't wait to see this setup."

"If you two are done jacking your jaws," Carl

Lyons said, "I want to get the hell out of this flea trap."

"What do you mean?" Grimaldi said. "This is one of the Middle East's better airports. You should try to fly into Damascus."

"We do need to get moving," Rosario Blancanales pointed out as he glanced at a pair of Egyptian troops watching them. "We're drawing attention, and I'm about out of ready cash for paying bribes."

"All aboard," Grimaldi called out as he opened the door to the rear compartment of the JetRanger.

ONCE THE CHOPPER was back on board the *Roxalana*, Mustapha had the captain steer for Port Said and the Suez Canal. It had been a long time since Yakov Katzenelenbogen had last seen the mouth of the canal blocked by the rusting hulks of blasted, sunken ships, but he hadn't forgotten the sight. He had seen it during both the Six-Day War and the Yom Kippur War. Now, there were no signs of the bitter combats that had raged over control of the critical waterway for so many years.

Occasionally the odd warship still took passage down the canal, but it was a rarity. Instead, a steady stream of commercial traffic, including tourist-laden cruise ships, sailed peacefully down the waterway cut through the sand dunes.

Once past the town of Suez, the canal ended and the Gulf of Suez led into the Red Sea. With Saudi Arabia on one side of the northern Red Sea and the

Sudan on the other, the *Roxalana* was in a perfect position to block any attack coming from the Sudan or Uganda, headed toward the Middle East.

The problem was that even if a strike force flew right over them, they had no way to destroy it. Mustapha had defensive weaponry hidden on his boat, but it wasn't an antiaircraft cruiser. Neither was the Stony Man team the type to fight with missile-launch buttons as they tracked images on radar screens.

If Betancourt's threat was to be stopped by Stony Man, it would be fought man to man on the ground somewhere. And that was the element that was still missing, where they would fight next.

Mustapha had ordered his captain to cruise in the international waters off the coast of the Sudan while the Americans worked to come up with a plan to recapture the nuclear weapons. They let him sit in on their planning sessions, and the Turk fully realized that the Americans were putting their lives on the line for people they owed no allegiance to, and it amazed him. He was no coward; he had fought many times in his life, but it had always been for him and his. Fighting for another man, a perfect stranger, was foreign to him.

Even so, he wanted to help these new friends, but there was little he could contribute to this phase of the mission, and it frustrated him. He was good at what he did, but his experience wasn't in this arena. Even his vast organization of contacts and agents in the region was of little use now.

AARON KURTZMAN was making good use of the information he had been able to recover from Sanders's computer. Not only did he have Stony Man's exclusive spy satellite on the job, but he also had stolen another K-12 from the NRO and put it to work. While his own 39D bird was watching the Wagner Metals mining operation in Uganda, the other one was loitering over the sprawling refugee camp in the Sudan. He had also dragooned a pair of NSA Comint birds, planting one of them over each target to listen in on the communications traffic.

The only thing he was having trouble getting online was the NRO nuclear-alert satellite. It was a specialized recon bird that picked up the neutrino emissions from nuclear devices. Anything from a handheld hospital scanner to a fifty-megaton warhead nestled in the launch tube of a Boomer one hundred feet under the ocean could be pinpointed. As yet, there was only one of these very expensive satellites in existence, and it was protected by more layers of cyber security than anything he had ever seen.

He could run the mission against Betancourt with just the recon and Comint birds, but he would still need to locate the warheads before the threat would be ended. Even with Betancourt dead, the nukes had to be recovered. In the mood Kurtzman was in, if he could have gotten his hands on the Russian criminal who was responsible for playing loosey-goosey with his country's nuclear arsenal, he'd have gladly beaten him to death with a Geiger counter.

Uganda

GRANT BETANCOURT'S flight to Africa had gone off without a hitch. Again, he had flown to the Caymans and had taken on his David Brown persona before continuing over the South Atlantic. Again he landed at Entebbe, Uganda, and boarded one of the Super Frelons for the flight out to the mine.

At the Wagner Metals mine site, he found the mercenaries growing bored guarding against threats that hadn't materialized. They had been recruited as a strike force, and they expected to get their chance to fight. After telling their leaders that there had been a minor complication, he assured them that they would be launching soon. That done, he opened his command center in the headquarters building and got to work.

Before he could launch anyone, though, he had to take a couple of precautions. One involved the problem Derek Sanders had left him. With the Vatican off the target list, he needed to disband the Arab unit that had been targeted against it. He knew that wouldn't be easily done. But, fortunately, Bernard Hart was on hand in the Sudan. The South African mercenary had proved to be a resourceful man, and he could be counted on to deal with it. And, in hindsight, it might have been better if Betancourt had given him the overseas command of the operation instead of Sanders. But, as always, he would work with the circumstances he had been given.

The other thing he needed to do was to get the Wagner mining engineers off the premises. Things were going to get busy, and he didn't want them as witnesses.

Sudan

MAJOR BERNARD HART had served a number of paymasters in his long career as a professional soldier. Few of them, though, had paid as well as his current employer, whoever he really was. But he also had to admit that none of them had been such a right proper bastard to work with, either. Since the pay was commensurate with the difficulties, he could bear it. Even so, the most recent order he had received wasn't going to be easy to implement at any price.

Apparently, there had been a major change in his employer's operational plan. The target list had just been reduced from three to two. By itself, that didn't matter to him one way or the other as long as his pay didn't change. It did, however, leave him with a problem, a fifty-four-man problem to be exact. He had been ordered to neutralize the Arab unit he had been training. He had been ordered to disarm them and turn them loose. That, however, would be much easier said than done.

He had never liked the idea of using an Arab unit for this mission, and had argued strongly against it.

The employer, however, had been adamant that the Vatican strike force had to be composed of Muslims. Faced with losing a lucrative contract, Hart had had no other choice but to go along with it. And now it had turned out to be as bad a decision as he had feared it would be.

The men who made up the Arab unit weren't the quality of men he usually worked with. If it had been up to him, the men he would have recruited would have been those who made up the ranks of Hamas, Hezbollah or the Brotherhood. The recruits he had gotten, however, were little more than street thugs from Cairo and the Gaza Strip. They were men who couldn't be trusted enough to be allowed to join one of the major Islamic terrorist groups.

Not only was it going to be almost impossible to disarm them, but it would also be dangerous to turn them loose, even here in the remote desert of the Sudan. They knew too much and suspected even more.

The mercenary commander had been forced to walk a fine line with the training of the three units when it came to divulging their ultimate missions. The Americans had only been told that they would be hitting a target associated with Arab terrorism. Even though all of them had expressed negative opinions about Jews, they hadn't been told the country that they would be attacking was Israel.

The Israelis, though, had been told their exact target right from the beginning. Almost every one of them had suffered a personal loss from Arab terrorism over the years, and they burned with vengeance. In fact, they had cheered when they had learned what they were to attack the very heart of Islam.

The Arab unit had been told that they would be striking a major holy site of the hated Christian infidels. When one of their leaders asked if the site was in Israel, he had been assured that it wasn't. Since most of the land now claimed by Israel was also sacred to the Muslims, slaughtering the population was quite all right with them. But they had qualms about causing major damage to sites in the territory they fully intended to recover one day.

Since they knew little of Christianity outside of the Holy Lands, they immediately fixated on the Vatican as being their target. As the center of the Roman Catholic Church, it was the only place they knew that would be worth attacking, and they were overjoyed. Late at night, they brought out all the old tales from the Crusades and every man claimed descent from a victim of the Christian knights. They were as fired up to launch as the Jews were, and now he was going to have to try to disarm them.

The only way he could see to do it was to use gas on the bastards. And, fortunately, he had access to a South African army chemical-weapons depot that had a stock of a nonlethal crowd-control, knockout agent. In the last years of apartheid, global intervention in their politics had reached a point that the government had hardly been able to even protect itself without being condemned by the international community. The blacks could go on a rampage in front of a CNN news camera, and if the police as much as whacked a rioter on the head, it made headlines all over the world. This nonlethal gas had been formulated to control such mobs and had proved to be quite successful.

A few canisters of that gas and troops from the American unit should be able to handle the situation quite nicely. Once the Arabs were knocked out and disarmed, he could worry about what he would do with them then.

THE CADRE SERGEANT found the man he knew as W. L. Burton cleaning his already immaculate M-203 grenade launcher. He could well believe that the man had once been a Ranger. Burton's attention to detail and his professionalism had elite unit written all over it, and he wondered what had driven him to sign on as a hired gun. If he had a hundred men like him, though, he'd be able to take any target in the world.

"Burton?" he called out.

"What's up, Sarge?" Hawkins asked as he looked up from his weapon.

"I've got a local mission for you and your men."

"What's that?"

The sergeant hooked his thumb toward the tent opening. "Come on over to the major's tent and he'll brief you."

Hawkins was more than curious about this, but he was also ready for any break in the routine. The training had become so repetitive that the men were losing their edge instead of becoming more proficient. The problem was that the attack plan was very simple and straightforward. A good troop of well-armed Boy Scouts could be taught to go through the motions, and the mercenaries had gotten bored. If this unit didn't get sent into action soon, it was going to start falling apart.

Major Hart's tent wasn't all that different from the ones his men lived in. This and many other leadership details the South African had shown had been effective in creating unit cohesiveness.

"Burton's here, sir," the sergeant announced.

"Burton," the major said. "Come in and stand at ease."

"Yes, sir."

"The sergeant major tells me that you have the best squad in the unit now."

"Thank you, sir."

"I have a problem I need to take care of, and I need a few good men to help me with it."

That wasn't the usual way a mercenary commander went around issuing his orders, so Hart had Hawkins's complete attention. "We're ready to help, sir."

Hart stared at the squad leader for a long moment. "I'm sure that you have heard that there is another contingent of troops close by here."

"Just heard rumors, sir."

"There are a group of Arabs that the principal contracted with to do a specific job. Now, however, the need for their services no longer exists. Do you follow me?''

Hawkins knew that this was a major development, but wasn't sure of the causes or the ramifications. "I'm not sure, sir.''

"They need to be disarmed and returned to their homes of record.''

"Home of record'' was military jargon for wherever those yahoos had come from before they had signed on to be money soldiers.

"They are having their contracts paid in full, of course,'' Hart hurried to add. Telling a mercenary that his fellows were being cheated wasn't the way to get his cooperation.

"Of course,'' Hawkins echoed.

"I'm going to use your squad to help the cadre with this job.''

"When do you want us ready?''

"It will be a couple of days,'' Hart said. "The sergeant major will keep you informed of the assembly time.''

"Yes, sir.''

"And, Burton...''

"Sir?''

"Keep the details to yourself until we're ready to move out.''

"Yes, sir.''

"Dismissed.''

Hawkins did an about-face, exited the tent and walked back to his squad.

Stony Man Farm, Virginia

AARON KURTZMAN'S hard work finally paid off when he got the stolen nuclear-alert satellite on-line and it worked exactly as advertised. On its first pass over Africa, it sent back indications of three nuclear devices large enough to be the fugitive Russian warheads. One of them was in Uganda and the other two were in the Sudan. That matched up perfectly with the mercenary camps they had been tracking.

The hard copy from the sensors was immediately faxed to the *Roxalana* in the Red Sea.

Sudan

THE BELL JetRanger bearing blue-and-white UN markings flared out for a landing in the open area outside of the main gate of the mercenary camp. As the two mercenaries on duty watched, two men quickly stepped out and walked up to the gate.

Major Bernard Hart stepped out of his tent to see who had arrived. He had no idea who in the hell these two were, but the UN had never been anything other than bad news for him. His employer had assured him, though, that the proper payments had been made to the Sudanese government in the region to give his operation sufficient cover.

Straightening his beret, he marched to the gate and signaled for the sentries to open it. "May I help you gentlemen?" he asked the two men.

CHAPTER TWENTY-FOUR

The Sudan

Rosario Blancanales bowed slightly to Major Hart. "Count Alesandro Orsini," he said as if his name would be recognized. He was wearing a expensively tailored safari jacket with khaki cotton slacks, chukka boots and an Aussie-style brush hat. It was the perfect kit for a wealthy visiting dignitary.

Hart hesitated for a moment before bringing his hand up to the front of his beret in a stiff salute. "Major Bernard Hart."

Blancanales glanced at the major's beret badge. "I do not recognize your regimental insignia, Major."

"It's the South African Rifles, sir."

"I see." Blancanales smiled as his eyes looked past the officer into the mercenaries' camp. Several of the troops had gathered to see who had come to break the monotony of their routine. "And those men?"

Hart didn't glance over his shoulder. "They are contract employees."

"As you are?"

"Yes, sir."

"I see," Blancanales replied again. "I was not aware that the UN Relief Office had contracted for refugee-camp security forces."

"I am under contract with the Sudanese government," Hart responded stiffly.

"I see."

Blancanales turned to Yakov Katzenelenbogen. "Were you aware of this development, Doctor?"

"I can't say that I was, Excellency," Katz answered in a clipped British accent. He was wearing a version of Blancanales's costume, but his was more rumpled. "But anything can happen out here, you know."

"And you are?" Hart had to ask.

"Terribly sorry, old chap," Katz said, extending his good, left hand. "I'm Dr. Simon Burgess, the queen's representative to the UN Relief Office."

Hart was no fan of modern England nor of the royal family, but he also knew when he had been trumped. Hart's first impulse had been to dispose of these two unwelcome visitors in the desert, but that was obviously not going to happen now. What the hell these two Ruperts were doing in a place like this he had no idea.

T. J. HAWKINS NOTICED the excitement by the main gate and joined the onlookers. He was stunned to see Rosario Blancanales and Yakov Katzenelenbogen talking to the major. They were the last two people he had ever expected to see in this hellhole. The blue-and-white markings on the JetRanger, though, gave him a clue to the scam they were working this time—the old UN ploy. More often than not, though, it worked. Particularly in a place like this.

All he had to do now was to get them to notice him, and he'd have his ride home. He'd enjoyed about all of this mercenary bit that he could stand, and he was ready to get the hell out.

He started to work his way to the front of the troops who were gawking at the unexpected visitors.

"I MUST ASK what your business is here, gentlemen," Major Hart said, trying to regain the initiative. "I'm afraid that I was not informed of your visit."

"It's rather spur-of-the-moment, actually," Katz said. "The count is here in Africa on a Vatican mission to coordinate a new refugee relief effort the Holy Father is planning. We heard about this camp and thought we'd drop in and see if it might be included in the program."

This was the last thing in the world the major wanted to have to deal with right now.

"I'm afraid that's quite outside of my commission, gentlemen," Hart said. "So I'm not sure that I'll be able to help you."

"Oh, we don't need much help," Blancanales said. "But perhaps you could spare a small detachment from your group here as an escort?"

There was no way that he could wiggle out of that one gracefully, so Hart gave in. Looking at the crowd of troops the visitors had gathered, he spotted Hawkins standing in the front row.

"Burton," he called out, "take two men, suit up and escort these gentlemen."

Hawkins stiffened to a position of attention. "Yes, sir."

"It will be just a minute," Hart said.

HAWKINS WAS BACK in a flash with two of his squad mates. All three mercenaries were in full assault harness and had their assault rifles at the ready. "W. L. Burton, sir," Hawkins reported to Katz.

"Good to meet you, old boy," Katz said, keeping his face completely neutral. "Dr. Simon Burgess."

"I'm Count Orsini," Blancanales stated, introducing himself. "What do you suggest we see here first?"

"I really couldn't tell you, sir," Hawkins replied, keeping his eyes fixed. "I've never been out of the camp before."

"Well, then," Katz said, "I guess we should take a bit of a walkabout, what?"

Hawkins had to keep from smiling at Katz's mixed British accent and Australian idioms. The tactical adviser was getting off on this charade.

"You two stick tight to the count," Hawkins told his squad mates as he fell in with Katz.

"How long have you been here, Burton?" Katz asked.

"We're not much on calendars around here, sir."

"It must get a bit tedious, what?"

"We keep busy, sir."

The two mercenaries chuckled at the obvious evasions. There was no way that their squad leader was going to break the mercenary code of silence to these two outsiders.

Blancanales led the parade past the makeshift shelters jammed with starving old men, women and children. The refugees were so beyond hope that most of them didn't even expend the energy required to follow the visitors with their eyes.

Hawkins knew that one of the escorts had also gotten out at night, but this was the first time that any of them had walked through the camp in the daylight, so it was an education for them, too. They couldn't help but be moved by what they were seeing.

When Katz spotted the tattered tent that served as the camp's dispensary, he turned to Blancanales. "You go on ahead, Excellency. I want to drop in on the clinic and have a look-see."

"Certainly," Blancanales said.

As soon as the two mercenaries were out of earshot, Hawkins broke into a big grin. "It's about time you showed up, Katz."

"We've been busy."

"If you're tracking a couple of nuke warheads," Hawkins said, "at least one of them's here."

"The satellite-recon run says that there are two, actually."

"And from the rehearsals we've been running, I think we're targeted against Jerusalem."

"That's what Aaron thinks, as well. We busted the operation that smuggled the weapons and got a computer hard drive out of it he was able to read."

"What's the plan to bust this up?" Hawkins wanted to get to the bottom line.

"That's the problem," Katz said. "Right now, we're on a boat in the Red Sea where we're still trying to put something together. Since we're still going this one alone, we can't call on Uncle Sugar to lend us a hand with firepower, transport or all those other goodies we've been able to call upon him for in the past."

"You do know that there's an Arab mercenary camp on the other side of this place?"

"We do," Katz said. "There's also a third mercenary company in Uganda, so we're a bit outnumbered. We have Able Team with us, but that's still not enough firepower to take all of these guys on head to head."

"You may not have to deal with the Arabs," Hawkins said. "Apparently, something's come up with them, and they're no longer needed on the trip. The major's planning to gas them, take their guns and leave them in the desert."

"Where'd you hear that?"

Hawkins grinned. "Well, I've been such a good

boy that he made me a squad leader, and he picked my squad to assist him with his housecleaning.''

''That will even up the odds a bit.''

''Can you get me out of here with you today?'' Hawkins asked hopefully. ''That'll help boost the odds.'

''Well...'' Katz hesitated. ''I was hoping that I could convince you to hang around here a little longer. Now that you're Hart's go-to man, you're more help to us here.''

''Dog bite my ass,'' Hawkins said.

''It won't be too much longer.''

Katz reached into the pocket of his safari jacket and came out with a com link. ''Here,'' he said. ''It has fresh batteries, and Aaron has a comsat parked right over you. You should be able to reach us with no problems.''

''Other than being caught with a contraband radio.''

''If Hart decides to move on the Arabs, give us a call. We might be able to use that as a diversion.''

WHEN HAWKINS RETURNED to his compound, he found the major waiting for him. ''How did your inspection tour go?''

''All pretty much routine,'' Hawkins reported. ''Our guests just walked around and took in the sights like all visiting dignitaries do.''

''What questions did they ask?''

"Not many," Hawkins said. "They wanted to know how long we've been here and what we do."

"And your answers were?"

"I didn't know anything, sir. I'm just a soldier who follows orders and doesn't think about it a hell of a lot."

Hart laughed. "Good man."

"Did they get over to the Arab compound?"

Hawkins shook his head. "No, sir. As soon as they got their noses full of the stink, they decided that they'd seen enough. You know how those kinds of people are," he said, sneering. "It all looks pretty on film, but once they get into the stink, they can't get away fast enough."

The major laughed. "Good work, Burton."

"Thank you, sir."

HART TRUSTED his employer, but he also knew how much trouble the UN could be when it decided to stick its nose into things that didn't concern it. Of all the UN agencies, the refugee-affairs people tended to draw upon the big names of the member nations. Every out-of-work count or baroness or has-been actress in Europe who was too old to make the disco report in the tabloids, signed up to work for the UN. And, for some unaccountable reason, most of them ended up doing their good deeds in Africa.

The aging actresses he could deal with, but the minor nobility usually had political connections that could be troublesome. He couldn't say that he had ever heard of this Count Orsini before, but if he was connected with the Vatican, he was trouble. So was that snotty doctor from Buckingham Palace. Damn all do-gooders! This was the last thing he needed.

Their visit, though, meant that he had to move on the Arabs quickly. They had to be gone before the UN came back with an entire do-gooder team and discovered them here. It would also get their mission warhead back under his sole control, which made him happy. He had been a little uneasy about issuing it to them in the first place, but again the employer had been adamant.

What had started out as a well-thought-out plan was rapidly turning into a classic cockup, and he had to get that turned around. Fortunately, the gas he needed to take care of the Arabs was coming in on the evening supply chopper. And he had a handpicked squad to take care of the job.

There would be a slight change in the operation as he had planned it, however. With those two refugee wallahs nosing around in the area, he couldn't risk leaving the Arabs alive. They knew entirely too much. Fortunately, though, the gas that was coming worked as a riot gas in one concentration. But double the amount, and it became a lethal agent. There would be a little fallout among the refugees, but that couldn't be helped. And, since they were all going to die soon anyway, it was no great loss to anyone.

T. J. HAWKINS WASN'T surprised when the cadre sergeant sought him out at sundown. It looked as if he had become the major's go-to guy for his dirty work, a DLJO in Ranger terminology.

"Burton," the sergeant said, "I need you and your squad to be suited up and ready to go by 2200 hours tonight."

"What's the mission, Sarge?"

The sergeant checked to make sure that no one was within earshot. "That job the major talked to you about the other evening."

"No problem," Hawkins replied.

As soon as the sergeant left, Hawkins walked to the latrine area. As with everything else in the camp, it was primitive, a field latrine rather than a building. But it had a waist-high canvas screen around it so he should be able to talk without being overheard.

Finding the latrine deserted, he dropped his pants, took a seat and pulled the com link from his pocket. "Katz," he said softly as he keyed the mike, "you'd better be there."

He knew that his radio signal was being transmitted to deep space, where it would be bounced back down to the ship in the Red Sea, but he couldn't wait. "Dammit, Katz, I need to talk to you!"

"You have to wait for the satellite delay, T.J.," he heard David McCarter answer.

Hawkins didn't have time for chitchat. If he was caught on the crapper doing something other than emptying his bowels, he'd really be in trouble.

"The major here is planning to gas the Arab mercenaries tonight and disarm them. He thinks it's going to be a walk in the park, but I'm not that sure.''

''What's the timetable?''

''I'm supposed to have my men ready at 10:00 o'clock tonight. I don't know how it's going to go after that.''

''Wait one,'' McCarter said. ''I want to talk to Katz.''

Hawkins glanced around. ''Don't make it too long.''

The moments seemed to stretch into hours, but Hawkins kept his seat. He did hitch his pants up a little higher in case he needed to move fast.

''We'll have you covered tonight,'' McCarter said, coming back on line. ''Be on the lookout for us.''

''Are you going to come in shooting?''

''That'll depend on the opposition. But stay loose.''

When Hawkins walked out of the latrine enclosure, he was stunned to see that another soldier had been waiting for him to finish his business. Fortunately, he had given him plenty of room for privacy.

''Jesus, man,'' the mercenary said. ''I thought you were going to shit yourself down to nothing.''

Hawkins grinned. ''That's what I get for eating MREs as a midnight snack.''

The merc laughed. ''I hear that.''

CHAPTER TWENTY-FIVE

The Red Sea

"We need to use your helicopter again," Yakov Katzenelenbogen told their Turkish host. "But we might not be able to bring it back in one piece this time."

Mustapha laughed. "What kind of friend would I be if I did not give you anything I have. As for the helicopter—" he shrugged expressively "—it is an old one anyway."

"We will pay for it," Katz assured him. "Although it may take a few weeks to process the payment."

"You have paid me enough already, my friend." Mustapha clapped him on the shoulder. "You have given me stories I will be telling my grandchildren for the next fifty years."

"I didn't know that you had grandchildren."

"I don't." Mustapha sighed. "But that is another story."

Katz laughed. "You'd better get her married off soon."

"I know."

EVEN WITH THREE PEOPLE jammed into the rear seats of the JetRanger, it would take two trips to ferry the Stony Man team to the LZ. Grimaldi landed his first load a mile from the camp so the sounds of his rotors wouldn't be heard.

"Back in a flash, guys," he said as he dropped off Bolan, McCarter, Encizo and James.

"Don't be long," James said. Even at full throttle, it was almost an hour back to the ship, so they would be on the ground alone for at least two hours. With eighty-plus mercenaries in the camp, they wouldn't have the chance of a snowball in a microwave if something went wrong.

As soon as the JetRanger disappeared into the night sky, the four men snapped down their night-vision goggles and set out for the refugee camp. According to the satellite-recon photos, the mercenaries weren't running patrols in the area so they moved quickly, but with their weapons at the ready.

HAWKINS MARCHED his squad to the major's tent at the exact time he was expected to report. Anything else would have been out of character for his Burton persona. Leaving his men outside, he went in to get his orders.

"Burton," the major greeted him. "Good. The

chopper will be here any time now with the gas you'll need."

"How does that stuff work, sir?"

"It's just riot gas in a canister," Hart said casually. "Just turn them on, start fogging the place, wait a few minutes and move on through. The good thing about it is that it dissipates rather quickly. Once they've been knocked out, you will be able to move right in and disarm them."

"What if they're not completely unconscious?" Hawkins asked.

"You just give them a little more gas," Hart said. "And I'll have the rest of the company standing by, too. So, if there is any resistance, just pull back until you can be reinforced."

This had to be the most half-assed mission Hawkins had ever been given. But, until his teammates showed up, he had to play along with it. Anything less would be hazardous to his health.

"One more thing," the major added. "There's a special package in that camp that needs to be recovered as a priority. It's in a stainless-steel container, and it needs to be safeguarded until you can get it back here."

Giving a nuke warhead to an Arab mercenary force didn't sound like too smart of a move to him, but this entire thing had been on the fringe from the very first.

"How will I identify it?" Hawkins asked, playing dumb.

"The sergeant major will point it out to you."

This was the first time that Hawkins had heard that the sergeant would be going with them. The cadre sergeant was a trainer not a fighter, so that showed the importance the major was placing on this mission. Beyond eliminating the Arabs, it was apparent that he, too, wasn't comfortable with their having one of these warheads, and he wanted it back under his control immediately.

"Yes, sir."

ON HIS SECOND TRIP, Grimaldi set down only half a mile from the camp. Once Lyons, Blancanales, Schwarz and Manning had been dropped off, he took off again and went into a high orbit several miles away to wait the outcome.

"Striker," Carl Lyons transmitted over the com link, "we're down about a thousand yards from the camp."

"Roger," Bolan replied. "As long as you don't get too close to the mercenary camp, there are no guards so you're free to move up. Come in from the south and call when you get in closer."

"Roger."

Taking off at a tactical run, Lyons led his Able Team partners and Manning toward the camp.

BACK OUTSIDE the headquarters tent, Hawkins walked up to his squad. "We're waiting for a chopper to come in and bring us some goodies," he said. "Our mission tonight will be to use a knockout riot gas on those Arab mercenaries on the other side of the camp.''

"All right!" One of the men sounded jubilant.

"Will this stuff kill them?" another one asked.

"The major says it won't," Hawkins answered.

"Damn."

"Here it comes." One of the men heard the beat of approaching rotors.

Just then, the cadre sergeant appeared with a flashlight in his hand and a submachine gun slung over his shoulder. "Bring your people, Burton," he told Hawkins.

"Yes, sir."

The Super Frelon touched down outside the mercenaries' perimeter wire. The pilot kept the turbines running while Hawkins's squad retrieved a wooden crate and carried it back to the major's tent.

The sergeant opened the crate in the light from the kerosene lantern. Inside were a dozen gas masks and two dozen yellow steel canisters marked in a language that looked like German. Since Hart was a South African, it was likely that the writing on them was in Afrikaans, the language of the Dutch Boers in South Africa. They were known for innovative riot-control measures.

The sergeant picked up one of the canisters. "This is a no-brainer as you Yanks say. We go to the upwind side of their compound, crack the canisters and wait for the gas to do its work. Once they're down, your job will be to secure their weapons and toss their bodies into the chopper.''

"Where we taking them?'' one of the mercenaries asked.

"Out into the desert. We're going to let them walk home.''

"All right!''

HAWKINS'S SQUAD MOVED through the crowded refugee camp with their weapons at the ready. Each man had his gas mask on his assault harness and two canisters of the gas. The markings on the canisters didn't mean anything to Hawkins, but he sincerely doubted that the gas was as harmless as the major had tried to tell him that it was. Most riot gases he knew of didn't knock people out immediately. More than likely, this stuff was lethal and his men were on hand to load the bodies once it had done its work.

Since there was no way that he could wear his com link openly, Hawkins had stashed it in his fatigue jacket breast pocket with the volume turned all the way up and the mike hot. That way he could hear when the team called him, and they could pick up the sounds coming from around him. It wasn't much, but it beat nothing at all.

"We're in the camp.'' Hawkins heard McCarter's faint voice from his pocket.

"How much farther to that Arab compound?'' Hawkins called over to the sergeant.

"It's on the western edge of the refugees, another five hundred meters."

"I got that," McCarter said. "We'll be in place there waiting for you."

Hawkins had no idea what McCarter had in mind, but he trusted him. He had more tricks than a magician's convention.

SINCE HE KNEW what to be on the lookout for, Hawkins spotted the shadows, blacker than night, moving in behind the mercenaries. Hoping to give his teammates a little more information, Hawkins moved up to the sergeant. "How many of them are there, Sarge?" he asked.

"Fifty-eight," the Sergeant answered.

"And you think that the ten of us are going to be enough to deal with them?"

That was one question too many. The sergeant stopped and turned to Hawkins, his hand on the grip of his submachine gun. "What the fuck's wrong with you, Burton?" he snapped. "I thought you had more balls than this. Don't tell me that you're going to—"

The black-clad arm that came over the sergeant's left shoulder clamped down on his mouth and jaw, jerking his head around. At the same time, a knife drove into the right side of his neck all the way to the hilt. As the Phoenix Force warrior eased the sergeant's limp body to the ground, Hawkins recognized Bolan.

"Dub?" the merc closest to Hawkins said. "What—"

The thunk of a solid object impacting the back of his skull sounded clear on the night air.

As if that were a signal, each of the mercs found himself being taken down silently. One man, though, was giving Manning a bit of a workout. As the man launched a karate kick at the Canadian, Encizo took his other leg out from under him with the butt of his M-16. When the man went down, Manning was on him and coldcocked him with the butt of his fighting knife.

Plastic riot restraints quickly immobilized them, and they were disarmed.

"What the hell's going on, Burton?" one of the mercs asked.

"I'm sorry, guys," Hawkins said, "but this party's over. You signed on to detonate a nuclear weapon in Jerusalem, and you just can't be allowed to do that."

"You're shitting me," one of the mercs said. "No one said anything about that. They told us that we'd be killing Arabs."

"You know that 'special package' we've been lugging around in training? It's supposed to be a nuclear device. And the ground we've been training on is supposed to be Temple Mount in Jerusalem."

"Shit, man, I don't need anything like that."

"Believe me," Hawkins said, "you guys've been lied to big time. Instead of being heroes, you were being sent to murder a million or so people and destroy the holiest city of three religions, including yours.''

"Carl," Katz said, turning to Lyons, "how about Gadgets keeping an eye on these guys while we call on the major."

"I never get to have any fun," Schwarz said.

"We need to secure that big chopper, too," McCarter pointed out. "We can all fit in it, and we won't have to shuttle to our next target."

"Good point," Katz said.

"I'll take care of it," McCarter answered.

THE REAR DOOR of the Super Frelon was open, so McCarter stepped inside. His rubber-soled boots made little noise on the deck plates. And even with the turbines at idle, their muted roar and the beat of the rotor masked any sound he made. A lone pilot sat in the right seat, looking out the canopy.

In a flash, McCarter was beside the pilot's seat and had muzzle of his pistol jammed into his ribs. "Easy, lad," he said. "Hands off the collective and feet off the pedals."

The pilot shot him a startled look, but complied. Holding his pistol in place, McCarter reached down and took the pilot's Beretta Model 92 out of its holster. He then reached out and cut the fuel feed to the turbines.

When the rotor started to wind down, he backed up and motioned for the pilot to get out of his seat. "Careful, lad," he warned.

The Australian pilot was an aerial mercenary and had no desire to die for his paycheck. Something had obviously gotten screwed up, but as long as he didn't have to die for it, he really didn't care what happened. He could always get another flying job.

"Not to worry, mate," he said.

"Just keep your hands high where I can see them."

As soon as he was out of the cockpit, McCarter slammed him up against the bulkhead for a search. "Assume the position," he snapped.

When the pilot put both his hands up high and spread his feet, McCarter patted him down.

"Okay," he said when the man was clean. "Slowly bring your hands around behind your back."

"You don't need to do that," the man protested.

"Oh, yes, I do," McCarter said. "We haven't been properly introduced."

The pilot laughed and put his arms behind his back for the riot cuffs. "Okay, mate, what's the drill now?"

"The drill is that if you're a good lad, you'll be able to walk away from this," McCarter said as he slipped a plastic restraint over the pilot's wrists. "You know what happens if you're not."

"I don't know who you are, mister, but I have no argument with that."

"Just see that you keep it that way."

"Not to worry."

MAJOR HART WAS surprised to hear the turbines of the helicopter shut down. Grabbing his Beretta submachine gun, he hurried out of his tent and headed for the main gate. He was almost there when he saw Burton running through the gate.

"Report," he said.

"Sir," Hawkins said, stiffening to attention, "there's been some kind of fuckup. The sergeant says he needs to see you ASAP."

"What's the problem?"

"That gas, sir."

"What about it, dammit!"

Two men suddenly stepped out of the shadows with submachine guns at the ready. "Stand easy, Major."

Hart almost didn't recognize the Italian count and the British doctor who had visited the camp earlier. Both men were dressed in black combat suits and assault harnesses. Behind them were at least a dozen more commandos. One of them swiftly relieved him of his subgun before stepping back. Only now did Hart realize that the sentries at the gate were missing.

"Call your men out," Blancanales said, "and tell them to ground their weapons. Your mission is being canceled."

This was the worst personal disaster Bernard Hart had ever experienced in his long career as a soldier. He had fought all over Africa and the Middle East for the past thirty years, and he had never encountered anything like this. Bloody, lying bastard politicians! This was supposed to have been his big finale, the job that would insure his comfortable retirement. Now he'd be lucky to escape going to prison for the rest of his life.

Screaming his rage, his hand went for the hideaway pocket Mauser in his boot top. The pistol was halfway up, and he was charging for Blancanales when Carl Lyons fired a single round into his head.

"That's the second time we've lost the man we needed to talk to," Bolan said.

"We don't need him," Katz replied. "We know where his paymaster is."

HAWKINS LED THE WAY into the first barracks tent, followed by half of the Stony Man commandos. The men were so accustomed to their fellow mercs getting up in the middle of the night, the faint sounds of movement didn't wake them. After collecting their individual weapons, Hawkins went into the second tent and did the same.

Stacking the retrieved M-16s in the late major's tent, the commandos then recovered the heavy weapons from the armory and added them to the pile. By the time everything was under guard, first light was breaking when Katz sounded the camp siren to awaken everyone.

Confused, half-dressed mercenaries poured out of their tents to face the guns of Phoenix Force. Most of them hadn't even noticed that their weapons were gone. The few who dashed back into their tent found another black-clad commando waiting for them, motioning with the muzzle of his subgun. In less time than it took to tell, it was over.

As soon as the mercs were corraled on the parade ground, Katz and Bolan went looking for the first of Hart's two nuclear weapons. The seals on the transport case were intact, so it was carried out and loaded onto the Super Frelon.

"Now we have to disarm that Arab bunch and get their warhead," McCarter said.

"If we wait till the sun's up," Katz suggested, "it'll be a lot easier."

"Good point." McCarter grinned.

CHAPTER TWENTY-SIX

Sudan

Taking down the Arab mercenaries turned out to be almost as easy as it had been to disarm the Americans. Waiting until the hour of morning prayer, the Arabic-speaking Katz led the Stony Man warriors into the compound and surprised them while they were gathered for their devotions. One or two of them had to be hammered into submission with gun butts, but that was all it took. Without their weapons in their hands, they were surprisingly submissive.

After their Russian warhead was secured, their small arms were collected and disabled by removing the bolts from the machine guns and AKs and smashing the firing mechanisms of the RPG launchers.

Katz then told them that the UN would be in to evacuate them soon and cautioned them about causing any trouble with the refugees. There were a few questions, but the mercenaries knew better than to argue with black-suited men with guns in their hands. Most of them felt lucky to still be alive.

"WHAT ARE WE GOING to do with these guys?" Hawkins asked Katzenelenbogen as he watched the confused American mercenaries huddling under the guns of Phoenix Force. "They're our people."

"We're going to leave them and the Arabs here for the UN to police up," Katz replied. "We don't have time to mess with them, and I don't think we owe them anything. They sure as hell weren't defending the red, white and blue by signing up to work for Betancourt."

"All except for the pilot," Grimaldi broke in. "I want to take him with us so I can have a little chat about where he gets his gas and a few odd flyboy things like that. If we're going to fly to Uganda to finish this thing up, we're going to need the fuel."

"Good point," Katz said.

IT TOOK a while before the Stony Man team was ready to move out with their prizes. Both the nukes and the Americans' small arms had to be loaded on the Super Frelon for the flight back to the Red Sea. Hawkins's squad members had been released from their riot cuffs and marched back to join the others.

Since it was light now, Hawkins was recognized when he led his men to the holding area.

"Hey, Burton, you sorry fuck!" one of the mercs from another squad called out. "What're you doing working for those UN bastards?"

"I'm not with the UN," Hawkins replied, "and neither are they."

"Don't give me that shit," the man said heatedly. "We saw you go out with them when they came in earlier to recon us. What did it cost them to get you to sell out to the New World Order, anyway?"

"I'm not with the UN," Hawkins restated, "and neither are any of the rest of us. We're part of a U.S. strike force working against nuclear proliferation."

"That's a likely story."

Hawkins then went over the real reason they had been recruited and what their target was to have been.

"If there's anyone here who can read Russian," Hawkins concluded, "I'll let him tell you what the markings on the transport case for that thing says. If nothing else, the radiation-warning signs on the damned thing ought to tell you something. You guys were suckered big time, and if you had carried out this mission, you'd be hunted down and executed for crimes against humanity."

That sobered the hotheads a little and started them thinking about what was going to happen to them next. "What are you going to do with us?" one man asked.

Blancanales took that as his cue to get into this discussion. "Now that you've been disarmed, you'll remain here until we can get someone in to evacuate you. You have food and water for at least a week."

"Aren't you going to leave us anything to defend ourselves with?" Being just another refugee wasn't something that sounded good to them. They had food, and without any way to guard it, they'd quickly become prey.

Blancanales looked over to Katz, who nodded. "We'll leave you enough to keep the refugees away, but that's it."

"What's going to happen to us when we get home?"

"To be honest with you," Blancanales said with no sympathy at all in his voice, "I don't know. But the next time someone offers you a chance to kill people, you might want to stop and think about it before signing on."

Stony Man Farm, Virginia

HAL BROGNOLA WAS relieved to get Katzenelenbogen's report that two of Betancourt's Russian warheads had been recovered. If Hawkins's assessment of the targeting was correct, it meant that Jerusalem and the Vatican wouldn't be attacked. A lesser man might have been satisfied with recovering just the two weapons out of the three. A lesser man might feel that Betancourt could be safely contained where he was in Uganda, and that even if he somehow was still able to take out Mecca, it would be no great loss.

But Brognola wasn't a lesser man. To him, even a single nuclear weapon in the hands of a man like Betancourt was a threat that couldn't be ignored. Also, the destruction of Mecca would be no less an abomination than an attack on the Vatican or Jerusalem. Beyond that, though, this had become a personal affair with Brognola. Betancourt was threatening the existence of something he held very dear to his heart, and he wasn't going to let him get away with it.

He was aware, though, that delivering on that vow also had its risks. So far the team had again managed to emerge unscathed from this far-ranging, long-running gun battle. But to bring this to a conclusion, they would be going up against a man who knew that he was being hunted and who would surely be prepared to defend himself. The real question was would he be willing to use his nuclear device in a suicidal gesture against his tormentors?

There was little doubt that Betancourt was a certifiable megalomaniac, and that mind-set usually went hand in hand with grand last gestures. Brognola knew that there was a good chance that he would set off the bomb so he could go out in a blaze of glory and take his tormentors with him.

In their favor, though, was the fact that Betancourt was holed up at the Ugandan mine. Both Kurtzman and Katzenelenbogen felt that he would stay there and would still try to find a way to use his last warhead to make at least one of the attacks. To a man who was as fixated on nuclear devastation as he was, even a little Armageddon was better than none at all.

The Red Sea

HAVING THE WARHEADS in custody was good, but it wasn't the end of the Stony Man team's problem. The big question now was, what they were going to do with them? Since this mission was off the books, they couldn't just fly to the closest U.S. base and off-load them for the military to dispose of.

The Super Frelon was too big to land on the chopper pad of the *Roxalana,* so it was flown to a desolate spot on the shore of the Red Sea. After ferrying everyone else to Mustapha's boat anchored right offshore in the JetRanger, Gadgets Schwarz and Gary Manning stayed behind to neutralize the two warheads. Both men were experienced with explosives and booby traps, but these destructive devices were safer to work on than the average high-school boy's pipe bomb. The disarming procedure did, however, take time.

First, they carefully removed the outer casing of the first missile warhead. The heart of this type of implosion nuclear weapon was actually rather simple. All it required was a certain amount of a particular refined radioactive material in metallic form that had to be squeezed very hard. The squeezing process was the technique that had to be finessed, though. Not enough squeeze, or a squeeze that didn't apply the force equally, simply wasn't good enough.

The core of this weapon was a hollow ball of fissionable material only about eight inches in diameter, which was covered in thick hexagonal plates of a specialized rapid-detonating explosive. This was all shielded within a seamless sphere of stainless steel pierced with a pattern of precisely located holes containing detonating wires controlled by the world's most accurate electrical timers.

Since this warhead had been mounted in a tactical rocket, it had a complicated detonating device able to sense speed, acceleration and outside air pressure. The first step to making it safe was to remove the power pack. Even though the detonator was switched off, Manning was tense as he removed the power pack. Laying it on the ground, he crushed it under his boot.

It wasn't difficult to render the bomb safe. Simply cutting all of the detonating wires or removing the timers known as microswitches would do it. When that was done, the core became simply a mass of deadly radioactive metal surrounded by plastic explosives. The explosive could still be detonated, but all the explosion would do would be to scatter the radioactive material. Without the microswitches to control the precision detonation of the individual blocks, it wouldn't go into a nuclear reaction.

By the end of the second hour, both warheads had been disabled and packed back in their transport containers. Schwarz grinned as he locked the last latch. "Miller time."

"You got that right," Manning replied. "Call Jack to come and get us."

WHILE THE WARHEADS were being worked on, Kurtzman had been engaged in a long-distance skull session via the Internet with Katz and the Phoenix Force commandos. Now that they had taken out the two Sudanese mercenary camps, they had to keep the pressure on Betancourt. Part of that plan was to take out his private air force. The mercenary pilot had been more than willing to tell everything he knew. As long as they kept him alive, he would continue helping them any way he could.

"This shouldn't be all that difficult," McCarter said as he looked at a faxed satellite photo of the secret air base. "We fly in there, round those people up and burn the choppers. Piece of cake."

"You know," Blancanales said, "we might try working the UN dodge again to provide a little diversion on the insertion. It might not affect the outcome, but the confusion might buy us a little time."

"Considering that this is Africa," Katz said, "it just might work. I'll see if Mustapha will extend the loan of his chopper."

"After giving him the weapons we captured, he shouldn't have a problem."

"We have to pay him for his efforts somehow, and I figured he could make a nice profit from them."

Uganda

BETANCOURT'S SECRET air field was nestled in a small valley surrounded by tree-covered hills and looked to have been a military field at one time. It had the wooden hangar, fuel dump and control tower so common to remote African colonial military operations. It also had the barracks one would expect and a small building that had to be either the headquarters or flight operations.

In the trees off to the sides of the runway was a derelict C-47 on collapsed landing gear, and a couple of smaller wrecked single-engine aircraft. The markings on the planes had been sunburned to the point of being unreadable, so there was no telling whose they had once been.

Six Super Frelons and four Mi-8s were lined up on the runway as if ready for inspection. A dozen mechanics were performing maintenance on the aircraft while another crew had a Super Frelon nose first in the hangar with its engine cowlings off.

"You notice the markings on those birds?" Grimaldi asked. "Two of them are wearing Israeli markings and two have Saudi air force. Those have to be their primary mission aircraft, so we're still in time."

As they flew closer, Katzenelenbogen could see the machine-gun emplacements their captive pilot had mentioned. No one was manning the weapons right now, but he knew that could change in a flash. From just the men he could see in the open, the Stony Man commandos were going to be outnumbered two to one, and that didn't take into account anyone who might be in the barracks or the headquarters building.

"Okay, guys, here's the drill," Katz radioed. "Jack's going to fall back into trail position behind the Frelon. David, you have your boy put down at the end of that flight line, but keep buttoned up. Then Jack will set down but will keep his turbines burning. They're going to want to know who in the hell we are, but they shouldn't start shooting immediately because we've been escorted in.''

"As soon as all eyes are on us, we'll get out and see how this thing goes. David, you then off-load your people and start working your way to the main hangar. Hopefully, we won't have to start shooting, but if we do, it's got to be quick and deadly. Any questions?''

As he expected, there was none. "Remember," he added, "don't shoot up the fuel dump. We need it to continue on to the mine.''

MCCARTER'S CAPTIVE pilot did exactly as he was told. He was an airplane driver and desired nothing more than to continue in his chosen profession. He had no desire to die for his ex-employer. He made the radio call that he was coming in and put down the big chopper close to the end of the flight line.

After shutting down his turbines, he submitted to having his wrists bound again. "Not that we don't trust you," McCarter said, "but I want you here when I come back.''

"I understand.''

With the pilot secured, Bolan, Katz and the Phoenix Force warriors quickly deplaned and ran for cover behind the flight line.

GRIMALDI FELT a bit exposed as he came in low and slow for a landing in front of the hangar. But the UN markings on the JetRanger should at least give the opposition reason enough to pause until they found out what was going on instead of just opening fire.

Flaring out carefully, he touched down on the oiled red dirt tarmac without dragging his skids. Dumping the cyclic to bring the rotor blades to flat pitch, he rolled back on his throttle to the flight idle setting.

Sliding open the side doors, Lyons, Katz and Blancanales stepped out and cleared the spinning rotor. Their unexpected appearance brought two men out to see who they were. Both of them were well tanned and had the look of the expatriate Europeans who ran so much of Africa's Western technical infrastructure. They also didn't look happy, and one of them was wearing a big semiauto in a well-worn hip holster.

"Gentlemen," Blancanales said.

"Just who the hell are you?" the man with the pistol asked in accented English.

"My name is Orsini," Blancanales said, "and I'm with the UN Refugee Commission."

"My name is Smith," the man growled, "and you're bloody well trespassing, mate. If I were you, I'd get back in that bloody chopper and get the bloody hell out of here."

"WE'VE GOT COMPANY," Manning called out over the com link from his position covering the team's rear. "I've got two trucks inbound with at least a couple of dozen troops, and these guys are armed. I need some backup here ASAP.''

McCarter and his team had worked their way half-way up the line of parked choppers and were almost to the hangar, but this new threat clearly took precedence.

''Roger,'' McCarter replied. ''I'll send Calvin and Rafe now, and the rest of us will be there as soon as we can.''

''Make it quick.''

Unslinging his sniper's rifle, Manning moved to the opposite side of the road to an outcropping that looked like a good sniper's nest. For this to work, they were going to have to hold the convoy long enough for the rest of the commandos to secure the landing strip.

James hurried forward with his M-60 and a pair of 250-round ammo assault packs slung over his shoulder. Encizo had swapped his M-16 with Hawkins for an M-203 and couple of bandoliers of 40 mm grenades.

''I'm in the rocks,'' they heard Manning say over the com link. ''Take up positions to my left where the road comes close.''

''On the way.''

CHAPTER TWENTY-SEVEN

The Airfield

Katzenelenbogen was monitoring the team's com link traffic, and since he was the only one of the three at the hangar wearing his earpiece, he flashed an alert sign to Carl Lyons. The big former LAPD cop nodded and subtly shifted his grip on the MP-5 slung over his shoulder and stepped off to the side to clear a better line of fire.

Rosario Blancanales also caught the signal, but he didn't openly react. "Mr. Smith," he said smoothly, "as I'm sure you must be aware, the Sudanese government has invited the UN Refugee Commission in to assist them with evacuation and redistribution of refugees. We are making a survey of places that we might use as stopover points in this process."

"I don't give a flying leap who you are, mate," Smith said, stepping closer to Blancanales. "This airfield is a private operation, and the UN has no jurisdiction here. Get back in that bloody bird and bugger off."

"But, Mr. Smith—"

"I said bugger off!"

CALVIN JAMES and Rafael Encizo found a perfect ambush spot along the road and quickly slid into position. Manning hadn't been joking about what was coming at them. It was a full platoon of infantry, and they looked like somebody's regular troops, not mercenaries. The trucks were coming on fast, and there was no time for complicated attack plans.

"And a one, and a two, and a three," James whispered over the com link as he lay behind his M-60 with the cab of the lead truck locked in his gun sights. "Rock and roll!"

His first long burst of 7.62 mm NATO rounds swept the cab from one side to the other, shattering the windshield and the three men behind it. He was just coming off the trigger when Encizo triggered his M-203, sending the 40 mm HE grenade into the radiator.

With the driver dead at the wheel, the lead truck drifted off the road, its radiator blowing steam, and ended up crashing against a tree.

AT THE HANGAR, Calvin James's countdown was the signal for Lyons to bring up his H&K sub gun while Katz and Blancanales each drew a Beretta model 92 from their bush jacket pockets.

"Stay right where you are," Blancanales commanded.

The merc with the pistol on his hip went for his piece, and Katz simply shot him through the head.

His partner stood stunned and instantly put his hands in the air.

"Good man," Lyons said as he moved in to pat him down.

The gunfire had gotten everyone's attention now, and the mechanics ran out to find men with guns waiting for them. After seeing the body leaking blood on the tarmac, most of them followed their boss's example and put their hands up. Two broke for the bush, and Lyons let them go.

WHEREVER THE LOCAL troops had come from, they were good. When James and Encizo opened the ambush, they didn't turn and run as the Phoenix Force warriors had hoped they would. The driver of the second truck immediately took his vehicle off the road, turning it sideways to give the men in the back unimpeded room to return fire.

James had a clean line of sight at the troops bailing out of the first truck and rapped out several long bursts, slashing into their numbers. Encizo used his grenade launcher to further bust them up.

From his perch in the boulders, Manning sighted in on the man from the second truck who seemed to be giving all the orders. At least he was the one who was waving his arms and doing all of the shouting. Since an open mouth made a good target, he ranged in on it and fired. The 7.62 mm round smashed through his lower face and blew out the base of his skull. The man who looked at his leader in stunned surprise was the next to take a round.

With those two kills, the other troops hit the dirt and scrambled for cover, which was what Manning had wanted them to do. Now he switched to targeting the men who had been in the lead truck.

Even with the surprise ambush and taking initial casualties, the troops were responding well. This hilly terrain of scrub brush was their home turf. They had fought hundreds of battles in this land, and they knew how to work it to their advantage.

No three men, no matter how good, were going to hold them back for very long.

IN THE JETRANGER, Grimaldi rolled his throttle against the stop. It took a few seconds for the turbine to spool up again, but when the rpm were in the green, he pulled pitch to the blades and the chopper almost jumped up into the sky. Snapping the tail around, he aimed his M-60s in the general direction of the hangar. The mechanics and ground crewmen reached as high for the sky as they could to make sure he noticed they had surrendered.

With his makeshift gunship in the air, Grimaldi held the trump card for the moment. As long as no one tried to do anything heroic, this should work. But, with mercenaries, one could never tell what they would do.

MANNING, James and Encizo were still holding their own, but just barely. Their opposition was skillfully using fire and maneuver to work their way around to their flanks.

"Jack, if you're not doing anything useful," Encizo said, "we can sure as hell use you over here doing your thing."

"Do it," Katz broke in. "We're secure here."

"The flight line's secure, too, Rafe," Bolan cut in. "We'll join you."

"Take your time," the Cuban shot back. "There's only two dozen of them left."

WITH THE CONTACT only a half mile away, Grimaldi was on them in a flash. He made his first run down the road to spot out the friendly positions. His first two targets were the trucks and one cluster of troops.

Whoever these troops were, they were veterans and they'd obviously been under fire from helicopters before. As he started his second strafing run, Grimaldi spotted ground fire that quickly turned into a serious firestorm. A burst of AK fire cut though the canopy in front of him, sending shards of plastic slashing across his face.

Since Grimaldi's machine guns weren't mounted in a turret as on a real gunship, he had to aim the entire chopper to bring the fixed guns to bear on the target. It also meant that he couldn't traverse the turret to the side and fire to cover himself as he banked away from an attack. A lot of the metal making up any helicopter was actually noncritical and could be shot up without affecting its ability to fly. But soaking up fire wasn't the safest thing in the world to do.

"Hey, guys," he called out, "this shit's getting serious up here. I could sure use a little suppressive fire to cover my ass when I make my break."

"We're on it," James sent back.

Swinging wide, Grimaldi was coming in on a gun run parallel to Phoenix Force's front line when his earphones came to life.

"Jack!" James yelled. "Break! Break! They've got a 12.7 on you."

That call was enough to freeze the blood of any chopper pilot. Grimaldi stomped down on his right tail-rotor pedal and let the torque of the main rotor snap his nose around. Dumping his collective, he dropped the nose and headed down for a little belly-to-the-ground E and E.

The heavy coughing chunk of the 12.7 was a sound that no one who had heard it ever forgot. The sound of the heavy, half-inch-diameter slugs punching through the airframe was also a sound no pilot ever forgot. The JetRanger didn't have any armor plate around the pilot's seat, but he hunched himself as small as he could anyway and silently recited the pilot's combat prayer, "Dear God, please don't let me fuck up today."

The heavy gun continued chunking at him and scoring hits.

MANNING WAS STILL in his sniper's nest, but a pair of attackers had been able to crawl up close enough to become real bothersome. Every time he popped up to do his thing, they were right on him. Hearing the panicked call about the heavy machine gun, he knew he had to find a way to help Grimaldi or watch him die. Grabbing a flash bang grenade from his harness, Manning pulled the pin and lobbed the bomb at his two tormentors.

The bright flash and thundering detonation spooked one of the pair and when he turned to run, Manning put a bullet in his back. His partner shouted in rage and charged the boulders, so Manning put a bullet in his chest, as well.

He got on the firing crew right as the JetRanger started smoking. The gun was obscured by the brush, and he didn't have a clear shot at the crew, but he kept pumping round after round into what he could see.

"Mayday, Mayday," Grimaldi called out calmly over the com link. "Will someone please come and get me as soon as I finish crashing."

EVEN FIRING BLIND, Manning was able to take out the 12.7 mm gun and, when the other Phoenix Force warriors hit the enemy's flank guns blazing, that was enough. With both of their trucks burning, the surviving troops disappeared into the brush to walk back to wherever they had come from.

When the commandos arrived at Grimaldi's crash

site, the pilot was still sitting in his seat. Much of the sturdy JetRanger had been shed in the crash, but the cockpit, minus the Plexiglas, was more or less intact.

"You okay?" Calvin James asked as hurried up to him.

"My foot's trapped."

Using one of the shattered skids, the commandos bent back the fuselage that had been pushed in and was trapping him. With the jagged metal out of the way, they helped him from the cockpit.

"It doesn't seem to be broken," Calvin James announced as he felt the pilot's foot. "But you're going to be hobbling around for a while."

"Wrap the damned thing," Grimaldi growled and looked at his ankle as if it had betrayed him.

"It's going to hurt."

"Wrap it, dammit," he snapped. "I don't want David trying to fly that Super Frelon. He'll just crash the damned thing and then we'll have to walk."

McCarter didn't have the total flight hours of Stony Man's ace pilot, but he more than knew his way around with a stick and rudder. In the mood Grimaldi was in, however, no one was going to bring that up. He always got a bit testy after being shot down.

WHEN GRANT BETANCOURT wasn't able to get through to either Major Hart at the mercenary camp or the tower at his airfield, he was forced to reassess his situation. It was obvious now that Derek Sanders's death hadn't been a fluke and that whoever was responsible for it was coming after him, as well.

He still didn't understand how he had come to be in this situation. He wasn't a man who was accustomed to making many mistakes. Mistakes were something he exploited when someone else made them. He was one of the world's wealthiest men and a close personal friend of the President of the United States. Tens of thousands of men and women worked for him, and tens of thousands more looked to him for leadership. He had brought down governments with a single phone call from his Phoenix office, and dozens of politicians owed their seats to his support. He had grown accustomed to being a powerful man, but he was being stymied everywhere he turned now.

The latest report from Security Plus in Phoenix had also been bad news. One of the teams he had sent after Brognola had been intercepted. One man had been killed and the other had simply disappeared. Further, Brognola hadn't been seen in his usual D.C. haunts since then.

That meant that his plan to use Brognola to get this crazy persecution of him stopped wasn't going to work. All he had left to try to take care of this situation was an ex-Soviet RD-45 nuclear warhead.

He wished that he had all three of his Russian warheads here instead of just the one. One was more than enough to relieve him of his attackers, but all three going off at once would be so much better. Even better would be having some way to transport the warheads to their intended destinations as he had planned. If he were doing this all over again, he would have found a way to appropriate three ballistic missiles to deliver them with.

He had made one mistake, but he wouldn't make another one. Whoever was coming for him wouldn't find him unprepared to deal with them.

WHILE THEIR Super Frelon helicopter was being re-fueled, the Stony Man warriors took the time to disable the choppers at the airfield. Rather than destroy so many valuable machines, they opted to simply destroy their tail rotors. After finding what he called a "bloody great hammer," David McCarter walked down the flight line giving the blades of each tail rotor what he called a "bloody great whack." The composite tail rotors of the French machines shattered nicely and the metal blades of the Hips bent.

"Having fun?" Carl Lyons asked him.

"Quite." McCarter grinned and held out the hammer. "Up for a bit of a whack?"

"Don't mind if I do," Lyons replied politely. "Where should I whack to get the best effect?"

NOT KNOWING the extent of Betancourt's radar system, Grimaldi brought the Super Frelon in low and fast, keeping under the radar horizon. Five miles out from the mine, he found a clearing in the jungle and put the aircraft down. After securing the area, David

McCarter and Bolan headed out immediately to recon the objective.

When they arrived, they saw that the jungle had been cleared away down to bare dirt for a quarter of a mile around the mine head. Since it was on a small hill, the complex dominated its surroundings like a castle. And, like a castle, it was well defended with a tall berm, bunkers and wire barriers. Betancourt had made sure that this complex wouldn't fall.

"This place is a bloody fortress," McCarter said.

Bolan could only agree with that assessment. Someone had thought out these defenses thoroughly and had spent a lot of time and effort hardening the site. Considering where this mine was located, that wasn't surprising. Even without an ongoing civil war, Uganda wasn't the most stable place in the world to try to conduct business.

"We've seen worse places than this, David."

"I was afraid you were going to say something like that, Striker." The Briton shook his head slowly. "How do want to try to do it?"

"We don't have enough force or fire support to storm the place," Bolan replied, "so we're going to have to go for an infiltration."

"Then what? Aaron says that there's at least fifty troops in there."

"We'll go for the command post and try to take out the leadership."

"When?"

"As soon as it gets dark."

"I was afraid you were going to say that, too."

Bolan chuckled. "Some things never change."

"I'll call them forward and we can wait out the dark here."

CHAPTER TWENTY-EIGHT

Wagner Mining

Hawkins was good at what he did and, this night, he really needed to be at his best. Making a one-man recon against a place like this wasn't for the faint-hearted. Even with the sensor detector he had borrowed from Gadgets Schwarz, it was dangerously slow going. Fortunately, it hadn't rained for several days so he didn't have to contend with mud, but he was leaving a clear track in the soft red earth. If he couldn't clear the wire before daybreak, he'd be as good as dead. But his only chance to survive was to keep going.

Emerging from under a section of razor wire tanglefoot he had cut his way through, he paused to again check for sensors. When the red LED on the bug sniffer didn't light up, he moved out again. Wire and electronic sensors were only part of this place's defenses. There were more than enough trip wires and booby traps laid out that the sensors were redundant.

"THIS ISN'T WORKING," Katzenelenbogen told Bolan. Hawkins had a tracking bug on his uniform, and his progress was being monitored from the woodline where the Stony Man warriors waited. "By the time he gets through, it's going to be too close to daylight for us to follow him."

"What do you want to do?" Bolan asked.

"With the JetRanger down, we can't do the UN thing. But we might try a Super Frelon insertion at first light and just fly in like we own the place."

"Why not?" Bolan agreed. "All they can do is shoot us down."

AS SOON AS it was light enough for him to see without night-vision goggles, Grimaldi brought the Super Frelon in fast and low from the west. Skimming right over the top of the wire, he set down with the tail ramp facing the barracks. Keeping his rotor rpm up, he stayed in a ground effect semihover. That close to the ground, the course pitch of the blades sucked up enough dust to create a localized windstorm.

Under that cover, Phoenix Force and Able Team left the chopper by the side doors in front and quickly spread out to take the sentries around the berm. The guard posts on each side of the main gate would be the first to be neutralized. Lyons and his Able Team partners took the right-hand bunker while Encizo, James and Manning did the left.

First light was always a bad time for standing guard duty. The guards had made it through the hours of darkness and were ready to rest their tired bodies, and the faint light also gave them a false sense of security. It was barely light enough to see, but not light enough to make out details until it was too late. The chopper was the only thing moving this early in the morning, so both guards were watching it. Since the machines flew in and out of the mine all the time, they weren't startled to see it, only curious.

They were equally curious about the black-clad man who appeared out of the artificial dust storm and was headed toward them. He wasn't armed, but even if he had been, that would be no big deal. Everyone in the camp was armed. The sentries' weapons were still slung over their shoulders when the man got close enough for them to see the big blond guy clearly.

"Good morning, gentlemen," the man said as he pulled a large-caliber pistol from behind his belt. "Please keep your hands where I can see them."

One sentry automatically obeyed. But, when the other one tried to unsling his weapon, another black-clad man coldcocked him from behind. Suddenly, there were six armed men and they quickly disarmed the two guards and secured their hands and feet with plastic cuffs.

"You boys stay quiet now," Lyons said as he slapped a piece of duct tape over their mouths.

After moving the machine guns in the bunkers so they were aimed into the camp, one commando stayed with each of them while the rest of them moved out to clear the other guard posts. They were halfway though when they came upon Hawkins in the wire, still three yards from the berm line.

"T.J.," Manning whispered over the com link. "Lay low for a second and we'll get you out."

"'Bout fucking time," a very weary Hawkins growled.

After clearing the berm-line bunkers and guard posts, the Stony Man warriors then gave the mercenaries an early wake-up call. Faced with a battery of machine guns and a dozen hard-faced men with their weapons at the ready, the mercenaries meekly came out with their hands in the air.

THE SOUND of the Super Frelon's rotors finally woke Grant Betancourt from a deep sleep. Looking out the window of his quarters, he saw dark-clad figures moving in the half light of dawn. Glancing at his watch, he saw that it wasn't time for a guard change, and he knew that the camp had been invaded.

Dressing hurriedly, he grabbed his hard hat and fled out a side door. Keeping under cover by going from one cluster of machinery to the next, he reached the elevator at the mine head unseen.

WITH THE ISRAELI mercenaries being guarded by James and Encizo behind their machine guns, the other Stony Man warriors stormed the Wagner Mining headquarters. It was still several hours before the first shift of workers was due at the mine face, so only a single technician was on duty in the control center. Everyone else was asleep.

The sight of weapons in the hands of these hard-faced men prompted the technician on duty to be very helpful.

"Have you seen Grant Betancourt this morning?" Katz asked.

"I don't know any Mr. Betancourt," the man said, "but if you mean Mr. David Brown, I saw him heading for the mine head a few minutes ago."

"Damn," Katz said. "Now we have to go down there and find him."

"The safety helmets have coded tracking chips in case of an underground accident," the technician stated, "so we can follow him from here."

"Show me."

The technician punched up a screen on his menu. "It looks like he's heading down to the lowest level."

"He's mine," Bolan said.

"Striker..." Katz started to say.

Bolan silenced him with a look. "Get everyone as far from here as you can, as fast as you can."

"I've got it, Striker." McCarter slung his assault rifle around over his back. "How much time do you think you'll need?"

Bolan looked at the computer-generated 3-D map the network of tunnels and caverns of the mine w their feet. "I don't know," he said, "but don't ....ke it too long. He's got that nuke down there."

The Briton met the eyes of his comrade-in-arms. "Good luck, Striker."

Bolan nodded. "Take care."

"Wait a minute, you two," Katz said.

Bolan's face was set. "You need to get these people moving, Katz."

The Israeli knew that look well. It meant that his friend was in the Executioner mode. Grant Betancourt had stepped across the line far too many times, and it would end here, this day. No matter what else happened, Betancourt's bill had come due, and Bolan would extract the payment.

"Okay, okay," he said. "But be careful."

Manning held back when the others turned to go. "You're going to need someone to run the elevator, Striker," he spoke up. "I've spent some time around mines, and I know how to get around down there."

"Are you sure?"

Manning nodded. "Let's do it."

"You'll need this." The technician held out an electronic tracking device. As long as these men were going to let him live, he was going to help them in any way he could. He had a family in England he wanted to get back to.

"Can you print out a hard copy of the tunnel map?" Manning asked.

"No problem, sir."

As BOLAN and Manning hurried for the elevator leading into the mine, Katz and McCarter started the evacuation. The first people flown out on the Super Frelon were the remaining mine employees.

As soon as the chopper was full, Grimaldi didn't even bother to raise the rear ramp when he lifted off. His destination was a road junction five miles away. The jungle had been cleared away there, and it was the nearest place he could get into quickly and off-load his passengers.

When it came time to load up the disarmed mercenaries, Katz took center stage for a moment. "Here's the drill," he told them in Hebrew. "You're getting out of here alive. What happens to you after that, I really don't care. However, at the first sign of trouble out of any of you, my men have orders to shoot to kill."

Katz's eyes scanned the men in front of him. "Are there any questions?"

A man raised his hand. "How will we get home, sir?"

Katz allowed a smile to form on his face. "Frankly, I don't give a damn. But if you boys ever want to see Jerusalem again, you'd better do exactly as you're told."

The smile suddenly shifted into a look of pure death. "I'm a Jew myself, and I gave my blood for Israel more than once, but I'll kill every one of you bastards in a flash if I have to."

THE MAIN MINE SHAFT descended almost a thousand feet into the earth. The elevator ride down took several minutes, and it wasn't long before Bolan and Manning felt the temperature start to rise and the air grow thick and damp. When they reached the bottom of the shaft, it would be like being in a sauna.

The elevator cage opened into a brightly lit large chamber whose ceiling was held up by huge square pillars of bedrock that had been left in place when the chamber had been carved. Half the size of a football field, the chamber was the terminus for half a dozen tunnels that radiated from it. All but one of the tunnels had the electric cars that transported the miners still parked at the rail head.

After checking as much of the cavern as they could see from the elevator platform, Bolan flashed a signal to Manning to move out. The tunnel with the missing cars had to be the one Betancourt had taken, but calling the cars back to pick them up would be a dead giveaway that they were in pursuit.

"You know," Manning said, "we don't have to go in there after that damned warhead. We can safely leave it right where it is and still take care of this."

"How's that?"

Manning pointed at several hand trucks by one of the tunnel openings loaded with wooden crates. "The powder monkeys were getting ready to shoot one of the faces, and I can use their stuff to collapse this whole thing on top of it. From the size of the pumps they have working down here, once this place fills up with water, they'll never be able to reopen it."

"Do it quickly."

"Where are you going?"

Bolan glanced over at the tunnel. "To finish this mission."

THE END OF THE TUNNEL Grant Betancourt had taken refuge in was brightly lit. The electric car he had used to carry the warhead was parked under one of the lights, and Betancourt was opening the stainless-steel transport case when he heard the whine of the elevator coming down the shaft. He hadn't expected anyone to try to follow him down into the earth.

His first instinct was to run back down the tunnel to see who had come down, but he knew better than to waste the time. He hadn't expected to be followed, but he was prepared for whoever was coming for him. He had brought the warhead down to the tunnel for safekeeping, but it could also be used to protect him.

With the glare of the lights around him, Betancourt had to squint when he looked up from his work to look down the tunnel. He still hadn't opened all of the case's locks when Bolan emerged from the darkness into the light.

The Executioner didn't waste time talking to this man. Far too much air had already been wasted talking about him. His first shot took Betancourt in the right shoulder, shattering it.

The industrialist screamed, and the wrench he had been using to open the warhead case dropped from his nerveless fingers.

Bolan's second shot took Betancourt's left kneecap

out, and the man fell to the ground by the rail car writhing in pain.

"You forgot this," Bolan said as he holstered his Beretta and took a good grip on the warhead case with both hands. Giving a heave, he rolled the warhead over the side of the car. The heavy case crashed down on the wounded man, trapping him under it.

"Don't leave me here!" Betancourt screamed.

Bolan turned without a word and walked away.

MANNING HAD BEEN so focused on wiring the demolition charges he hadn't paid much attention to what was going on in the tunnel behind him. He had found plenty of explosives, but they weren't what he usually worked with. It was all slow, rock-busting charges, not the faster RDX explosives he preferred for this kind of work. Nonetheless, there were also two five-hundred-foot rolls of det cord, and that would make the job possible.

He was running the det cord to the last charge when Bolan rejoined him "Are you ready to shoot?" he asked.

"Just about," Manning replied. "But I couldn't find a remote detonator, so I had to rig the charges with regular time fuses."

"Light them and let's go."

"I just hope I timed that elevator ride properly," Manning muttered to himself as he pulled the time fuse igniters and waited to make sure that the fuses were all smoking.

GRUNTING AGAINST the pain, Betancourt used his good leg to roll the warhead case free of his wounded right leg. Grabbing the rail car with his good hand, he pulled himself up to his feet. Dragging his shattered leg, he used his good arm to balance himself against the wall of the tunnel as he limped forward as quickly as he could.

When he made it to the main chamber, he heard the elevator clank to a halt at the top of the shaft. He was limping over to the bank of elevator controls when he spotted something he didn't recognize at the base of the main pillar in the chamber. When he got closer, he recognized the markings on the bundles and saw the smoking fuse leading into it.

"No!" he yelled when he saw the burning fuse disappear into the bundle of explosives.

The end of time came for Grant Betancourt, a thousand feet beneath the earth.

THE STONY MAN commandos were waiting in the clearing five miles from the mine. Since the com links couldn't transmit underground, all they could do was wait. They had armed the mine employees and had them guarding the ex-mercenaries while this final act was being played out.

Even from five miles away, the blast that shot up from the mine's elevator shaft showed over the tops of the trees. It was quickly followed by a rumbling, rolling roar as the mine collapsed. Forty-foot-tall trees swayed like stalks of wheat in the wind, and the earth shook under their feet as if they were in an earth-quake.

"It's not a nuclear detonation," David McCarter shouted. "They caused the mine to cave in."

"Get that thing in the air," Katzenelenbogen shouted over his com link to Grimaldi as he raced for the chopper.

Grimaldi's gloved hand shot out to hit the start button for the Super Frelon's starboard turbine. As soon as its tach was registering, he bunched in the port-side engine. Overhead, the five-bladed rotor seemed to take forever to wind up. As soon as he had even minimum rotor speed, Grimaldi started feeding in pitch, trying to nurse the big machine off the ground.

"Come on, you piece of junk," the pilot muttered as he watched his tachs slowly move out of the red. "Don't puke out on me now."

When he felt the blades biting the air, he came up on the collective and the chopper rose in the air. Dropping the nose to get forward momentum from his lift, he headed straight for the mine. A cloud of dust hung over the mine, totally obscuring his vision, so he swung wide to come in from the windward side. Reaching the perimeter, he started to drop down slowly, letting the rotor wash clear the dust away for him to see. Spotting the open main gate, he dropped down to land beside it.

Leaving the rotor turning to blow away the dust, Grimaldi jumped from the cockpit and joined the others running for the mine elevator. Under his feet, a chasm suddenly opened in the earth and he had to leap across it to keep from being sucked down. The Wagner buildings lay in ruins; even the concrete block headquarters had partially collapsed. The ore-crushing machinery had toppled over, and a sinkhole had appeared to swallow up half of it.

The Stony Man warriors were making their way around the debris when Bolan walked out of the dust cloud. His arm was around Manning's shoulder, and the Canadian was limping.

"Striker!" Katz called out.

Bolan sketched a salute. The mission was over.

CHAPTER TWENTY-NINE

Stony Man Farm, Virginia

Hal Brognola was strangely subdued when the satcom call came in from Uganda. He congratulated the Stony Man warriors and concurred with how they had disposed of the warheads. Armageddon might still flash brighter than the sun some day, but for now the end had been put off yet again.

When he hung up, he left the Annex and went back to his office in the farmhouse. Sitting at his desk, he pulled out his prepared resignation letter and read over it again. There wasn't a word that could be improved upon, and not a comma was out of place. He put it back in the folder and put the folder back in his briefcase.

Brognola's office was sparse in personal appointments; a family photo and a couple of certificates from his law-enforcement career were about the extent of it. His memorabilia collection was kept in his mind and in the archives of the Sensitive Operations Group.

Clicking on the intercom, Brognola called over to the blacksuit com center in the Annex. "I need a ride," he said.

"Where to sir?"

"Washington."

HAL BROGNOLA DISMISSED his driver and walked out of the rear entrance of the White House compound alone. He desperately needed to get out and rub elbows with the common American on the street to recharge his batteries. The halls of power had drained him dry, and he needed a reminder of why he did what he did for a living. The best way he knew to be reminded that he ran Stony Man Farm for the good of the many, not for the good of the few or even for the good of the Man, was to walk among the people he really served.

Behind him, he had left an uncommon American going through a very complicated revision of something he had held very dear to his heart for most of his life. The current occupant of the Oval Office was having a personal crisis that few in his position had ever had to deal with. Even though he hadn't known what he been doing, he had nurtured a viper and had almost caused the Apocalypse to visit the earth. It was a heavy burden for a proud man like him to bear.

It was a statement of the President's character, though, that he hadn't accepted Brognola's offered resignation. A lesser man might have done that, a man who wanted to strike out at the messenger who had brought him the bad news. Instead, he had sincerely apologized for not having been willing to listen to Brognola earlier.

The President had also thanked him for having taken care of the matter without allowing it to leak to the media. Since the late Grant Betancourt had controlled a large portion of the nation's defense industries, it was too easy to see him as an arm of national policy. If the extent of his insanity had made it onto the six-o'clock news, it would have caused the United States untold trouble on both the domestic and the international scenes. The private crimes of a madman would have been seen as deliberately aggressive American actions.

It also went without saying that had any of this been made public, the President's tenure in office would have been thrown into turmoil. The hearings and investigations into his relationship with Betancourt would have hamstrung Washington officialdom and brought the nation's legitimate business to a screeching halt for as long as he remained in office. And, considering the closeness of that relationship, charges of influence peddling and financial improprieties would have been the least of the President's problems.

The media would have certainly, and rightfully, wondered if the President in any way had shared Betancourt's bloody dreams of nuclear genocide. And therein would have been the real problem America would have faced from the rest of the world. Religion had always been a hot-button issue, and it would continue to be so for much of the world's population.

If Betancourt's plans had been made public knowledge, the Muslim world would more than likely have declared jihad against the United States. The Catholic vote would have permanently deserted the President's party, and the American Jewish community would have been rightfully outraged. Instead, as the poem went, the Stony Man warriors had once more ''saved the sum of things for pay.''

Brognola almost wanted to laugh. For a meager federal paycheck and, this time, the chance of going to a federal prison, they had put their lives on the line to end a nuclear nightmare. And, he knew, they would do it again the next time they were called upon.

As long as he had been the head of SOG, he should have been blind to the sacrifices of the men of Stony Man, but he wasn't. Even after all this time, he was still in awe of what they did routinely. He liked to think that if he were called upon to do what they did, he would have their zeal and dedication. But he wasn't sure that he had the raw courage necessary to be one of them. Few men did.

Someday, the world might be a kinder, gentler place for everyone to live. But even though this was the dawn of a new millennium, there were no signs that universal peace was about to break out anytime soon. And, until it did, the warriors of Stony Man would be needed time and time again.

Readers won't want to miss this exciting new title of the Super Bolan series!

DON PENDLETON's

MACK BOLAN®
SCORCHED
EARTH

Three acts of terror against America prompt
Hal Brognola to ask Mack Bolan to look into the
possible existence of a Serbian Mafia operating out of
Pittsburgh. Not only does he find a Serb-Russian Mob
connection, but he also discovers a plot that pits the
Serbs with ADMs—nuke backpacks—against NATO.

Available in January 2001 at your favorite retail outlet.

GOLD
EAGLE®

GSB76

James Axler

OUTLANDERS®

TIGERS OF HEAVEN

In the Outlands, the struggle for control of the baronies continues. Kane, Grant and Brigid seek allies in the Western Islands empire of New Edo, where they try to enlist the aid of the Tigers of Heaven, a group of samurai warriors.

Book #2 of the Imperator Wars saga, a trilogy chronicling the introduction of a new child imperator—launching the baronies into war!